Trust No One

Mel Parish

ALSO BY MEL PARISH

Motive for Revenge

The Anniversary

Ulterior Motives

Silent Lies

Trust No One

By

Mel Parish

ISBN 978-1544724621

Cover design: Jonny Gillard

For the ladies at the Charity Knitting Bee

in Mamaroneck, NY

Keep up the good work!

Chapter 1 - Monday evening

Maggie Cumberland froze a split second before her outstretched hand made contact with the kitchen door, her plan to announce her momentary return home to her husband fading at the urgent tone in his voice. It had an unrecognizable edge to it, cold and dispassionate, but it was the subject of his conversation that made her hesitate.

Shipments and delivery dates were not unusual topics for someone in the distribution business but unless Maggie's ears were playing tricks on her the cargo he spoke of was human. Why else would the words "young women", "twenty-five" and "Eastern European" belong in the same sentence about shipping?

She shook her head as if to reset her hearing. What was wrong with her? Mastersons Distribution specialized in high-end luxury goods including art and antiques. Daniel could be talking about portraits or other works of art depicting women, perhaps by Eastern European artists or part of an Eastern European collection.

Still, some instinct kept her rooted to the spot, afraid to

fully open the door and reveal her presence. She didn't like to eavesdrop, considered it a transgression which more likely than not would have a regrettable outcome, but she could hardly avoid hearing Daniel's side of the phone call as his voice grew louder and more animated.

She stifled a gasp as he answered some unheard question with, "They've been drugged so they'll cause no problems in transit."

She started to tremble. So, no inanimate objects excuse. Her eyes widened as the full implication of what she'd overheard sank in. But it couldn't be her husband talking. It had to be some stranger, some monster.

She backed quietly down the hallway, terrified the kitchen door would open before she could escape. Thankfully, in her rushed return home to collect the tennis balls for her club league match that evening, she'd left the front door open on her way in. She eased it gently closed behind her with only the slightest telltale click. Hopefully Daniel wouldn't hear it from the kitchen.

She dashed to her car, drove around the corner before pulling over again. If someone she knew saw her she didn't know how she would explain why she was sitting in that spot, but she didn't dare drive any further. Not until she got herself under control. She gripped the steering wheel tight and pressed her feet hard against the floor in an effort to stop her limbs shaking. Snippets of Daniel's words replayed in her mind.

Shipments. Girls. Drugs.

She tried desperately to view them in a different light, to turn them into something innocent, but to no avail.

What was she supposed to do? Should she go to the police? But with what? A few overheard words? They'd think she was crazy. And what if the police did believe her but she was wrong? Think of the havoc she'd cause. Daniel would never trust her again and with good cause. What kind of wife rats on her husband of over twenty years based on a few minutes of conversation she wasn't meant to hear?

She shouldn't have been there. Nor, for that matter, should Daniel. He rarely came home early, especially if he knew she would be out, her absence giving him an excuse for working late. The forgotten tennis balls were her excuse, but what was his?

She wished she'd slammed the front door on the way in. He would have heard it and come out of the kitchen to check who was there. They would have exchanged their mutual excuses and she wouldn't have heard any of the awful conversation, which the more she thought about, the more she believed she must have misunderstood. It was the only explanation. Instead of sitting there like an idiot she'd be on her way to her tennis match, a match which, given her opponent's inability to hit back any ball that didn't bounce right at her feet, she was guaranteed to win.

She glanced at the dashboard clock. If she was going to make the match on time she needed to leave now. So what to do? Police station or club? Spend the next hour playing tennis, or spend it denouncing her husband as a potential monster to the police?

Daniel, a monster? No, no, no, he wasn't like that. He was a kind, honest man. There had to be some perfectly innocent explanation which she'd now never know because she could hardly admit she'd been eavesdropping and then fled. What would he make of that?

She should have sailed straight into the kitchen, caught him mid-conversation, let him explain. But it was too late now. So she should put it out of her mind, accept she was making a mountain out of a molehill, and go and play tennis. Sue would be waiting for her. It was too late to back out now. Besides, she couldn't go home early while Daniel was there and whacking tennis balls would be the perfect way to get rid of all the tension she'd built up inside.

She started the car.

Yes, tennis first, and then home again, and somehow she'd try and raise her concerns with Daniel over dinner.

Chapter 2 - Later Monday evening

Daniel's car was no longer in the driveway when Maggie got home. Nor was it in their two-car garage. The discovery spooked her. She'd convinced herself on the way back that his explanation for his early return would answer all her concerns regarding the strange phone call, but now she had to assume he didn't even want her to know he'd been home.

She drove into the garage but made no effort to get out of the car. Monday evenings, she played tennis from six until seven and then came home and made dinner. Daniel would return sometime between eight and eight-thirty. A regular, predictable routine, or at least, that's how she'd thought of it. But for all she knew this might not have been the first time Daniel had been home while she was out. If she hadn't come back for the balls, she'd still be none the wiser.

Where would he have gone? Presumably not all the way back into the city. She pictured him sitting in Starbucks waiting for eight o'clock so he could pretend he'd just come off the train. Or maybe the bar nearby the station. Though the latter would be risky.

He might bump into someone they knew who might later happen to mention it to Maggie. She was tempted to drive into town and see if she could spot him or his car, except what excuse could she give for being there if he saw her? The local stores would be closed.

No, far better to act normal and give him a chance to explain when he came in. Which meant she needed to get started on the dinner.

She hurried into the kitchen via the connecting door from the garage. Glanced around for any sign Daniel hadn't tried to hide his presence, a coffee cup on the bench, crumbs from a pre-dinner snack, or a discarded water glass. A doodle on the scratch pad they used as a grocery list, a date, a number or something, anything that hadn't been there an hour earlier. The kitchen was as spotless as she had left it.

She filled a large pot with water, set it to boil for the pasta. Put the rich meat and tomato sauce she'd made earlier on to simmer and started preparing a salad while she waited for the pasta to cook. Her hands shook as she chopped, forcing her to concentrate on the task more than usual. When the pasta was ready she mixed it into the sauce, poured it into a casserole dish and topped it with a hefty layer of grated cheese, and put it in the oven to bake.

Her movements were automatic, an often followed routine, but this time sloppily performed leaving a pool of water by the sink from the drained pasta, tomato splashes all over the hob, and flecks of cheese on the counter. She'd taken her frustrations out on the food.

She wiped up the mess and headed for the shower. On the way she snuck a glance into Daniel's closet, rattled by the sudden memory of an acquaintance whose husband had packed up and left while she was out shopping. A woman who'd believed she was happily married. It had been the focus of local gossip for weeks.

There were no noticeable gaps in Daniel's hanging garments or empty spaces on the shelves. His electric razor was on the bureau, his toothbrush in the bathroom. So it was safe to assume he would come home.

She had to reconsider that assumption when eight-thirty

came and went and he still wasn't back. She called him, got his voicemail, and left a message, but only because under normal circumstances he would expect her to do so. At nine she ate some salad, left the casserole untouched. She paced the floor, poured a glass of wine, and paced some more.

She couldn't decide whether she wanted him to come home or not. If he did, what would she do? But if he didn't, what would she do?

She tried his number again. Again it went straight to voicemail. She stood at the living room window, watching the deserted street for signs of his headlights.

It was uncharacteristic of Daniel to be late without warning her. He hadn't said anything that morning to indicate this Monday would be any different from previous ones. She double-checked the calendar to make sure he hadn't scheduled some event she'd forgotten about. Stared at the single entry for the day, tennis at six, and wondered how a day could start so ordinarily and end in such confusion.

The longer she waited the more her mind raced, examining trivial events for deeper meanings, for an understanding of how the man she thought she knew so well could be the same man she'd overheard earlier. She never claimed great intelligence, but she couldn't believe she would be so easily duped. If someone was living a double life there had to be signs, didn't there?

She sniggered. A double life? Did she really think that was what Daniel was doing? The guy might be bright and excel at his job, but when it came to the rest of his life he'd be at a loss without her to keep him on track. If he had another life, there'd have to be another woman and...

No, she refused to go down that line of thinking. She was one hundred percent certain there wasn't another woman. Not one who did his laundry or cooked his meals.

She jumped at the sound of the phone. Snatched up the receiver and uttered a breathless, "Hello?"

"Hey, Maggie, I am so sorry." Daniel sounded it. "I got called into a last minute meeting and it went on way longer than expected."

The relief at hearing his voice drained away in the face of his blatant lie.

"Maggie, you there?"

She managed to make an indecipherable sound. Daniel read it right.

"I really am sorry. I would have phoned earlier but I couldn't. I know you've probably been worried, but I just want you to know, I'm on my way home now. Should be back in an hour."

An hour? So where was he? Not in Starbucks, it would have been closed by now. And if he had gone to the bar why would he say he wouldn't be home for an hour?

"Maggie?" She could hear the growing concern in his voice. "You okay?"

"No." She managed to squeeze the word past the growing lump in her throat. Then wished she'd said yes.

"Why? What's wrong?"

Wrong? She wanted to scream at him. Everything was wrong. This was wrong. They were wrong. Lying was just downright wrong. She tried to clear her throat to vent, managed only a coughing sound.

"Are you coming down with something?"

How about a bad case of deceiving husband, she wanted to say, but instead she croaked out a "yes."

"Look, don't wait up for me. Get yourself to bed, have a good night's sleep. Hopefully, you'll feel better in the morning."

Maggie doubted it, but the idea of not having to face him and his lies until morning held appeal. She needed time to process this confirmation of his dishonesty.

She managed to find her voice.

"I think it's the bug that's going around. Been feeling off all day. Maybe it would be best if you slept in the guest room tonight. I don't want to pass my germs on to you."

She was surprised how easy the lie came out.

"A good idea. Means I won't disturb you when I come in. So, see you in the morning. Love you."

"Goodnight." Maggie cut off the call.

Would Daniel notice she'd failed to return his endearment?

She couldn't bring herself to say it. She hoped he'd be too caught up in whatever he was doing to realize. Or he'd put it down to her not being well. Whatever, until she decided what she was going to do she'd have to be careful how she behaved toward him. He mustn't realize she was onto him.

Chapter 3 - Tuesday morning

Maggie pretended to be asleep when Daniel came into the bedroom the following morning. She sensed him hovering by the bed, presumably debating whether he should wake her to see how she was. He must have thought better of it because she heard movement, a gentle click of the bathroom door, followed by the faint drum of the shower.

She really did feel lousy, but not from illness. She'd barely slept, her mind refusing to stop tormenting her with 'what ifs' and 'if only' while, no matter how hard she tried, her conscience wouldn't let her dismiss what she'd heard as a figment of her imagination. As much as it hurt to admit it, she knew what she'd heard. But she didn't have a clue what she was supposed to do about it. How much easier it would be if it didn't involve Daniel, the one person she'd normally turn to first for advice on something as serious as this.

The shower door rumbled on its track. Another few minutes and he'd be back in the bedroom. Should she pretend to have woken or wait to see whether he tried to wake her?

She clenched her eyes shut as the bathroom door opened. Flinched a few seconds later as his hand brushed her forehead.

"How you feeling?"

She rolled onto her back, feigning the first moments of wakefulness, and forced a weak smile.

"Awful."

"Really?" Daniel sounded surprised. He put his hand on her forehead again. "You don't look sick. And your forehead's not hot."

She turned onto her side, pulled the sheet up over her face and muttered, "Tell that to my insides."

He chuckled. "You poor thing. Do you want me to get you anything before I go? A cup of coffee? Some medicine?"

She moaned in response. Then wondered whether she was overdoing it.

He kissed the top of her head. "I'll give you a call later. See how you're doing, okay?"

Maggie made a positive noise. Lay still and listened as he took an interminable amount of time to get dressed. She just wanted him to go.

Finally she heard the bedroom door shut. Or had he merely closed the closet? She strained to hear any other sound, aware she was being ridiculous, but she didn't feel capable of keeping up an act in his presence. Once she felt confident he'd gone she pulled the sheet off her face.

Six-fifteen. He'd still be downstairs. He left the house promptly each morning at six-thirty. She couldn't remember the last time he was late for work or took a day off sick. And even on those rare winter days when the weather forced him to stay home, he'd be at his desk in his study by eight and put in a whole day's work.

She'd given up trying to persuade him to enjoy an impromptu day off or even half a day, but he insisted he had all the information he needed to work at home so there was no justification for it. She never came out and said it but she thought he was taking dedication to the extreme, especially when he was foregoing the opportunity to spend some unexpected quality time with their son.

She slid out of bed, crossed to the window and peered through the thin gap where the drapes met. A few minutes passed before Daniel's BMW appeared in the driveway. He reversed it into the road and set off for the station in one fluid, confident movement that always impressed her.

She lingered by the window, glad he was gone but reluctant to make a start on her own day. She rarely ventured into Daniel's study, had no reason to, but short of asking Daniel outright it was the only way she could think of confirming one way or the other whether she had anything to worry about.

To delay the inevitable further, she took a shower, dressed, and tidied up the bedroom. Then she remade the bed in the guest room and collected up the clothes Daniel had left lying on the floor. Twenty-two years of marriage and she still hadn't managed to train him to put his dirty clothes in the laundry hamper.

In the kitchen a half-drunk cup of coffee and an empty cereal bowl stood on the countertop. Maggie sighed. Was it really too much to ask him to put them in the dishwasher?

She opened the appliance door. Felt a twinge of guilt. The washer was full of clean dishes, dishes she'd forgotten to remove the previous evening. She'd have been doubly annoyed if he'd stuck his dirty dishes in with the clean ones. Though of course she had no way of knowing whether he'd bothered to look inside, because if he had, what were the chances he'd noticed the dishes were clean and not dirty? His domestic abilities were non-existent, a fact which sometimes she found endearing but increasingly, like today, downright frustrating.

She slammed the door shut. The dishes could wait. She gulped down a lukewarm coffee—for some reason Daniel had turned the coffee maker off—and headed for his study.

Chapter 4 – Tuesday morning

The study was as neat as ever. Despite Daniel's domestic shortcomings, his organizational approach to his work verged on obsessive. The top of his L-shaped desk was bare save for his computer. Only the accounting texts on the solitary narrow bookshelf hinted at the profession of the occupier. A four-drawer hardwood filing cabinet and an ergonomically designed chair were the only other pieces of furniture. At first glance a stranger could be forgiven for thinking the room was unused, but Maggie knew Daniel could lay hands on any information he needed in seconds from his well-maintained filing system.

She, on the other hand, had no idea where he kept anything. There'd been no need. He managed it all so well. She took care of the house, he looked after the finances. So where to start? And what was she even looking for?

She opened the top drawer of the desk. Pens, chargers, a calculator and a disused cell phone, nothing out of the ordinary. She moved on to the lower drawer, found neatly marked tabs listing files of household bills, insurance and their bank accounts.

She pulled out a couple, flipped through, but neither contained anything unexpected.

She sat down, leaned back in the chair. What she needed to find was an innocent document, an invoice or a delivery note, which would explain what she'd heard. The kind of document Daniel would probably keep with his work files in the filing cabinet. All she had to do was look. But what if she found something else, something confirming her fears? The possibility made her terrified to look.

Too terrified to look. She had no business doing so. These were confidential work files, for Daniel's eyes only. She leapt up. He probably kept the cabinet locked anyway. She yanked on the handle of the top drawer of the cabinet to prove her point. Stumbled back as the drawer easily slid open.

It was empty.

She frowned. Remembered a conversation when Daniel had mentioned he was running out of filing space. So where were all the files?

She opened the next drawer down. This one was half full, the tabs labeled with names of various companies, some of which Daniel had worked for. She fingered through them, found one marked Mastersons. She inhaled hard, gingerly pulled out the file as if it were toxic.

As she opened it she let out a sigh of relief. It contained a single letter, a contract of employment. She skimmed the text. Saw no mention of types of cargo, human or otherwise, merely a list of responsibilities of the job. A list so lengthy, no wonder he worked such long hours.

She put the file back. Closed the drawer and moved on to the third one. This was full, the tabs marked with quarterly dates. She took out the most recent, realized it was merely an accounting report for the first quarter of the current year. She snapped the file shut. It was confidential information which she should not be looking at. Daniel would be furious if he found out.

The bottom drawer contained tax files, personal tax files. She checked the latest one, in case Daniel had used it as a cover for shady dealings, but it contained nothing but tax forms. Her eyes widened as she noticed the size of the figures on the main form. She had no idea their income was so large. She merely signed the forms at Daniel's request, never paid much attention to the detail.

She was about to close the drawer when she noticed some of the older files at the back had thick brown envelopes squashed between the covers. Receipts probably, from the days before Daniel did most of his banking online.

She started to close the drawer. Hesitated. If she didn't check them out she'd probably have to come back later and satisfy her curiosity. But if the envelopes were sealed she wasn't going to tamper with them. No matter how curious she was.

The envelopes were closed with metal clasps. She gently unfastened one, reached in and pulled out the contents.

Or at least half the contents.

She gasped at the sight of the wad of cash in her hands. She put the envelope down, shakily fanned through the wad. All fifties, as far as she could tell, held together by a thick rubber band. She put the cash on the desk, reached back into the envelope and pulled out another similar size bundle.

She dropped the cash and envelope onto the desk and slumped into the chair.

What the hell was going on? Daniel didn't use cash. Said using cards gave him more control. He could tell exactly where he'd spent every penny, had even tried to persuade her away from using cash. But she didn't necessarily want a reminder of how she spent money, every coffee or cosmetic she bought listed for Daniel to see.

So why would he have bundles of cash hidden away?

She looked down at the open drawer. There were another three envelopes. Did they contain cash too?

She picked out the middle one. Saw how easily it bent in the middle as the contents separated. Her fingers shook so much she could barely open the clasp. She emptied the contents onto the desk, hardly daring to look. Two more identically-sized bundles fell out, this time of twenty dollar bills.

Practically in a trance, she opened the remaining two envelopes. Two more bundles of fifties, two more of twenties.

Daniel had thousands of dollars stashed away in the house. And he hadn't told her. But why? Why would he not want her to know about it?

She grappled for an explanation. Her eyes filled with tears as she forced herself to accept the only possible explanation. He was involved in something underhand. Something he didn't want her to know about.

She picked up one of the bundles of fifties. Slipped off the band and counted the notes. Fifty. Two thousand five hundred dollars. She assumed each bundle had fifty notes, but counted them anyway. Fourteen thousand dollars. She'd never seen so much cash before in her life. Somehow the eight bundles looked small compared to what they represented.

But what did they represent? Other than dollars? His share of profit from ruining the lives of others?

The tears flowed fat and fast, rolling down her cheeks, dropping off her chin, as her anguish demanded to be released in breath-catching sobs. She, who had donated her free time to help abused women, was married to someone who perpetuated abuse. The very thought made her want to vomit. Made her limbs shake.

She laid her forearms on the edge of the desk, bent forward to rest her forehead on her hands while she struggled to breathe. Her tears plopped onto her knees as she willed herself not to be sick. Daniel must never know she'd been in his office. Not now.

Chapter 5 – Tuesday midday

Maggie stood outside the non-descript building that served as the police station, the gravity of the moment rendering her motionless. Decision time. Once she walked through those doors there'd be no going back. This was the moment when she could either save her marriage or blight it forever.

The temptation to walk away was strong. All it would take would be to pretend she'd never heard the phone call. No one else knew. She could go on living her life as she always had done, safe and comfortable. It wasn't her job to root out criminals. She couldn't be the only wife who knew her husband was involved in shady dealings. She shuddered. Disgusting dealings. Inhumane dealings.

If you see something, say something. Wasn't that what the signs in the subway and train stations said? But they were referring to possible acts of terrorism, acts which could cause devastation and kill or hurt many people. This was different, wasn't it?

She could wait and hope justice caught up soon. Act the shocked and surprised wife when the police turned up at the door.

Daniel would back up her claims she was ignorant of what he was up to. There was nothing to tie her to the crimes.

She glanced over her shoulder, back the way she'd come. She'd parked her car in a municipal lot down the road, afraid for it to be seen outside the station house.

Afraid. There was so much to be afraid of now. She'd been flung into a no-win situation, dire consequences whether she followed through with her plan or not, a life of fear the only guaranteed outcome.

She sighed. She'd been over and over this in her mind, bouncing back and forth between her options, but the truth had gnawed at her. If her suspicions were correct, for every day she kept quiet she would be inflicting misery on untold numbers of girls. Her fear surely paled in comparison.

Suddenly, one of the double doors swung open. A uniformed officer breezed through. He stopped abruptly as he noticed her and caught the door before it started to close.

"Ma'am."

Maggie took it as a sign.

"Thank you." Head high she strode into the building.

Her courage didn't last long. Her mind emptied and her mouth dried up the moment the stern-faced officer behind the desk asked how he could help.

He waited a moment while she stood speechless, his expression softening. "Ma'am?"

"I... I'd... I'd like to speak to a detective, please."

"You want to report a crime?"

"No. No."

The officer frowned.

"Well, sort of." She leaned close to the glass separating them. There was nobody else there to hear her but she couldn't bring herself to raise her voice. "I think I have some information about a possible crime."

The officer narrowed his eyes. "What kind of crime?"

"Please, if I could just speak with a detective."

"A robbery? An assault?"

"Please." Maggie broke off. This wasn't how she'd

imagined dealing with the situation. She probably came across as a crazy woman.

She noticed the officer eyeing her up.

A crazy woman in an expensive suit. Maybe she'd overdressed, but she wanted to be taken seriously.

"Your name, please?"

"What?"

"Your name. So I can tell Detective Abbot you'd like to see him."

"Oh." Maggie surveyed the still empty lobby. Whispered, "Cumberland."

"Mrs. Cumberland," she added before the officer could ask for her full name.

The officer picked up a phone, punched in a couple of numbers. Told someone named John about Maggie's request.

"No, she wouldn't say what crime."

He grinned as if he'd heard something funny.

"Probably. Thanks."

He hung up. The grin disappeared. "Detective Abbot will be with you in a few moments." He began tapping away at a keyboard.

Maggie bristled at the apparent dismissal. She was expected to wait there in full view of anyone else coming into the building? Why couldn't the officer let her in through the coded-entry door? Find her a seat out of view. Surely the detective wasn't going to conduct the interview in the lobby.

She coughed.

The officer didn't look up. "He won't be long."

Maggie peered through the entrance door to check for any sign of someone else coming in. She couldn't imagine there was a lot of crime in town, but it would be just her luck for someone she knew to turn up while she was there.

Her agitation increased as the minutes passed. She jiggled from one foot to the other trying to hide the fact she'd started to shake.

This was a big mistake.

She jumped at the sound of a door opening behind her.

"Mrs. Cumberland?"

A hulk of a man approached and offered a handshake. "Detective Abbot. Would you follow me please?"

Wordlessly, Maggie followed him back the way he'd come into a brightly lit, narrow hallway.

He opened the door of a sparsely furnished office, switched on a light and gestured for her to sit down in front of a battered wooden desk.

"Can I see some ID please?"

The brusqueness of his request startled Maggie. And the way he loomed over her while waiting for her to dig her license out of her wallet unnerved her, made her feel as if she had something to hide. She struggled to suppress a sigh of relief when he finally moved around to the other side of the desk. He copied some details from her license onto a pad of paper, slid the document back over the table and settled back in his chair in such a relaxed fashion Maggie doubted he'd take her seriously.

He stared at her, his emotionless expression giving little indication of what he might be thinking. Was he categorizing her? Well-dressed, possibly wealthy, white, middle-aged, probably a stay-at-home wife based on the time of day she'd shown up. What other labels was he attributing to her?

He smiled. In an instant his whole demeanor changed. The thin line of his mouth softened, his steely stare took on a kinder, gentler look, the combination taking a good five years off Maggie's estimate of his age.

"So what was it you wanted to tell me?" he asked after what seemed like an interminable wait.

Maggie realized he'd been waiting for her to speak.

"I think…"

She tried again.

"My husband, I…"

The carefully rehearsed speech vanished, words stuck in her throat. Abbot was looking at her as if she was a gibbering idiot, which she probably was.

"I'm sorry."

Abbot held up his hand. "Take it easy, okay."

Maggie nodded rapidly, grateful to be able to respond without words. She hadn't even started explaining her situation and already she was being told to calm down.

Abbot smiled again. "Nothing to be nervous about."

Maggie gaped at him. Well, if informing on your husband was nothing to be nervous about, she wasn't sure what was.

"You're here to report a crime, yes?"

Maggie swallowed hard. "I think so."

Abbot squinted. "You think so."

She could hear the doubt.

"I think my husband's company is involved in human trafficking." The words tumbled out so quickly they barely sounded decipherable.

There was a moment of silence. Abbot's smile disappeared.

"Human trafficking."

Thank goodness, he'd understood that part.

Abbot straightened in his chair, picked up the pen, pulled the pad toward him again.

"What makes you think that?"

Maggie chewed on her lip. There was no going back now.

"Take your time. Tell me what you know."

Maggie told him.

Abbot listened. Jotted down the occasional word in an illegible scrawl, at least from Maggie's perspective, though she'd never been particularly adept at reading upside down.

Each pen stroke felt like a knife in Maggie's soul. She was betraying her husband, her best friend, the one person who'd made her life so happy, and her traitorous words were being reduced to a few salient points.

She stopped short of telling Abbot about the money. She'd damned Daniel enough. Let the police find out the rest. Abbot took her through her story again, checking he'd got it down accurately.

He hadn't. Or she thought he hadn't until she corrected him and realized he didn't amend what he'd written down. He was testing her. She almost called him on it, but decided to play along. Consistency in her story had to work in her favor.

"I hope I haven't wasted your time." She shrugged. "I didn't know what else to do. I tried convincing myself I'd misheard, but I know I didn't. I know what I heard."

Abbot tossed his pen down.

"No, it's good you came in and let us know your concerns." He gave her a reassuring smile. "It can't have been easy. Not many people would have the courage to do what you've done. Especially since it involves your husband."

"Will he know?"

Abbot frowned. "Sorry?"

"Will he have to be told I made this report?"

"That'll depend on whether you are willing to testify against him if necessary."

Maggie gasped.

"Testify! No, I couldn't do that." The very thought unnerved her. "I won't have to, will I?"

Telling an unknown detective her concerns was bad enough, sitting across from her husband in court, something else altogether.

"By law you can't be forced to testify against your husband."

Relief washed over Maggie.

"So what will happen now?"

"Now?" Abbot sighed. "Well, now I have to ask you some more questions, but if you mean going forward, first we'll have to check out your statement, see if we can find some corroborating evidence."

"But what about my husband? And the company directors? Will they be arrested?"

Abbot shook his head. "We can't arrest people on the basis of one suspicious phone call."

Abbot's words sent a shiver down Maggie's spine. And not just because of her concern for the potential victims. She'd imagined the police would act immediately to prevent whatever was being planned from happening.

"But what about me?"

"You?"

"Yes, me! I've just… just ratted out my husband. What am I supposed to do?"

Abbot took a deep breath. "Mrs. Cumberland, you're not going to like this, but what we need you to do is to go home, act normal, don't give your husband any reason to suspect you. In the meantime, we'll look into the matter as quickly as we can."

Maggie felt the blood drain from her face. She'd come to the police partly because she couldn't face Daniel, couldn't pretend everything was okay between them, and now this detective was telling her that was exactly what she'd have to do. Except now she'd be doing it with the added knowledge she'd betrayed him. Was Abbot joking?

"I can't," she stammered.

"You have to. If what you told me is true, Mrs. Cumberland, this could be the tip of a much bigger iceberg. Guys who deal in this kind of crime, they're not petty criminals. Chances are you're talking about a major crime organization."

"You're scaring me."

"I don't mean to."

Maggie looked to see if he was joking. He wasn't smiling.

"Look, you said yourself this could be a complete misunderstanding. How would it be if we charged in on the basis of what you've said and discovered there's a perfectly innocent explanation?"

"I don't think I'm a good enough actress. He's going to know something's wrong. And if he is arrested he's going to know. Know I had something to do with it." She hid her face in her hands and groaned. "Why did I even think this was a good idea?"

Abbot spoke softly. "Even if you hadn't, you'd still have to live with your suspicions. Would that be any easier?"

"At least I'd know in my heart I was innocent."

"Innocent of what?"

Maggie moved her hands from her face. "Innocent of betrayal of my husband. And perhaps some seriously scary people."

"And you could live with yourself?" Abbot hesitated. "Live with the knowledge you did nothing to stop a potentially horrific crime?"

Maggie covered her face again.

"Do you have children, Mrs. Cumberland?"

Maggie nodded.

"How would you feel if it were your children who'd been trafficked?"

Maggie burst into tears. Why did he think she'd come here in the first place?

Chapter 6 – Later Tuesday afternoon

Maggie barely remembered driving home. She rushed into the house, threw her purse onto the kitchen table, crossed straight to the refrigerator and poured a generous glass of wine. Normally, she didn't drink during the day, but given she'd just erased the idea of normality from her life, what did it matter? She needed something, anything, to relieve the rigid tension that had invaded her body, making the smallest movement a robotic parody of her former self.

She kicked off her shoes, peeled off her jacket and padded out onto the deck with her glass. A fresh spring breeze tickled her bare skin. She shivered but instead of returning indoors sat down in one of the oversized wicker chairs and mindlessly surveyed her surroundings.

The grass needed mowing. Daniel should have done it at the weekend, but work in the form of a game of golf with his bosses had got in the way. It had always been their son's job, a job Craig had done willingly all through high school, but she should have known Daniel's claim that he'd take it on when Craig left would prove unworkable. There'd always be something more pressing. She would have to call up a lawn service, relieve Daniel of the obligation.

Relieve Daniel of the obligation.

She took a large gulp of wine and set her glass down heavily on the table. An arrest would certainly remove any obligation to mow the lawn for the foreseeable future. Remove any obligation at all. Everything would be down to her. Not just the practical side, but all the decisions, financial and otherwise, decisions she'd never had to make.

She shivered violently, but not from a chill.

And those decisions would have to be made without a regular source of income to fund them. The mortgage? The bills? Where would the money come from without Daniel's regular paycheck?

There might be savings. There would be savings. Daniel would have ensured there were, but how much and how long would they last if used to pay the mortgage? She'd be a fool to think that even if she could find a job it would cover anything but the most basic necessities. They'd have to downsize, and dramatically.

How could this happen to her? Forty-eight hours ago her most complicated decision was what she should do now she was an empty-nester, a happily married and well-off empty-nester, and now she was facing a future of poverty, divorce and no nest at all.

She wanted to rush back to Abbot, tell him she'd made a terrible mistake. She was just a paranoid, crazy woman, not to be believed, and she was sorry for wasting his time.

She glanced at her watch. He'd hardly had time to put any investigation into motion. Assuming he was planning to do so. Maybe he'd been humoring her, as soon as she left, tossed the piece of paper with her story into the garbage or some dead-end file. Was that why he'd been so blasé about her going home and acting normal? Because he knew she had nothing to worry about?

She leapt up.

But he couldn't do that.

Just as she couldn't take back her story. She was convinced this was real, would be convinced until someone proved otherwise.

If necessary, she'd be a nuisance, call Abbot—he'd handed her his card as she left—every day until she knew for sure some action had been taken.

Her thoughts startled her. All her life she'd gone along, anything for the easy life, never quite brave enough to make a stand. And now look at her, deliberately standing on the precipice of financial ruin and marital disintegration, not to mention the possibility of falling foul of some dangerous characters.

She shuddered at the recollection of Abbot's use of the term organized crime. Her meager knowledge of the problem came from movies and novels, and if they were to be believed, there was nothing sportsmanlike in their attitude if they believed they were losing in the war on crime. A loss generally meant a betrayal, a betrayal which, no matter how long it took, needed to be avenged. Daniel might be sentenced to prison by the courts, but she'd be sentenced to a life of fear, a life of looking over her shoulder.

She grimaced. She hadn't thought this through properly. She shouldn't have gone in person. She should have made an anonymous phone call or sent an anonymous letter.

But would anyone have paid attention to a vague suggestion of wrongdoing? Any specific mention of Daniel or his phone call would automatically implicate her, but without concrete evidence what would the police have to work with?

She shivered again.

How long would it take the authorities to investigate her concerns? She'd pressed Abbot for a timeframe but he'd been non-committal. Told her to be patient.

Ha, patient! Easy for him to say. He'd mentioned possible complications because Mastersons Distribution was based in the city which would mean involving other police departments and possibly even the FBI given the high chance the crime crossed state lines.

Whatever vestiges of confidence Maggie had felt had disappeared at that news. Her imagined private disclosure to one detective suddenly didn't seem so confidential. Once the relay of information started who knew where it would be handed over to next. Suppose the Mastersons had a link to the police, someone who could give them a heads-up on possible investigations and also finger the source.

Abbot had promised her name would be kept secret, but he'd written her details down and unless he was going to carry the piece of paper with him at all times, she couldn't see how he could make such a promise.

She'd got so scared she'd asked whether she needed police protection, but Abbot pointed out it would be difficult to explain to Daniel why she needed protection. A valid point, but not particularly reassuring. As it was she had no idea how she would be able to face Daniel at the dinner table or over breakfast. She couldn't pretend to be sick for too long, he'd soon see through that ruse. There was a reason she'd always volunteered to work behind the scenes at her high school plays. She couldn't act to save her life.

Except now she was being told she had to, and without the benefit of any preparation or coaching, which meant she had to keep interactions with Daniel to a minimum. Not so difficult during the work week but as far as she was aware his diary for the weekend ahead was free of golf commitments, meaning he might suggest they go for a walk or a drive upstate. All options which gave them plenty of face time.

She went back indoors, switched on the weather channel as she uttered a quick prayer for rain in the forecast. If it rained she could suggest they go see a movie or she could find some jobs around the house which required her to be in another room.

Of course, there was no rain forecast. She switched over to the local channel hoping they knew something the national channel didn't. No luck there either.

She called a few friends. If Daniel had no commitments for the weekend maybe she could make some for herself. True, it would be unusual, but she could say she got confused and thought he would be out and it was too late to cancel.

Lies, lies, so many lies. Would this be how it was from now on? One lie after another?

Unfortunately, her friends weren't going to help. They all had other plans. Some suggested the following weekend for a get-together, but by then, chances were, they wouldn't want to know her.

She wandered back out onto the deck, idly dead-headed a hanging basket of petunias while she considered her options. Ha! As if she had any. All she could do was wait. Wait for the police to take action. Wait for the shame that would accompany the news of Daniel's arrest. Wait to find out who her real friends were. Wait to see how she could eke out a life on her own without the love of her life.

Assuming she didn't meet a grisly end before then.

She snatched at the remaining withered petals. She had to stop these stupid thoughts. Accept she'd read too many mysteries and thrillers. This wasn't a novel requiring suspension of belief as the fear and tension were ratcheted up to create the necessary satisfying moment when good eventually overcame evil. This was real life.

Except, elsewhere, girls were being kidnapped, transported to far away cities and probably forced into sexual servitude. That was no fiction. For them life was a horror story lacking in heroes ready to rush to their rescue, a story without a fairytale ending. Why should she assume she was exempt from the vagaries of life, that her story of quiet domesticity wouldn't conceal a deadly twist?

She heard the faint trill of the telephone. By the time she got indoors her voice was telling the caller to leave a message. She grabbed the handset, desperate to hear Abbot's reassuring words.

"Maggie! Are you okay?"

Daniel sounded anxious.

"I've called several times to see how you were. Didn't you get my messages?"

The red light on the base blinked, backing up his claim.

"I must have been out." As soon as the words left her lips she realized she should have said she'd been sleeping.

"You're feeling better?"

She hesitated. "Not really. But I needed to go to the supermarket."

"You should have called me. I could have picked up what was needed on my way home."

"Cold medicine. We were out of cold medicine." She made

a mental note to check their supply before Daniel returned. "I needed it now," she added lamely.

Daniel's sigh was unmistakably apologetic.

"Look, I'm sorry, but I'm going to have to work late tonight. Something's come up that needs to be dealt with immediately. Don't worry about dinner, I'll order in a pizza while I'm working. You just take care of yourself."

"Is it serious?"

She imagined the police swooping into the office demanding to see records.

"What? No. Just a report one of the bosses has decided he needs tomorrow rather than next week."

Or an urgent need to get rid of incriminating records before the police did swoop.

Truth or lies? She didn't know. She'd always believed him before, because that's what you did, trusted the ones you loved. And you got trust in return. Except now she was lying, forced to lie because of his lies. Anger welled up inside.

"I'd better let you get on with it then."

Daniel didn't reply.

"I'll probably be in bed when you get back."

Definitely be in bed when he got back, she'd make sure of that. And hopefully he'd put the out-of-character abruptness down to her not feeling well.

"Bye," she parroted in response to his tentative sign off before she slammed the phone down.

She replayed the messages. Three, all from Daniel. Each sounding more concerned than the last. Yet he hadn't challenged her as to how it had taken over two hours to go to a supermarket less than five minutes drive away. Over three hours, if he assumed she'd just got back in. He knew she always checked for messages after she'd been out, an instinct as automatic as taking off her shoes. An instinct which had failed her today.

Act normal, Abbot had said.

Ha! She'd left the police station less than an hour ago and had already failed. But what did he expect? She was a suburban housewife not some undercover agent. Normal wasn't normal anymore when you had to think about it.

Missed messages, drinking mid-afternoon, outer garments strewn where they fell. All signs of an orderly life fraying at the edges, but none as great as the overwhelming urge to scream at the unfairness of it all. Scream and, ideally, make it all disappear.

Disappear.

If only she could. Just until this was over. If nobody knew where she was she'd be safe. Or would she? Or would she be committing herself to a life-long disappearance? Initially there'd be a manhunt, someone would care she'd vanished. Daniel for sure. Craig. Or her sister Jane at the very least, if not also some of her friends and neighbors. There'd be publicity: in the media, flyers in local stores and on telegraph poles. For a brief period of time she'd be the most famous person in town, until the scandal about Daniel broke. But eventually interest would die down. Days, weeks, months, she had no idea, but eventually she'd fade from memory.

But any reappearance would cause another big story and not necessarily a positive one. The authorities might not be too forgiving of the expense she'd put them through with the manhunt. Her family would be furious about the worry she'd caused, although at that moment she cared little about Daniel's concerns. If he ended up in prison, which he fully deserved, she wouldn't be interacting with him in person anyway. But Craig and Jane were another matter. What if they never forgave her? What if they didn't understand why she needed to disappear in the first place? How could she admit she'd turned her own husband in?

No, disappearing wasn't an option. She'd have to get through this somehow.

Chapter 7 – Tuesday night

Despite exhaustion and a desperate desire to slide into the oblivion of unconsciousness, she couldn't sleep, her senses on high alert for the slightest change, a sound, a shape, a smell, any warning of imminent danger.

She heard a car pull into the driveway about ten o'clock. Daniel, she assumed, but as the sound of the engine cut off other more frightening possibilities came to mind. She lay rigid, the blankets pulled tight, and strained to hear confirmation of her initial belief.

A car door closed, followed by a second. She held her breath. Daniel and another? Or two strangers?

She relaxed. Or Daniel removing his briefcase from the back seat as he always did.

She pictured him walking toward the front door, heard the faint thud as he closed it behind him. Would he come and check on her? The outside light went off, a signal that all occupants were home for the night. What had once been reassuring suddenly struck terror into Maggie. What if someone was watching, waiting for her to lower her guard?

She listened for footsteps on the stairs, knowing the plush carpet deadened all but a stampede. She focused on the thin rectangle of hallway light outlining the bedroom door knowing a break in the continuity would indicate someone approached. Five minutes, ten minutes, thirty minutes, he wasn't coming, was probably catching up on the late night news before turning in. He'd said he wouldn't disturb her and he'd meant it. So she could relax until morning at least. And if she pretended to be asleep if he checked on her in the morning, she might be able to put off seeing him until the following evening.

But lying alone in the dark gave free rein to all the conflicting emotions. The initial fear vied with guilt, overwhelming guilt. What kind of woman betrayed the man she loved? What had she done?

She pictured Daniel's expression when the police showed up to arrest him. The distress, the devastation, a devastation borne of guilt at what he'd inflicted on her and Craig, though surely he must have been aware of the potential consequences of his actions. Would he try to explain why he'd done what he'd done? More likely he'd hug her, if they let him, and tell her everything would be alright. Daniel always made everything alright.

Or he had until now. There wasn't anything he could say which would make this alright.

The rectangle of light disappeared. Daniel had gone to bed. Maggie rolled onto her back, reached out to the empty space where Daniel usually lay. Hard to imagine they might never share a bed again.

A noise startled her. She jerked upright searching the dark room for the source. Heard it again, the low rumbling sound of an engine, and realized it came from outside. She crept to the window, twitched the drape aside a fraction and peered out. A patrol car slowed in front of the house.

She gasped.

Had they come to arrest Daniel already? In the middle of the night? Abbot must have worked fast.

As far as she could tell there was only one person in the car.

That seemed weird. She thought they'd have more for an arrest in case the person they'd come for made a run for it or the people in the house out-numbered the police.

But the car hadn't actually stopped. It merely crawled past the house and sped up as it reached the neighbor's property.

She sat back on the bed, listened for sounds of other vehicles. Had Abbot taken her fears to heart and ordered local officers to keep an eye on the house? Or were the police more interested in Daniel's whereabouts? They might have followed him home and, now the house had gone dark, assumed it was safe to leave for the night.

She gulped. Or was the patrol car connected to Mastersons? A rogue or fake cop, checking out a potential target?

She shook her head. She definitely read too many mysteries and thrillers. There was a simple solution. Call the station house and ask them. If it was legitimate someone there would know, right? And if it wasn't?

Then the police might really turn up. Feel they had to reassure a nervous woman. And how would she explain their presence to Daniel without revealing everything?

She pulled a basket chair up to the window, tweaked the drape so she could see through a sliver of window without being seen from the outside, and waited, her cell phone and Abbot's number by her side as a precaution.

She struggled to keep her heavy eyelids open. She wished she'd never heard the car, never heard the phone call. She wasn't cut out for any of this. She just wanted to be a wife and a mother. Do what made her happiest. Intrigues, deceit, they made her want to run away.

Run away.

How enticing the prospect sounded.

Run away and disappear.

Chapter 8 – Wednesday morning

As soon as she was sure Daniel had left for work, Maggie pulled a battered brown leather suitcase down from the topmost shelf of her closet. The case had belonged to her great-great-grandfather or possibly his father before him. It had passed down through the family to her mother who had continued her mother's tradition of using it as a repository for old family documents.

After their mother's death Maggie had suggested getting rid of the case and its contents. She couldn't see much use for the old passports, certificates, letters and occasional diary. Jane had been horrified, pointing out it acted as an archive of half their family history. How could Maggie suggest such a thing? If Maggie didn't want it, she certainly did. Except at the time Jane had nowhere to keep it. So, along with several other boxes of Jane's belongings which she didn't want to throw away but couldn't take with her, the suitcase ended up in Maggie's closet.

The case had been there so long Maggie had almost forgotten about it. Until the previous night when her idle wish that she could run away from her problems had resolved into a scary decision to do just that. To disappear. The more she thought about it, the more obvious it seemed. She wouldn't have to lie to Daniel or worry about the Mastersons learning of her role and if they did they'd have to find her first to exact revenge. She wouldn't have to face her friends and neighbors after Daniel's arrest, their ostracism or, worse, their condescending sympathy. Or deal with the demands of a relentless media.

Pack a bag and go. All it took was the courage to carry it out. Walk away from everyone she knew and everything she owned. Or rather, drive. She could load up her car with her favorite possessions and be far away by nightfall.

The euphoria from making the momentous decision lasted about ten minutes. Until she realized she couldn't take the car. Not unless she could come up with some super fast way of getting new license plates. It would be too easily identifiable, make her vulnerable to being tracked down. If she was going to do this she had to cover her movements as much as possible. She needed another plan. Except every plan she came up with created a trail. The use of credit or debit cards would give away her whereabouts. And even if she paid cash, she'd need to show her driver's license or passport to rent a car, travel by plane or check in to any decent hotel.

She was a fool to think she could get away with it. Within twenty-four hours the police or, worse, the Mastersons would have tracked her down. And she'd have to explain why she'd run. Unless the Mastersons and Daniel had already been arrested, in which case it would be obvious why.

No, if she was going to disappear she'd need money and forged documents, neither of which she had. She had no choice but to stay and face whatever came her way.

Disheartened, she'd stared out into the deserted street. There'd been no traffic since the patrol car. One by one the neighboring houses had gone dark. The bedside alarm showed it was after one a.m. It was futile to sit there any longer.

She'd got back into bed. Fell into a chaotic dream of running. She was being chased, except when she checked back over her shoulder there was no one following, merely a trail of twenty and fifty dollar bills. Horrified, she ran back, snatching up the notes and stuffing them into the torn brown envelope in her left hand. As fast as she put them in, more fell out of the bottom.

"Need some help?"

Startled, Maggie looked up to find her grandmother smiling down at her.

"Whatever are you up to now, Jane?"

"It's Maggie, Granny." The old lady was as forgetful as ever.

"Maggie. Jane." Granny laughed, totally unperturbed at the sight of the money. "I never could tell you two apart, except when one of you got up to no good. Then I'd know it was Jane."

Granny had a tendency to be long-winded. If Maggie didn't stop her, there'd be no chance of getting away from her enemies.

"Sorry, Granny, I can't stop." She glanced back over her shoulder. Discovered she was kneeling on the floor of her granny's living room. She stared back at Granny. The woman appeared sprightly given she'd been dead for over twenty years.

Dead. They'd had a funeral. Sold her house. The house Maggie was now sitting in.

She gasped and jolted awake.

It had taken a moment to get her bearings. She was at home, in bed. Nobody was chasing her. And Granny was definitely dead. They had the death certificate to prove it, in a suitcase in the closet.

Maggie used a tissue to wipe a thick layer of dust from the top and sides, an indication of how long it had been since the case was last opened. Meaning the document she hoped would be inside might already be out-of-date.

She flicked the lock openers. Nothing happened. She tried again with the same result. She pulled at the metal clasps, her trembling fingers unable to get a grip on the shiny surface. She picked up the case by the handle and shook it hard. Tried the locks again. Still no luck.

Had Jane locked it? But why? And how? Maggie didn't remember ever seeing a key. It certainly didn't make sense that Jane would have one.

Unbelievable. She slammed the top of the case with her palms. Just when she'd come up with a plan, thwarted by a locked suitcase.

She sat back on her heels, determined she wasn't going to let the case get the better of her. She could try ripping it open but she'd need something extremely sharp, like a box-cutter, but if they had one she had no idea where it was. They didn't have a tool box. If something was broken, they got someone in to fix it.

So who did you call to open a locked suitcase? Someone who wouldn't go to the police with a tale of how they'd helped the useless woman who'd recently disappeared open a case full of old documents? Her cover would be blown before she started.

She picked the case up and slammed it against the floor again and again. Was it too much to ask for something to work in her favor for once?

One of the clasps popped open.

Momentarily stunned, Maggie tentatively reached out and pushed the other lock. The second clasp sprung up. She mouthed "Thank you, God" even though she hadn't been praying—she'd needed a miracle.

She raised the lid, peered down at the haphazard piles of paper inside. The document she'd hoped to see on the top wasn't there. Her heart sank. It had been a long shot anyway. She rifled through the contents to see if there was anything else she could use. She found Jane's birth certificate. If she'd had more time she might have been able to use it to get some new ID, but she couldn't wait for the driver's license or passport to turn up. She debated taking it anyway. It might come in useful later. She put it to one side and continued her search.

It was the first time she'd really gone through the case. She began to see why Jane had been so adamant about keeping it. Here was the history of her family, a record of the joy of births, the grief of deaths, her grandfather's navy discharge papers after World War Two alongside her great grandfather's army papers from World War One. Had she even known they'd fought in the wars? She couldn't remember anyone talking about it.

As she studied the dates she realized both her mother and

grandfather were born during world wars, which meant her grandmother and great grandmother would have had to fend with a new baby while their husbands went off to fight. She couldn't imagine what that would be like. As hard as Daniel might have worked when Craig was little, at least he was there in the evenings and most weekends.

The phone rang. Without thinking Maggie leapt up to answer it. Daniel's number displayed on the caller ID. She hesitated, her hand over the receiver, too nervous to speak to him.

"Hi. Just thought I'd check in on you. You were fast asleep when I looked in on you this morning. Hope you're feeling better. Give me a call back, would you?"

The temptation to pick up was enormous. Daniel sounded so normal, so caring. She couldn't possibly be thinking of leaving him, turning him in.

Maggie pulled her hand back as if the receiver was too hot to touch. Too late, too late, she mustn't let Daniel's smooth voice, the image of his charming smile, disarm her.

The call ended. She looked back at the suitcase, half the contents now spread on the floor. She'd automatically sorted them into piles, one for each family member. Instead of a five minute job, she'd spent over an hour and still hadn't found what she needed. By the amount of yellowed paper visible in the case, what remained was too ancient to be of use.

She rifled through them anyway, resisting the temptation to read them in detail. Her initial assumption was correct. On the bottom of the case lay a stiff card embossed with elaborate script, a wedding invitation to her great-grandparents' wedding.

As she picked it up, she grinned. There, underneath, was the driver's license. When she shook the case she must have dislodged it. She scanned it for the expiry date. Yes! There was over a year before it expired, that should give her plenty of time to work something else out. And while the photo wasn't a perfect match it would suffice for a quick glance. All she'd have to remember going forward was her name was not Maggie Cumberland but, instead, Abigail Thornton.

Chapter 9 – Wednesday morning

She scooped up the other paperwork except the birth certificate, dumped it back in the case and stowed the case back in its original place in the closet. The chances of anyone looking in it after she disappeared had to be slim. And if they did, they'd only find documents from the past. There would be no reason for Daniel to think there should be anything more modern.

She hid the license and certificate in a drawer under her sweaters, an extreme precaution, but she didn't want to risk anything going wrong. She started sorting through her clothes, deciding what she should take with her. She pulled her favorite items out, piled them on the bed. Worked through the remainder piece by piece. Some items she'd forgotten about, hadn't worn for years, but even a few of those she decided she couldn't leave behind. Who knew when she'd be able to afford to buy new clothes?

When she finished working through the clothes she started on her shoes and bags. Too bad she couldn't take them all. She liked to match the color of them to her outfits. She chose a few pairs, set them aside and then reconsidered. And then reconsidered again.

She sighed. It was difficult enough deciding what to take on vacation, but at least then she was returning to what she'd left behind. This time she had one chance to get it right. Eventually, after she'd been gone long enough, someone would have to empty out the remains of her closet, send it to a consignment shop or donate it to charity. Jane wouldn't have much use for any of it. She could probably fit all her clothes into one suitcase and have room to spare. Getting her to wear a dress for a special occasion was a major achievement.

Maggie sighed again as she studied the enormous pile on the bed. She was going to need more than one suitcase. But how could she? A second case would hamper her movements. She had no choice but to go through it again and trim it down to what she could fit in one case, ideally a compact one.

But how to do that when she had no idea of what her new life would entail or what kind of clothes she would need? She idly wondered whether Daniel would be able to describe any of the clothes missing from the now half-empty closet. She doubted it, though he might be able to identify which suitcase she'd taken.

She groaned. So much to think about. She needed a break. She went down to the kitchen, put some coffee on and booted up her laptop. She'd check her e-mails for a few minutes and go on Facebook to see what her friends were up to. Too bad she couldn't ask their advice on the ideal wardrobe for someone planning to run away.

She grinned. That would certainly give the game away. She scanned the multitude of unread messages in her inbox, mostly enticements from stores to spend, spend, spend. She deleted them all with one click. She needed fewer clothes not more.

She switched to Facebook, viewed the latest posts. One friend had put up photos from a recent trip to Europe, another, the photo of her latest grandchild. There was the day's funny animal video—this one featuring cats—and a heated discussion about the appropriate punishment for a man on trial accused of murdering a woman several years earlier.

Maggie clicked on the news link. It was the only post that didn't make her sad. The others emphasized the growing gulf she was creating. Once she left she assumed her e-mail and social media accounts would be monitored for activity. She'd have to abandon them. She'd never see the growing grandchild or the next envy-inducing trip. Any future appearances in her friends' newsfeeds would most likely be as the topic of conversation rather than as a participant.

The news story loaded. Maggie skimmed the first few paragraphs. She couldn't remember reading about the original investigation into the woman's disappearance. It had hit the news again because after five years her body had been found and, along with it, evidence the police needed to tie the murder to a neighbor who'd been a prime suspect. Without a body, police hadn't been able to disprove the possibility the woman had merely run away. Tales of an unhappy home life and a potentially emotionally abusive husband had added to the uncertainty. The lead detective in the case claimed he'd never believed that theory for one simple reason. The woman's purse had been found in her abandoned car, her house keys and a full wallet inside. A search of her home suggested that apart from the clothes she was wearing when she was last seen by her husband, none of her personal belongings were missing. If she'd been going to run away, why not take some ID and cash with her?

Maggie reread the detective's claim. Read it a third time. She thought of the pile of clothes on the bed. A clear indication of her intended departure. She didn't usually believe in coincidence but, for some reason, she knew she was meant to read that particular article. It had been put there especially for her to see.

She closed down the open tabs. Raced back upstairs and put every piece of clothing back, taking care to ensure, by the time she finished, her closet and drawers were as ordered as normal.

She checked her wallet. Grimaced. She had some cash, but not enough. She hadn't planned on touching the money in Daniel's study yet, but she had no choice.

She slunk into the room, the enormity of what she was about to do overwhelming the certain knowledge she was alone in the house and would be for hours. She flipped through one of the wads of fifties, counted out a thousand dollars and started to slip them from the band. Hopefully, Daniel wouldn't notice one pile was thinner than the rest.

She hesitated. Pushed the notes back into place and peeled off five instead. From each of the other three bundles she took five more. Problem solved. Daniel would have no reason to suspect some of the notes had gone.

Still, her fingers shook as she closed the clasps on the envelopes. About to put the last one away in the drawer she noticed a tiny tear in the paper. Had it been there all along? She hadn't noticed it before. Surely she would have? The more she thought, the more she was positive the envelopes were pristine. She glanced around, hoping she may have missed Daniel's supply of envelopes when she searched the previous day. Her silent pleading failed to conjure up any.

She looked back at the tear, a clear sign the envelope had been tampered with. She felt a rush of panic. She'd have to buy some more envelopes when she was out, replace it later. There was plenty of time before Daniel came back. Plenty of time. So why didn't it feel as if there was? She stared at the crisp new notes on the desk. She'd never stolen anything in her life and look at her now, stealing money, dirty money. Given the suspected source of the cash, did using it make her complicit in the crime?

It probably did. But what could she do? She needed cash. She wouldn't get far without it and, if it really was the profit from illicit activity, Daniel could hardly file a burglary complaint.

She took a deep breath. She was over-thinking matters. Letting panic and lack of experience build the tiniest flaw into a potential catastrophe. The tear was miniscule, only noticeable by someone whose senses were on high alert. Besides, what chance was there Daniel would even take the envelopes out of the drawer in the near future? Providing there were four envelopes there, he'd hopefully have no reason to check the contents.

Maggie drove to White Plains. The city was far enough away to make it unlikely she'd bump into anyone she knew and it also had a wide range of stores so she'd be able to pick up what she needed in one trip. She started at Target, bought the basics and added the cheapest weekend case she could find. Next, she moved on to Staples where she resisted the sales talk about faster, brighter, better, and chose the cheapest laptop they had on offer. On the drive over she'd debated about going without a computer, but since she'd decided against buying a new cell phone—she wasn't savvy enough to know how to buy one that couldn't be tracked—the convenience of information at her fingertips was worth the expense.

The shopping complete, she stopped for a coffee, taking the break to mentally check she hadn't forgotten anything. Except she had. She still needed shoes and a bag to carry her laptop in. By the time she drove home there wasn't much of the thousand dollars left.

She carted the bags into her son's room. Took everything out of the packaging, tore off the labels and packed the clothes and toiletries in the suitcase. They just fit.

She gathered up the wrappings and squashed them into one of the plastic bags and took it straight out to the garbage can. As she raised the lid, she hesitated, the bag poised over the opening. The can was empty. The next garbage collection was not for three days. In the crime novels she read the police often sifted through the garbage looking for clues. Would her disappearance register as a crime before the next collection? She shut the lid. Put the bag on the passenger seat of her car. She'd have to find somewhere else to dump it.

She hurried back into the house, her mind racing, replaying her movements over the last twenty-four hours. If shopping tags and receipts could provide evidence, what else could? It could be something so innocent, so ordinary she'd never consider it might give her game away.

Except it was hardly a game.

She went back to Craig's room. Stowed the suitcase in his closet. Daniel had no reason to go into Craig's bedroom so it should be a safe enough place for the night. Now, all she had to do was get the laptop up and running.

She checked the time. Still several hours until Daniel would be home. She had no idea what footprints using a computer left, but caution ruled, so she drove to the library and used the internet service there to personalize the laptop and set up an e-mail account under the name of Abigail Thornton.

She also researched bus and train times, the only options for transport she could think of. True, with a driver's license she could get on an internal flight, but who paid cash for an airline ticket these days? It was a red flag she'd rather avoid.

On the drive home, she pulled into a shopping mall and dumped her garbage bag into the first trash can she saw. Back in the car, she slumped against the seat. Exhaled heavily. She'd covered her bases, thought of everything.

She was sure she'd thought of everything.

She switched on the engine. All she had to do now was get through one more evening with Daniel.

Chapter 10 – Thursday morning

Maggie eyed the tiny suitcase by the front door. Not much to show for twenty-two years of marriage. Tears welled as she took one last look around the elegant hallway of her home. She'd always loved this house since the moment they'd first seen it. It hurt to have to walk away.

She blinked hard, thrust back her shoulders. This wasn't the time for weakness or doubts. She'd made her plan, taken the first steps and now had no alternative but to follow through on her decision. The time to cry would come later.

She strode toward the door, her three inch heels clicking against the marble floor. In less than half an hour, Mila would be here, punctual as ever, and one of the few people she hadn't lied to yet. She didn't want to start now. Mila had been with the Cumberlands for most of their married life, coming in two mornings a week to clean and do the laundry and, unbeknown to Daniel, act as a confidant whenever Maggie needed a little one-to-one female advice that she didn't want to share with her friends. Maggie trusted Mila's discretion, but didn't dare tell her she was leaving. How could she, when she couldn't tell her why? Besides, surely the less Mila knew the better. She would be as puzzled by Mrs. Cumberland's disappearance as anyone.

Maggie opened the front door and peered out. Nine-thirty in the morning and most of the neighbors should be at work, school, the gym or Starbucks, leaving only the housekeepers, the nannies and the babies as potential witnesses to her departure. The street was as deserted as she'd hoped.

She grabbed the suitcase and pulled the door closed behind her, the click overly loud to her heightened senses, a solitary drumbeat heralding an end.

And a beginning, she reminded herself as she loaded the case into the trunk of the car while still scanning the street for any sign of life. An end also brought a new beginning. Well, apart from death, though even that was debatable depending on one's religious beliefs. She shuddered. Death. The reason she was running.

The slam of the trunk door, the thud of the driver's door closing, the snap of the seatbelt locking into place, each added to the sense of finality. She shuddered again, checked her rearview mirror and reversed the car down the short driveway and into the road.

She allowed one last look back at the house as she switched the car into drive. Once she'd imagined she'd live there until she died. She'd never imagined that one day it would be the fear of death that would force her out.

The roads to downtown were quiet. Only two cars passed her before she reached the village railway station, neither familiar. She could probably park there and take the train without anyone seeing her, but it would leave too obvious a trail. She needed time to get away before anyone connected the dots and figured nothing untoward had happened to her.

She bypassed the station, headed south and west until she came to a late-opening supermarket near a train station on the Hudson line. There was no logical reason for anyone looking for her to think she'd leave her car there, she only knew of its existence from research she'd done on her new laptop, and hopefully it would be a while before someone noticed it appeared to have been abandoned.

She found a spot between two vehicles on the crowded side of the lot nearest both the supermarket entrance and the exit to the road. To be seen wheeling her case away from the store might attract attention. Probably a groundless fear, but why take the chance? When she was sure no one else was around she got out of the car, retrieved her case from the trunk, and hurried toward the street.

Overcome with anxiety, her heart pounded way too fast and she had to gulp for each breath as the enormity of what she was doing finally washed over her. She wanted to go home. She wanted everything to be normal again. Her husband to be the man she'd thought he was until a few days ago. A few days! How could someone's life change so quickly? It shouldn't be possible.

A crowd waited on the platform for the first off-peak train of the day. The sight of others with suitcases made Maggie smile. She was just another traveler, one among many, unworthy of a second glance. The smile faded as she spotted a portly businessman eyeing her up. She hurried past him, her face turned from his as she pretended to watch for the train. Once she'd put a decent distance between them to prevent any chance they'd end up in the same car she kept her back angled toward him despite the overwhelming temptation to check back and see if he was still looking her way.

The station intercom crackled. An officious voice announced the train to Grand Central was running approximately ten minutes late. A collective sigh rippled along the platform.

Maggie grimaced. Why today of all days? She'd planned this stage so meticulously. It came with the greatest risks. She could have taken a cab into the city but even if the driver had picked her up from somewhere other than her home and dropped her off somewhere other than Penn Station, chances were he'd still remember her well enough to identify her as one of his passengers if anyone asked. And they would ask—maybe not today, but tomorrow or the next day—so much better to keep her movements as anonymous as possible.

Maybe she should have done more to change her appearance, but if she had been seen leaving the house or in her car that would have aroused curiosity in itself. She had a reputation for being a smart, if staid, dresser even if she was only going to the supermarket. Besides, why risk revealing her new persona of Abigail Thornton until she was well away from anyone who knew her as Maggie Cumberland?

Chapter 11 - Thursday morning

The journey to Grand Central took thirty minutes. Guilt and fear made it seem much longer. The likelihood of anyone she knew getting on the Hudson Line train was miniscule but still every stop stretched her patience to snapping point before allowing a few minutes of relief as the train headed for the next station.

She maneuvered her way among the throng of passengers exiting the platform into the lower level food court and stayed close to a group of middle-aged travelers wheeling their suitcases up the ramp past the Oyster Bar to the main concourse.

Outside, she ignored the line of taxis, crossed the street and headed south down Park Avenue. When she and Daniel traveled it was by car or plane. The idea of going somewhere by train would never enter his head, which is why it seemed like the perfect solution. True, once the police were involved—and he would have to involve the police, wouldn't he?—they would consider all options but as she'd left a purse with her driver's license and credit cards behind for them to find, hopefully they'd focus on other, more grizzly, explanations for her disappearance.

Would they suspect Daniel? Probably. Wasn't the closest relative always the first person of interest in a missing person's case? The thought induced a momentary sense of guilt as she waited for the lights to change at 35th Street.

Daniel didn't deserve it. He'd been a kind, loving husband. Yes, he had his faults—his inability to do anything domestic, the most frustrating—but he'd been a good provider allowing her to stay home and raise their son without having to worry about the financial side of life. They'd sailed unaffected through the recent recession, unlike some of their friends who'd faced down-sizing, foreclosure and relationships under severe strain. Sadly, she'd even witnessed the complete breakdown of the marriage of a close friend whose lifestyle Maggie had envied on those rare days of discontent until she discovered the lifestyle was built on credit.

She choked back a sob as she headed down 34th Street, ignoring cajoles from the ticket sellers exhorting the delights of a trip to the top of the Empire State Building.

She'd never voiced her thoughts, of course, but she'd been smug about how her reliable husband with his dedicated approach and charming personality had not only managed to keep working throughout the recession but had actually scored a new position as Chief Financial Officer for a small privately owned company that, with bonuses, would double his take home pay.

True, the job involved longer and longer hours, but Daniel assured her once he'd got himself established that would change, as too would the golfing weekends. He'd laugh and roll his eyes when he mentioned those because she knew how much he disliked golf, but at the early stage in his new role he couldn't politely extract himself from the invitations. "Be thankful," he'd say, "the wives don't come along too. You'd hate it." And Maggie would realize how lucky she was because her idea of hell was to have to hobnob with a group of wealthy women whose only connection was their husbands' jobs.

How could she have been so stupid? So blind?

She lowered her head, aware of the imminent tears that threatened to flow if she allowed her mind to continue on such thoughts for a second longer. Instead she forced her concentration onto navigating the oncoming crowds, weaving a path around the lower limbs appearing in her line of sight.

"Hey, watch it!" a gruff male voice yelled, presumably at her as her case bumped against something for an instant.

She charged on without looking to see the cause of the indignation. Why didn't people watch where they were walking? They could surely see she was in a hurry. Why should she be the one who always had to move aside?

Her pace increased as an overwhelming rage built inside. She was not a fool. She was not invisible. How dare people treat her as such?

Someone grabbed her by the arm, hard enough to yank her back a step. She spun toward the offender, ready to lash out, as the draft from a passing taxi brought her to her senses.

She gulped, shivered at the thought of how narrow her escape had been. She hadn't noticed the "do not walk" signal or even the crowd of pedestrians standing at the curbside. She'd allowed her anger to take her straight out into the road. She managed to clear the blur of tears from her eyes and face her savior.

"I hope I didn't hurt you," the young man said as he let go of her arm.

She almost laughed at the idiocy of the comment, but realized he appeared to be as shaken as she felt. And far from being invisible, she now had the attention of a crowd of people who must be wondering what kind of idiot she was to step out in front of oncoming traffic.

She managed a mumbled "Thank you." A paltry response given he'd probably saved her life. She shuddered again. For a second pictured herself lying broken in the road. And when the police finally connected the dots and linked Abigail Thornton to Daniel, what would he have thought? Would he realize why she felt it necessary to leave home under a false identity? Would he feel guilty? Blame himself? Because he should. This whole mess was his doing.

She could feel the tears well up again.

"Are you okay?" Her savior looked uncomfortable as if he

didn't know how to behave after saving a life. Who did?

"Yes." Maggie shook her head. "I'm sorry. I was miles away. Thank you again. You saved my life."

The man noticed her suitcase.

"You from out of town?" Before she could respond he added, "The traffic in this city is crazy. You have to be real careful crossing the roads."

How many times had she lectured Craig on the very same subject while he was growing up, his increasing forays into the city a constant concern? And now here was someone not much older than him lecturing her.

The light changed.

"Take care." He dashed off across the street before she had a chance to tell him she was a life-long New Yorker. She stood routed to the spot, watching him disappear into the crowd, suddenly aware of her vulnerability. Alone. Unable to reach out to anyone she knew. Not even a close friend who she could confide in. This was the path she had chosen. She glanced back the way she'd come. She could go back. It wasn't too late. Daniel wouldn't even be aware she'd been planning to leave. Life could go on as normal, or at least until the police turned up on the doorstep. And then she'd have to lie and fake surprise, disbelief, outrage, horror.

The light changed to red. Another group of pedestrians surrounded her. There was still time to go back. If she returned immediately nobody would be any the wiser to her intentions. She shuffled back from the edge of the sidewalk. Let those more impatient than her push in front.

Home, safety, security, beckoned.

Home, safety…

No. No safety. Daniel had made sure of that.

Daniel had ruined everything.

Chapter 12 – Thursday morning

Maggie checked the departure board at Penn Station. The North East Regional was expected to arrive on time which gave her thirty minutes after she purchased her ticket to complete the next stage of her plan. Luck was on her side. There was no line in the ladies room and the few women using the sinks and mirrors would hopefully be gone before she re-emerged.

She pulled her case into the disabled-access cubicle, grateful to see the floor was both clear of tissue and relatively clean. As she locked the door she exhaled hard, letting a rush of tension out. So far so good. It was unlikely anyone would be aware that the woman who went into the cubicle looked very different from the one who came out.

She opened her case. Slipped out of her heels and stripped off her navy linen suit and cream silk blouse, replaced them with a pair of pre-faded jeans and a simple navy T-shirt. Without the benefit of a full length mirror she could only imagine what she looked like. When was the last time she'd worn jeans or even sneakers for anything other than going to the gym? Sneakers so white, they screamed new. Maybe she should have worn them in a little or opted for the colored ones, but she didn't particularly like those, they were so hard to color coordinate.

Or maybe she was being paranoid. Why should anyone notice? Or care?

Still, with the compact mirror and the wipes she'd brought especially for the purpose, she removed the make-up she'd carefully applied as usual earlier that morning. She grimaced at the sight of her bare face, nearly harder to accept than the casual clothes. Was she being ridiculous? Maybe watched too many movies? She was just another face in the crowd. But it would only take one, one eagle-eyed observer to ruin her plans, so yes, this was necessary. Besides, she didn't have any make-up with her to reapply.

She raked her fingers through her auburn sleek hair, pulled it up from her shoulders into a high ponytail and wrapped the ends into a tight bun. Tendrils of hair brushed her neck and face confirming the haphazard attempt at hairstyling. Exactly the look she was aiming for.

She packed up her suit and shoes into the case, double-checked to make sure she hadn't left anything behind and exited the cubicle. She let out an involuntary gasp as she caught sight of her full reflection. She barely recognized the plain-looking woman who stared back at her. She moved slowly toward the mirror, half expecting her real self to suddenly materialize.

A strange glance from the woman who pushed past her to go into the now vacant cubicle jerked her back to reality. She washed her hands, taking longer than necessary so she'd have an excuse to stare into the mirror, and rearranged her hair, scooping up a few of the loose tendrils while she tried to act as if this was an everyday occurrence.

How could clothes and make-up make such a difference to a person's appearance? She'd always considered herself attractive enough, not a great beauty by any means, but presentable. But this vision before her—dowdy was the first word that came to mind. As if she didn't care to make the effort to present an attractive façade to the world, and yet, there was something else, something she couldn't quite put her finger on. She shook off the feeling.

Whatever it was, it would come to her eventually, and she didn't have the time to stand gaping at the mirror.

Back at the departures board she eased her way into the middle of the crowd. The train still showed as on time. A flood of people appeared on the escalators coming up from a lower platform. Some of the waiting people immediately moved toward Gate 9 even though a gate number had yet to be announced. Maggie assumed they were seasoned travelers who knew the routine and decided to follow them. Her instincts proved right as the announcement over the loud speakers brought a rush of people up behind her. She scanned the crowd for any familiar faces, barely able to breathe until she'd reassured herself there weren't any.

Despite her place in line the train car was almost full when she got on. She'd just settled into one of the few remaining window seats, her backpack on the seat next to her to deter anyone from sitting there, when she became aware of someone lingering in the aisle close by. She pretended not to notice, silently praying for them to move on.

"Excuse me, is this seat taken?"

Dare she say it was?

She sighed. Forced a smile as she moved her bag to the floor, first pulling out a novel as a signal she didn't want conversation. "No."

The guy swung a small carry-on bag onto the overhead rack and sank heavily into the seat. "Phew. Nearly missed it."

Maggie opened her book. Hoped he'd take the hint.

"That would have been a disaster. First big assignment and I mess it up before I even start."

The words sent a chill down her spine. An assignment. What kind of assignment? She could ask. Reassure herself he wasn't on the trail of a missing woman. But that would involve a conversation and she didn't want that. It would be too easy at this stage to say something inappropriate and raise suspicions. She needed time to acclimatize to her new identity, get her story straight. Besides, how could anyone be following her? Nobody knew about her escape. Not even Daniel. Or the police.

She ignored him. Pretended to read. The train pulled out of

the station. She wanted to look out of the window, catch her last glimpses of New York, but if she did the guy might try to strike up a conversation. As it was, she could sense him watching her so she made sure to turn the pages at reasonable intervals. Her thoughts were racing so fast no way could she take in the words. It was almost a four hour journey to Washington, DC. Was she going to have to keep this pretence up all the way?

After a decent interval of silence she tried to sneak a sidewise glance at her neighbor. He'd barely moved since he'd sat down and his rudeness at making her feel uncomfortable irked to the point where she was ready to take him to task for it. When she finally could stand it no longer she turned to confront him. His head was tilted toward her, his chin on his chest—she could practically guarantee he'd end up with a stiff neck—but he was asleep and likely had been for most of the time while she fumed.

She shook her head at her own stupidity. A polite exchange when he'd first sat down and she could have saved herself all this angst. She couldn't treat everyone as a potential enemy or she'd drive herself crazy. This guy would get off the train and never give another thought to the non-descript woman he'd sat next to. Just as if she were asked to describe him at a later date, she wouldn't get much past male.

Except the very thought made her take a second look at him. The first word that came to mind was average. Average height, average weight and average looks. Okay, the latter was a subjective judgment, but the guy neither made her heart beat faster nor repulsed her, so in her view that made him average. His clothes didn't set him apart either: jeans, a white shirt open at the neck and a slate-gray sports jacket. But put him in a business suit or a uniform or gym gear and, more than likely, she'd pass him in the street without a second glance.

And if that was true for him it should be true for her. Clothes were a convenient disguise, giving no real indication of the person within. The guy could be the sweetest man on the planet or he could be a serial killer. He could be a heart-breaker or a sad, solitary man. And even if they spent the rest of the journey talking, there'd be no guarantee he'd be telling the truth. She'd never know whether he was spinning a story just as she was. She'd opted for a life of lies to save her life but it came with a heavy price. Where previously she'd been trustworthy and trusting, now she had to face up to the idea of being deceptive and cynical.

Her heart grieved for her loss of innocence.

Chapter 13 – Thursday morning

Her neighbor slept most of the way to Washington. When he woke he went to the cafe car, first asking her if she would like a drink. Might as well save one of them the trek, he added and smiled. An attractive smile, the kind that would make most women look twice.

She declined his offer which was just as well as he didn't reappear until moments before the train was due to arrive in the capital.

"Have you been to Washington before?" he asked.

"No, have you?"

"Years ago. With my parents. Can't say I remember much about it. So are you going for business or pleasure?"

Maggie hesitated, reluctant to divulge even the smallest part of her plan. For all he knew she could be going on further than Washington, but he would see her get off the train there so it was time to begin the lies.

"Pleasure. I'm visiting friends for a few days."

He grimaced. "Nice. Unfortunately I'm here strictly on business."

"What kind of—"

She broke off as the guard announced the train would shortly be arriving in Washington, DC, and passengers leaving the train should gather their belongings.

The guy leapt to his feet and reached up to the overhead rack. "The blue case yours?"

"Yes."

"Here, let me get it down for you." He pulled his bag halfway off the rack. "Damn, the strap's caught."

He pushed the bag back, stretched up and fumbled with it for a few seconds before sweeping it down with a triumphant gesture. Maggie's case came off the rack with ease.

"This is it? I'm impressed. My ex-girlfriend used to pack for a weekend as if she was going for a month."

He slid her case into the space in front of his seat, hoisted his own bag by the shoulder strap and smiled down at her.

"Pleasure meeting you. Enjoy DC."

"You too," she hastily added as he sauntered off toward the end of the car. She allowed herself a moment to relax. All in all, the journey hadn't gone too badly. In future, she needed to tamper down her imagination, stop seeing potential threats at every turn. Accept that most people she met were simply ordinary people going about their normal lives with absolutely no reason to think she was any different.

Union Station buzzed with people who knew where they were going. Maggie stepped to one side to let them past while she debated what to do. She regretted the caution which had kept her from making any advance plans other than the one train to Washington, DC. She'd wanted to keep her options open, be able to react immediately to unforeseen events that gave her cause for concern.

Her plan to work out her next move while on the train had been cast aside by the irrational concern about her fellow passenger. As if he might somehow be able to read her thoughts. How stupid given he was asleep or in the cafe car for most of the journey. That was the problem with being on edge—it messed up her thought processes. She guessed for some people it might bring total clarity. Why wasn't she one of those?

The flow of passengers from the New York train thinned out. She needed to make a move so she meandered along the passageway until she spotted an Au Bon Pain cafe, as good a place as any to take refuge while she decided.

She bought a coffee and a pastry and found a seat at a corner table in the rear of the cafe. Hopefully no one would bother her. She switched on her laptop. If she was going to stay in the city she'd need a hotel. If she couldn't find anything reasonably priced she'd have no choice but to move on. Ideally she wanted something close to a metro station. As far as possible she wanted to avoid taxis.

She gasped at the prices of the first few options, the nightly rates way out of her league. When they'd traveled in the past, Daniel had always made the arrangements and she'd never enquired about the cost. If Daniel said they could afford it that was all that mattered.

She changed the search priority from distance to price. While she waited for the page to reload she checked out her surroundings. She was the only solitary traveler not in a suit.

The alternative options were much more reasonable, assuming she didn't mind going miles outside the city center. Which she did, she needed to be central though she couldn't explain why.

She scrolled down the list. Why didn't the site let her choose both price and distance? Suddenly, she noticed the sidebar with exactly those options. She selected the downtown area. The prices were still more expensive than she'd hoped but after all she'd been through she decided she deserved one night of comfort. Too bad she couldn't charge it to Daniel's credit card. She smirked. If she was going to do that she'd stay at the best hotel in town. But that would give away her location. Besides, she didn't have the secondary card with her.

She used Google Maps to check out the location of a few of the options in terms of distance from Union Station. Decided an independent hotel would be a less obvious choice than one of the chains. She found one which boasted of being a short walk from the White House and other major sightseeing attractions. She could play tourist to fill in the hours when she wasn't fretting about her future. By fleeing she'd launched herself into a strange limbo of having nothing which had to be done. Well, nothing except to stay out of the clutches of Daniel, the police or, more importantly, Daniel's employers.

She shivered.

Daniel's employers, a successful privately-owned company specializing in the international distribution of luxury goods. Goods so expensive, the extortionate shipping fee was inconsequential to the buyer. What mattered was the safe delivery of the goods in question whether it was a container of high end purses for a retail conglomerate or an exotic antique piece for a multi-millionaire's personal collection. Mastersons Distribution would make sure it arrived in perfect condition.

Daniel had shown her the beautifully designed website when he'd first been offered the job. She hadn't known he was looking for a new position, but he'd explained how a headhunter had called him out of the blue and been so persuasive he'd agreed to follow up on it, not expecting anything to come of it, which is why he hadn't mentioned it to her. And then to his total surprise he'd not only been offered the job, but on terms he'd have been an idiot to turn down.

And like an idiot, she'd believed him.

Chapter 14 – Thursday afternoon

Tears welled in her eyes. How could she have been so naïve? Yet how was she supposed to know anything was amiss? They were an ordinary family, perhaps a little more successful than others, but compared to some of their neighbors nothing to boast about. She'd given up work when their son was born, content to be a stay-at-home mom, making Craig her focus. When he started full-time school, she filled in her spare time helping out at a local women's shelter. They had a nice home, took yearly vacations, usually to the New Jersey Shore, and belonged to a local club with a pool and tennis. Why should she have had any suspicions all was not as it seemed? There had to be some element of trust in life surely or what was the point?

She sensed a couple at the adjacent table staring at her. Had she spoken out loud? She dabbed at her eyes and gathered up her belongings without looking in their direction. As she tossed her trash, she finally glanced back. They were holding hands across the table, laughing, engrossed in each other. She envied them their innocence.

She followed directions down to the metro. By comparison to the New York subway the station was modern and clean, but the ticket machines were archaic. She stood flummoxed, trying to work out how much she needed to pay and how to get a ticket. She wasn't alone in having problems. A man offered to help the couple at a nearby machine. She tried to listen in but the guy simply asked questions and pressed buttons so she still couldn't figure it out. When he'd finished he came over to her.

"Here, let me help. Where are you going?"

She told him. He pressed a couple of buttons and told her to insert three dollars seventy-five. She slid a five dollar bill into the required slot. As the ticket emerged the guy grabbed it and handed it to her with a flourish after she'd collected her change.

"That will be a dollar," he said before she could thank him.

She frowned as he held out his hand.

"For services rendered." He smirked, revealing a mouth full of tobacco-stained teeth.

"Aren't you…" Maggie left the sentence unfinished as she took in the torn jeans and filthy shirt of the man she'd assumed was a station employee. He was a panhandler who'd come up with an ingenious way to make money from unsuspecting tourists. And he knew she had a dollar in her hands.

She was tempted to refuse him, but she didn't like the way his expression changed as she hesitated. And now there was no one else at the machines to help her if he got angry, so she slapped the dollar into his hand and marched off.

She fumed all the way on the metro, ashamed she'd given in so easily. She was on her own now. She had to be strong, couldn't let others run her around. If she couldn't even deal with a panhandler in the station how did she think she was going to cope with all life's other challenges?

The rage receded as she walked into the hotel lobby. The gleaming marble walls, the huge floral arrangement under the glittering chandelier, the uniformed doorman who opened the door and the low hum of polite conversation offered a temporary respite to her insecurities. The receptionist greeted her with a huge smile, the smile turning slightly askance when Maggie told her she'd be paying in cash. The woman asked for ID anyhow, a request Maggie had been hoping she could avoid.

Fingers fumbling, she pulled the driver's license from her purse and passed it across the counter. She held her breath while the receptionist gave it a cursory glance, handed it back and informed her there would be a hundred dollar deposit to cover any extras.

"There won't be any extras."

The receptionist's smile came back. "Then you'll get your deposit back in full when you check out."

Maggie grimaced.

"If you pay by credit card, we'd use your card as a guarantee."

Maggie handed over six fifty dollar bills and waited while the receptionist checked each one.

They're not counterfeit, Maggie wanted to tell her. Who do you think I am? I'm a respectable, innocent woman who happens to be surrounded by crooks. No, not crooks. They're villains, evil villains who trade in the worst kind of business, but not me. I'm not like that, and my money is clean. Except she'd taken it from Daniel's filing cabinet so how did she know for sure and how could she insist she was innocent?

She wanted to snatch the money back and run. But it was the only money she had. What else could she do? The notion the money might be counterfeit had never crossed her mind. It looked genuine enough and the sleek efficient receptionist had no idea where the money came from. So she needed to hold herself together for a while longer, pretend all was well with her world until she got the key and could hide in the room and work out how to deal with the latest nauseating realization.

"Room 304. The elevator is around the corner to the left." The receptionist pointed in the general direction as she handed the key card over.

Maggie mumbled her thanks, gripped her suitcase handle and strolled as nonchalantly as she could over to the elevator. A few more minutes and she could drop the façade, if indeed she'd ever managed one. Her insides appeared to be at odds with one another. Chills tickled her spine even as a rush of heat swept through her. Her heartbeat pounded erratically, her stomach rumbled ominously. Even the act of walking felt unnatural, her legs threatening to give way with every step.

She glanced over her shoulder. The receptionist had turned her back. The doorman pulled cases from the trunk of a limousine. Nobody paid the slightest attention to her, had any idea of her internal chaos.

The elevator was empty. She sagged back against the wall for support. This had seemed like a great plan at the time, but now she had no idea whether she had the strength to cope.

Chapter 15 – Thursday afternoon

The temptation to hide away in her room proved overwhelming. Maggie didn't unpack. There wasn't much to unpack anyway and she couldn't afford to stay at the hotel another night so there was no point. She drank her way through the free coffee and tea the hotel provided, the latter black because she'd already used up the creamer.

She knew this wasn't the best use of her time. She should be planning out her next steps, but sitting alone in a strange hotel room, the enormity of what she'd done crashed down on her in alternative waves of guilt and fear that paralyzed her. Her mind focused only on the past, wouldn't let her consider the future. How could there be a future when everything she believed in and had worked for had crumbled away?

Except for her son.

She hadn't been too thrilled with the idea of Craig, fresh out of high school, volunteering at a school in Africa. It was too far away, too dangerous—the headline news from the region talked of rebel armies, kidnapping and bomb explosions—the very idea terrifying her. Craig had tried to reassure her. The school was in Botswana, a democratic country with a thriving economy. The reason she knew so little about it was because it was rarely in the news, unlike Somalia, Nigeria or Kenya.

Okay, safe, she'd wanted to protest, but still too far away. Why couldn't he volunteer at a school in America, somewhere he could hop on a plane and visit them for a weekend or they could visit him. What was the big attraction about Africa?

His answer stunned her. It was different he said. Different from the middle-class, mostly white neighborhood he'd been brought up in. He needed to experience diversity, see the world from an alternative perspective, or he'd end up just another middle-aged suburban guy who believed the world revolved around America or, worse, whatever city or small town he happened to end up in.

"You mean like us," she'd wanted to interject. She could hardly believe her son was criticizing his upbringing and even his parents. Neither she nor Daniel had traveled much outside of the northeast apart from the occasional vacation to some exotic resort in the Caribbean. They'd never felt the need, didn't really have the time.

To her surprise, Daniel agreed it would be good for Craig to travel. In fact, now she thought about it, he'd been overeager for Craig to take up the opportunity. He'd rebutted all her objections, paid for his plane ticket, ensured he had decent travel insurance, and deposited what he referred to as emergency funds into his bank account.

At the time she assumed the financial help was to reassure her Craig wouldn't be penniless in a foreign country, but maybe there'd been an ulterior motive. Had Daniel wanted to get Craig out of the way for some reason? Afraid his inquisitive son might discover the truth about his father's real line of work? Discover that the private distribution company not only transported works of art and luxury goods, but also girls and who knew what else?

Her flimsy resolve cracked. She slumped onto the bed in a fetal position. Tears streamed down her face, her gulp-inducing sobs unstoppable. She had no one to comfort her, no one to offer reassurance, and not the faintest idea of where to turn for support. She thumped the mattress. There had to be someone out there who could help, a group or something, a helpline for spouses of lying scum who were willing to put their families at risk for God knows what personal benefit.

True, Detective Abbot had mentioned the possibility of eventual witness protection if she testified, but the mere thought terrified her. Who knew how powerful the kind of organization her husband worked for was? How far their tentacles of influence had spread? They'd managed to corrupt her law-abiding husband, hadn't they? Who else might be in their pay? It would only take one rogue cop in the investigation to point the finger at her and give away her whereabouts. No. Far better to engineer her own disappearance and not have to worry that someone else would betray her.

But how could she explain this to her son? They had been a close family. How would he cope with the sudden news his mother had disappeared and his father was a criminal? What would it do to him? He'd have no one to turn to either.

Her first instincts had been to fly out to Botswana, tell Craig of his father's crimes personally, and explain why she needed to disappear. Even suggest it might be in his best interest to consider it too. But she would need to use her passport and that would leave a potential trail not only to her but also to Craig. She didn't dare risk it.

When the sobs turned to whimpers and the tears ceased, she pushed up off the bed and staggered into the bathroom. Her reflection startled her. It wasn't the blotchy face or the red-rimmed eyes that took her by surprise but the glimpse of her younger self, before she married Daniel, when jeans were her uniform of choice, albeit a choice made to fit in with her peers. Her figure had barely changed. From the shoulders down she could still be twenty-one years old.

She splashed her face with cold water over and over again as if she wanted to wash away the years from her face too. It didn't work, but it eased the blotches and with the coolness came a sense of calm. Who knew how long it would last, but she had to make the most of it. Lying, crying in a hotel would not achieve anything and it was too early to scan the internet and television for any mention of her disappearance.

She locked her laptop and all but a small amount of her cash in the room safe, grabbed her purse and headed out. She'd never been to Washington. She might as well make the most of this unexpected visit.

Chapter 16 – Friday morning

At daybreak Maggie sat propped up in bed against a multitude of pillows, yawning furiously while she waited for her laptop to access the hotel internet. The night had been torturous, the red digits on the alarm clock operating in slow motion, each chaotic dream-filled doze moving them on a mere ten or fifteen minutes. The miles she'd walked, past the White House and all the way down to Washington Harbor and back, plus the two glasses of wine she had after dinner had failed in their roles as sleep aids. Not that she'd had any grand illusions about a solid seven hours sleep but even an hour would have been nice.

One by one she scanned her local online news sites for the slightest mention of Maggie or Daniel Cumberland or Mastersons Distribution. Futile really, it was far too soon for the press to have got hold of any part of the story. But this was going to be her life now, gleaning vital information from news reports in her strive to stay safe.

As she checked each site she bookmarked it for future use. When she'd exhausted all possibilities she returned to the first, her heart skipping a beat at the latest headline, "Police issue alert for missing local woman."

She clicked on the link staring transfixed at the screen as the article took an age to load. The picture of an elderly lady snapped her back to reality. A ninety-year-old had wandered from her home late the previous evening dressed only in her nightgown. Her family was desperate to find her.

Maggie sighed. So nobody desperate to find her yet. How well had Daniel slept? She hoped he hadn't. She hoped he'd never sleep well again, the lying bastard.

She slapped the laptop shut and leapt out of bed. She had to focus her anger, use it to her benefit. Not let it eat away at the little self-esteem she had left. She checked the hotel guest guide. The fitness room and pool opened at six. She hadn't thought to buy a swimsuit or gym clothes, but she did have leggings and a t-shirt which would do.

The hotel corridors were deserted, the tiny fitness room empty. She switched on the television, surfed through the channels until she found an affiliate news show. Not that she expected to see anything about her own predicament but any police action against Mastersons Distribution might well hit the national media.

How long would it take the police to act on what she'd told them? She guessed they'd have to check she wasn't an aggrieved wife wanting to get her husband into trouble. But how would they do that without letting on to Daniel that she'd ratted on him and his employers?

She upped the speed on the treadmill, the need to run faster spurred by a sudden realization. What if either Daniel or his company got wind of what she'd done before the police could take action and they fled too? Then she'd have no idea where they were or what they were doing, or how close they were to finding her.

She upped the speed again. And again. Until all she could think of was putting one foot in front of the other fast enough so she didn't fall over.

When she slowed to a walk, hands on her aching sides, gasping for breath, she noticed a man had come into the gym. He sat on the stationery bike behind her, his movements languid, reminiscent of someone out for a leisurely ride rather than for a workout.

He grinned. "Did you get away?"

"What?"

He recoiled at the sharp tone in her voice. Raised a hand. "Hey, only joking. You were running as if you were being chased."

Maggie shook her head, her voice failing her. A rush of heat infused her already-flushed cheeks.

A look of concern replaced his grin. "You okay?"

Maggie bit her lip. The sudden desire to unload to a complete stranger threatened to loosen her tongue.She made to speak. Reason prevailed at the last moment.

"I'm fine. Thank you." She dashed from the gym before he could say anything else.

Back in the safety of her own room she sat on the bed and stared into space. She had no idea what to do next. She had nothing to do, nowhere to be. It was Friday. Normally she'd spend the morning at the shelter, have lunch with a friend, and the afternoon puttering around the house and garden. Even with Mila coming in two mornings a week there was always something that needed doing.

Sometimes she dreamed of having a completely free day, a day of no responsibilities which, even on vacation, she found hard to achieve. Now the day spread before her, its emptiness offering endless hours to worry.

At least the room had been a good choice. It was small but cozy with furnishings tending toward the old-fashioned rather than the modern. She liked it. It provided a much needed aura of comfort and security.

Where would she spend the coming night? She had no idea, only the vague plan she should keep moving on. So really her sense of having nothing to do was an illusion, one built out of fear, because she should be researching train times and possible destinations, checking out potential hotels even if she didn't want to reserve anything until the last minute. But she didn't want to do it, didn't want to admit the itinerant nature of her current life. To admit it confirmed that what had happened in the last few days had been real, not a horrible dream, and no matter how much she tried she still couldn't get her mind around that.

This was real. Real. Real.

Chapter 17 – Friday morning

She took a shower. Rechecked the headlines—they hadn't changed since an hour ago—and reluctantly pulled up the Amtrak map. Where to go? She could go to Chicago and, later, on to the west coast, to Los Angeles, San Francisco or Seattle. Or she could head south to Florida or New Orleans. There were too many options. If she wanted she could spend the next few days on the train, always moving. It would make it harder for anyone to track her down and if she slept on the train it would save on hotels. From the description online if she booked a sleeper she would have self-contained space to herself. She could hide away for the whole journey if she wanted to. Really, she couldn't ask for a better solution.

But which way? West or south? She sighed. She couldn't remember the last time she'd been free to make such a momentous decision. No one to consider, no need to compromise, the future was hers to create.

She paced the room.

It was a heady feeling, liberating, exhilarating and

downright scary. She'd give it all up in a second if she could just go back to her life as it had been a week ago.

How could it be so hard to make a decision? She stopped pacing, closed her eyes. Where would she like to go? She opened her eyes. She didn't have a clue. Had never considered it before. She wasn't a traveler. Not like her sister, Jane. Jane was the complete opposite. Loved to travel so much she'd rarely stayed in one place for long until two years earlier when she'd stunned Maggie by announcing she was getting married and moving to San Francisco.

Six months ago she'd announced she was pregnant and asked Maggie to come out for the birth.

It would have been her first trip to the west coast. Daniel had given his approval. The plane tickets had been purchased. They sat in the bureau in the bedroom, never to be used now. She hoped the news of her disappearance wouldn't devastate her sister, affect her pregnancy. They hadn't been particularly close since Maggie finished school, their lives so different in every respect. Jane couldn't understand how Maggie could settle into what she considered a mundane old-fashioned lifestyle while she'd wondered why Jane didn't seem to need someone else in her life.

With their parents both dead, Jane was the only immediate family she had. When she'd heard about the pregnancy she'd secretly hoped this might be a chance for them to become close again. Recent events had put an end to that hope. Their roles had reversed, except now she couldn't ever have her sister in her life again. If only she could go and hide out with Jane in San Francisco, but that would be one of the first places Daniel would check.

Then he'd check her friends from the shelter, her book club and tennis. Some of them might be more than willing to help her under the circumstances but it would only take one of them to say the wrong thing and give the game away. Far better to keep her plans to herself.

How would they react when they heard she'd disappeared? No doubt she'd be the center of gossip for the next few weeks. But then what? Gradually forgotten as more current pressing personal issues took precedence? Someone remembered only in passing or whenever the story of the case was resurrected? Though to be fair, there'd been nothing quite like this among her circle of friends. Divorces, infidelities, and recession woes, they were the roots of their gossip. Her disappearance without a trace would definitely be a first.

Without a trace. She had to disappear without a trace. So going west was out, at least at first, because of Jane. She knew nothing about the south. Had no friends or family in that part of the country so it would be the last place Daniel would think she'd go.

She pulled up the route map. From Washington there was a service all the way to Miami. She shuddered. It might be a popular tourist destination but from what she'd read and heard there was an undercurrent of crime, exactly the kind of crime she was fleeing.

She opened Google, typed Mastersons Distribution into the search box and waited. Sure enough, the results offered her a choice of offices other than New York including Miami, Las Vegas and Chicago.

Besides, Florida wasn't a sensible choice. Too many of her neighbors vacationed there or had second homes. It would just be her luck to bump into someone she knew.

She studied the timetable again. Most of the station names meant nothing to her. Should she just pick one at random? A late morning train from Washington would get her to North Carolina by afternoon. But Cary, Durham, Burlington, she'd never heard of those places. She googled some of them, checked out the town sites. They sounded pleasant enough and presumably offered the added bonus of being cheaper than big city prices, a factor which she could not ignore, but what would she do there? If she didn't have something to occupy her time she'd go crazy with worry. Besides in a smaller town her presence might be more noticeable, attract the wrong attention. She needed a decent sized city, one where she could fade into the crowd.

The train route ended in Charlotte. She knew nothing about it, but at least she'd heard of it. But the train didn't arrive until after 8 p.m. She didn't like the prospect of having to navigate a strange city alone in the evening. Maybe she should stay in Washington.

Except she couldn't afford to, her cash wouldn't last forever. She ran down the list of stations again. Charleston, the name conjured up an image of a genteel sedate city, no doubt the result of too many southern historical romance novels. And it had to be a decent size, surely?

She checked the schedule again. The train got in at 4.51 in the morning, barely better than arriving in the evening, though at least it would be light. Or if she stayed on the train longer, it would be seven before it got to Savannah. Maybe this idea of traveling by train wasn't such a great idea. A car would give her so much more freedom, but having to drive huge distances on her own would scare her. True, she'd have a GPS to guide her, but Daniel had always wanted to drive when they went on vacation and she'd been happy to let him. She'd never driven much more than fifty miles at any one time. Besides, without a credit card she probably wouldn't be able to rent a car anyway. Or if she could, there'd be a hefty cash deposit—not something she could afford.

So it had to be the train.

She closed her laptop. She had to go back to the station anyhow to buy the ticket so she might as well wait and see what was available. Perhaps the decision would be made for her.

Chapter 18 – Friday morning

Union Station bustled with activity, the morning commute still in full flow. In her hurry to take action, any action, Maggie hadn't even considered what time it was. She'd gathered up her few belongings and checked out of the hotel at record speed.

At the metro station she still hadn't been able to figure out how the ticket machines worked but this time she was helped by an impatient commuter in the line behind her. His brusque manner made her feel like an idiot, but at least he didn't demand a dollar for his efforts.

On the packed subway, she'd garnered hard stares from fellow travelers who obviously begrudged the tiny amount of room her suitcase occupied. She was squeezed in so tight she wondered how she'd ever get off at the correct station. Her worry proved needless. As the doors opened at Union Station, a surge of people pressed forward toward the platform sweeping her with them. How anyone put up with the journey every day, she had no idea. She couldn't remember the last time she'd had to deal with rush hour traffic, vehicular or human.

She berated herself for not thinking through her plan before setting out. A line of people snaked back from the ticket office window despite the availability of self-service machines. Fellow travelers without credit cards? Or others equally confused about their destinations? Could there be others fleeing for their lives?

As she didn't have a specific train to catch she decided to let the line go down while she had breakfast. She sat in the same cafe as the previous day, lingering over a coffee and croissant, watching the madness slowly dissipate. She allowed herself to relax a little. Time was on her side, there was nowhere she needed to be, no need to hurry.

Her thoughts drifted to Daniel, what he would be doing. Nine o'clock on a normal morning he'd be at his desk and would have been for nearly an hour. He liked to start early, said it made a good impression on his bosses and set a good example for his staff. As a secretary she'd considered herself a conscientious worker, always on time, but the job was a means to a paycheck and she'd never volunteered to start early or finish late.

Still, this was hardly an ordinary morning for Daniel. He surely wouldn't go to work as normal, not when his wife had disappeared. How long before he got in touch with the police to report her missing? She had an idea that forty-eight hours had to pass before the police would get involved. Forty-eight hours, a long time especially if the person was someone like her, who rarely deviated from her routine without leaving a note. Would Daniel have called the police anyway to express his initial concern at her absence? And if he had, how long before they made the connection between the missing woman and the nervous, shaken woman who'd come in a few days earlier to report that she suspected her husband was involved in a horrendous crime?

"Well, hello again."

The cheerful voice startled Maggie. She gaped at the speaker, the man from the train, her mind blank, even the word "hello" escaping her.

"Heading back already?"

Maggie frowned. What did he mean?

His eyes lit up with amusement. "You know, it's not that bad a city."

Maggie still didn't understand.

"Yesterday you said you were staying a few days." He nodded at her case. "Looks like you're making an early escape."

Escape?

She froze, the word reverberating in her mind. Escape. Did he know? How could he know? He couldn't know. She had to stop sitting there with her mouth open like a goldfish who'd just spotted a cat about to pounce. Say something. Anything.

"I... um...a change of plans." Her mind began to thaw. This guy was a stranger. She didn't owe him an explanation. Yet she felt she did. "Family emergency."

For a moment the expression in the guy's eyes changed, but too fast for her to label it before he wiped the smile from his mouth as if her words had finally sunk in.

"Sorry to hear that. Too bad. Washington's a fun city to visit." He glanced at his watch. "But I shouldn't keep you. The train back to New York leaves in twenty minutes."

She hesitated. This lying business was harder than she'd imagined. It required a degree of fast thinking, not one of her best skills. She could stand up and pretend she was heading for the train, but what if he was too? Maybe he'd completed whatever work he had here and was going back to New York.

Why had she added that about a family emergency? It was none of his business. Had she even told him she lived in New York? She could have come from anywhere. Which gave her an idea.

"Florida. My parents. They live in Florida." She waved him away. "But don't let me make you miss the train."

The guy shook his head.

"I'm not going back to the city either." He grinned. "Would you believe I'm headed to Florida too?"

Alarm bells rang in her mind. Was it merely a coincidence? She knew there weren't any trains to Florida until later that afternoon so what was he doing at the station this early? And if he knew the times of the trains wouldn't he be wondering what she was doing there?

"My boss called me first thing this morning. Said he wanted me to go onto Florida after I'd finished up here. Sometimes I think he thinks because I'm single I don't have any social life that matters." He sighed. "I mean, he's right, but would it do any harm to ask if it's going to cause any problems first? Common courtesy, that's all. Not that I'm sure the guy knows what courtesy means."

She offered him a sympathetic smile, but now her mind was racing. There were two overnight trains to Florida. If she could find out which one he was on she could take the other. Though if she remembered correctly, only the later one stopped at Charleston.

"Maybe we'll be on the same train. Are you on the afternoon or evening departure?" Whichever he said, she'd say the other one. It was that easy.

"I don't actually have a ticket yet. That's why I'm here now. To see what's available. The boss said I could take a sleeper so I guess it will be whichever train has one left."

She struggled to hide her dismay. She was probably being paranoid and this was a complete coincidence because, apart from reading her mind, how could anyone know where she was planning on going or even that she would be back in the station that morning, but she had to shake the guy off somehow because the longer he was in her company, even from a distance, the greater the possibility he'd recognize her when the missing woman stories emerged.

"Good luck getting the ticket." She made a show of looking at her watch and stood up. "I have to get moving. I've got a few chores to do before I catch my train."

She walked away before he had time to respond. She could sense him behind her. Following her? She resisted the temptation to look back. What should she do now? The line to the ticket office had disappeared. Up ahead she saw a sign for the restrooms. She sped up, snuck a glance back as she turned into the ladies room.

The guy stood at the ticket window, buying his ticket to Florida, no doubt, just as he'd said. Why did she think he was following her? These kind of coincidental meetings happened all the time. Many times she'd met someone new or even learned something new only to come across that person or information again in a short period of time. There could be several other people from yesterday's train from New York in the station too, but because she'd had no interaction with them on the journey, she had no idea. If she wanted to be really paranoid she should worry about the passengers she hadn't noticed because if someone was really following her, why would they make their presence known? A sure way to give the game away.

Still, while he was busy, she made a dash for the exit.

Chapter 19 – Friday morning

Maggie paced the streets outside of Union Station. She didn't want to go too far. She realized she should have left her suitcase at the hotel until the evening. As small as it was, it still hobbled her ability to get about. Hopefully the station would have lockers or baggage storage, but she didn't want to go back in until she felt confident the guy would have got his ticket and gone.

"Spare some change."

A middle-aged man huddled in a doorway. A cardboard placard in front of him read, "Fallen on hard times. Homeless. Please help. God bless."

Maggie shuddered. Walked on.

Homeless. Technically, she was too. Is that how she'd end up? Sleeping on the streets? The only thing separating her from this guy was that she had money. Some might say a large sum of money, certainly more than she should be walking around with, but it wouldn't last forever. And then what? She didn't exactly have marketable skills.

How could she have been so stupid? She should have

turned a blind eye. Pretended she didn't know what Mastersons Distribution was up to or what Daniel was involved in. She couldn't be implicated. She couldn't be blamed for not knowing her comfortable lifestyle was paid for by such an evil crime. She'd always trusted Daniel. To her, trust was the most important element of a marriage. Without trust, love was a sham, a mere illusion.

At the very least she should have waited, given herself a month or so to plan out her escape and possibly gather a bigger cushion of funds.

She blinked back tears. But how could she? How could she put her comfort over the safety and dignity of who knew how many young women? The idea was so abhorrent she'd had to act immediately. Her conscience wouldn't let her wait, wouldn't let her take the time to think through the consequences of what she was about to do.

Fallen on hard times.

She wondered what the homeless guy's story was. Where were his family and friends in a time of need?

She shuddered again.

On her way back into the station she silently put a twenty dollar bill into the guy's bowl.

His face lit up like a child's at Christmas. "Thank you Ma'am. God bless."

She swallowed back a sob. She wanted to speak but couldn't. Instead she offered him a teary smile and hurried away.

The ticket clerk's shake of her head as she checked her screen forewarned Maggie of what was to come.

"No sleepers available to Jacksonville, I'm afraid."

"Oh." Maggie was at a loss as to what to do.

"Plenty of seats available," the clerk said. "They're quite comfortable, you know. The backs recline and there's a footrest and a leg support. You can still get a good night's sleep."

When Maggie didn't respond, she added, "They are a lot cheaper too. A lot cheaper."

Maggie liked the sound of cheaper. She needed to preserve her funds for as long as possible, but she'd planned on hiding away in the roomette. And knowing her luck if she sat in one of the coaches she'd probably bump into the businessman again. Unless he'd somehow managed to get the last sleeper, he'd have to make do with a seat too.

She knew she was being too cautious, but she didn't want to risk it. She could sense the clerk's growing impatience.

"What about tomorrow night?"

The clerk shook her head. "No, no roomettes available tomorrow night either."

She could book a seat for the following evening. Not perfect but safer than going that night. But she'd have to find somewhere to stay. She could go back to the same hotel, though it was still pricey. Fine for one night but she would not have picked it if she'd known she'd be staying two nights. Could she afford it?

"Excuse me," the clerk's voice interrupted her musings. "But there are others waiting."

Maggie chewed her lips. Decisions, decisions. How was she supposed to know what was best to do? She stepped aside.

"I'll have to think about it. I'll come back later."

She wandered over to the nearest departure gate and sat down. She wanted to cry. She couldn't do this. She had no idea what she was doing. She could run a home, organize a party, manage contractors and decorators if need be, but in a controlled environment. This fleeing business, it was way beyond her abilities.

She scoffed.

Daniel would know what to do. He'd bring the same cool-headed logic he brought to his work to this situation and before she knew it, he'd have a master plan. So dependable, she'd never had to bother with the logistics. Even when it came to having work done on the house, he'd set out the parameters and she'd simply follow his plan.

She watched others go purposefully about their business. Men and women in suits knowing exactly where they wanted to go. A woman pushing a baby in a stroller, chiding two small children to keep up as they hurried toward one of the gates with only minutes to spare. An elderly couple sitting opposite, the man fussing with the zipper on his bag until the woman put her hand on his to stop him and smiled at him with such warmth and love it almost broke Maggie's heart. That was the future she'd always envisioned. Not one of shame and prison visits.

The women turned her attention to Maggie. "You okay, dear? You look distressed."

Maggie forced a clenched lipped smile. Her emotions were too close to the surface to speak. She took a couple of deep breaths to clamp them back down. The departure board over the gate was empty. Did the couple realize they were sitting at the wrong gate?

"Just a little tired," she said. "Early start."

The man started fiddling with his bag again. There was a slight tremor in his hands, but she put it down to age. A slender, short man with a full head of pure white hair and a well-lined face, he fit Maggie's idea of a grandfather perfectly. Her own had died while she was too young to remember them and her father had died at sixty-seven, but this was how she imagined they would have looked.

The man eventually noticed her. His eyes narrowed as he scrutinized her, his bewilderment as to who she was written in his eyes. He nudged his wife gently with his elbow and whispered something.

She gave Maggie an apologetic look and said, "This lady's waiting for her train, dear. Hannah will be along soon."

"Oh." The man switched his attention back to his bag.

The woman raised her eyebrows and exhaled wearily. "Arthur has problems with his memory. He's not too good with faces anymore, even his children's. Our daughter is coming to meet us. We're spending the day with her. He thought you were her for a moment."

Maggie marveled at the woman's strength. While she could well be several years younger than her husband she was by no means youthful, and having noticed the blank stare in Arthur's eyes, Maggie guessed it wasn't only faces he forgot. His wife must have to keep a watch on his every move.

"We're going to New Orleans tonight," the woman

continued. "To stay with our son for a few days. It's his daughter's sixteenth birthday and they are having a big family party for her."

Maggie felt a pang of envy. Would her son ever want to speak to again when he discovered what she'd done? Could she ever even tell him? Or would she have to remain disappeared?

"So your daughter's taking you down to New Orleans by train? Does she have any family?"

"Oh, no. Hannah wouldn't take the train. Says it's too slow. She'll fly down next week with her kids."

The woman leant toward her and lowered her voice. "Arthur doesn't like to fly nowadays. It unsettles him and I'm afraid of how he might react. So we take the train. He likes looking out the window, watch the scenery go by. Besides, it's not as if we're in a hurry to get anywhere. We lead a very quiet life." She cast a plaintive glance at her husband. "And it makes a nice change from being at home all day."

"There you are!"

A tall, elegant woman strode into view and planted perfunctory kisses on the couple. "I told you to wait at your arrivals gate. I've been searching all over the station. I thought something might have happened to you."

"Your father needed to go to the bathroom, dear." If the younger woman's tone, which expressed impatience rather than concern, bothered her mother she concealed it well. "And you know your father doesn't like crowds. There were too many people milling around when we came off the platform."

The daughter let out an exasperated sigh. Glanced at her watch.

The mother eyed the daughter from head to toe. A look of resignation replaced the initial spark of excitement at seeing her.

"You're not going to the office today, are you, dear? You said you'd be able to spend the whole day with us."

"Just for an hour or so. I need to brief John on some latest developments in a case we are handling." She gave her mother a petulant look. "Don't look at me like that. It's not my fault my boss doesn't know which way is up if I'm not there to tell him."

Maggie suppressed a snigger, taken aback by the daughter's

sense of self-importance. If she'd been her mother, she'd want to slap her.

Her astonishment must have shown on her face because the elderly woman gave her a smile too wide to be genuine and said, "My daughter's a very important attorney."

The daughter made no attempt to downplay her mother's boast. Nor even acknowledge Maggie's presence.

"There's a Starbuck's across the street from the office. You can wait there for me. Now, we really need to get moving."

Before the couple had barely stood up, the daughter had grabbed their suitcase and headed toward the exit.

The mother hesitated in front of Maggie. "Children nowadays, they're always in such a hurry. I've told her before, it's not healthy, but she wouldn't listen to me when she was little and she certainly won't now."

She sighed. "Well it was nice meeting you, dear. I hope you have a wonderful trip to…" She frowned. "Sorry, I can't remember where you said you were going."

Because I didn't, Maggie thought. Because I don't have a clue.

"Mother! Please, we need to get going."

Maggie watched as the couple dutifully followed their daughter. She smiled. Impatience did have its benefits.

Though really she could have said the first place that came to mind and what would they care? They were passing strangers, that's all, a few moments' interaction of no consequence, to be forgotten just as quickly.

Chapter 20 – Friday evening

As the evening train pulled out of Union Station Maggie settled back in her seat. Finally, for the next twenty-four hours she knew exactly what she was doing and all it involved was sitting on the train. One day at a time, that's how she'd get through this. She could handle one day. The future, well, that was just too scary to contemplate.

She glanced around the tiny compartment, her safe haven for the journey. Meant for two, it was more than adequate for one. It even had its own toilet and sink, and she'd stocked up with water and snacks before she boarded, so theoretically she wouldn't need to leave its confines.

She closed her eyes. Concentrated on the gentle motion of the train, the soothing hum as it raced along the tracks, whisking her away to safety. Or at least, to New Orleans. The idea tickled her. She couldn't remember the last time she'd been so spontaneous. One minute heading to Florida, the next to Louisiana. And as easy as walking up to a ticket office window and buying a ticket. True, she'd been lucky enough to get one of the last available roomettes, but as she handed over the fare to the genial ticket clerk—she'd gone to a different window than before, not wanting to raise intrigue as to why someone should have such a sudden change of heart as to their destination—she'd enjoyed a powerful sense of freedom. How crazy was that?

She jerked her eyes open at the sound of the compartment door being slid open. For a horrible moment she mistook the uniformed man in the doorway for a policeman.

"Good evening, I'm Brian, your attendant for the trip." His cheerful grin wiped away Maggie's concerns. "Have you ridden with us before?"

Maggie managed to shake her head.

"Okay. So someone will be along from the dining car shortly to take dinner reservations, and let me know when you want me to make up the bed. There'll be coffee, tea and juice available first thing at the end of the corridor, and if there's anything else I can help you with, be sure to let me know."

She offered out her ticket.

"The conductor will be along in a moment to check tickets. Please don't lock your door until he's been."

He moved away from the door. She heard him repeat himself to the occupants of the next roomette.

The next visitor was a tall, stout lady in the same style uniform as the attendant. Before Maggie could show her ticket, the woman spoke, her voice a soft southern drawl.

"Hi, hon, what time would you like dinner?"

"I'm not having dinner, thanks."

"You know it's included, right?"

"Yes, but," Maggie hesitated. The idea of a proper meal sounded tempting, so far that day her food intake had consisted of mostly unhealthy snacks. And the ones she had with her weren't much better.

The woman smiled encouragingly. "You don't have to worry about being on your own. We offer communal dining, we'll sit you at a table with others, give you a chance to get to know your fellow travelers."

Maggie gulped. A nice idea, except she didn't want anyone

getting to know her.

"Thanks, but I had an early dinner just before I got on the train."

"With my daughter," she added as an afterthought, not sure why she needed to explain her decision to a stranger.

"Okay, hon. Breakfast is between six-thirty and eight-thirty. No reservations, first come, first served. You have a good night."

As the woman moved on Maggie wanted to leap up and lock the door. How many more people would she be forced to interact with? Didn't they realize she wanted, no, needed to be left alone? And where was the ticket collector?

The attendant passed her room several times, each time glancing in as if he expected her to make some request. The lady from the dining room bustled past again too and a stream of passengers soon followed, presumably heading for their dinner. Most cast a look in her direction; some offered a nod of acknowledgement or a polite "good evening" if she made the mistake of catching their attention.

She tried staring out the window in the hope passersby would only see her profile.

"Well, hello, dear."

She took a deep breath and plastered a grin on her face as she turned to face the elderly woman.

"I'd forgotten you said you were going to New Orleans," the woman said.

Maggie didn't bother correcting her. Instead she willed her to move on.

"Look, Arthur. It's the lady from the station. She's going to New Orleans too."

Arthur either didn't register his wife's words or didn't give a damn, which was fine with Maggie. But when his wife showed no signs of moving on she felt forced to be polite.

"Did you have a nice day with your daughter?"

"Oh, yes. It was lovely. Wasn't it, Arthur?" She didn't give Arthur time to reply. "We don't get to see her very often. She's so busy with her job and the children, but she took us out for a nice lunch, didn't she, Arthur?"

The forced brightness in her voice made Maggie wonder if they'd spent most of the morning sitting in Starbucks waiting for their daughter. Why did people do that? Treat their families as afterthoughts to be fitted in as and when rather than given first priority? One day, that's all the couple wanted. One day with their daughter. What job could be so important the woman couldn't give them that? Didn't she realize those times were precious and, given their age, there might not be too many more opportunities like it?

Arthur stared at her as his wife launched into a myriad of excuses for their daughter's dereliction of duty, confirming Maggie's assumptions. When the woman paused for breath he muttered something about the television.

His wife laughed.

"No, Arthur, this lady is on vacation." She rolled her eyes. "He thinks you look like a woman he saw on television before we got on the train. Some breaking news report." She leaned toward Maggie, lowered her voice a fraction. "He's obsessed with watching the news. I don't know why."

Maggie felt the color drain from her face. She wanted to ask, "What news?" but her mouth wouldn't work and her instincts screamed not to, no matter how desperately she wanted to know. To know it wasn't her story that had been broken. That this doddering, old man hadn't had an untimely moment of lucidity. How could he? She'd changed her appearance, didn't look anything like she used to. At least, she didn't think she did. Which photograph would Daniel give the police or the press? Surely, he'd have picked one of the more recent formal ones.

She watched the woman's mouth move, registered only the occasional word. She tried to glance at Arthur without appearing obvious. To check whether he was still staring, somehow matching the image in front of him with the image he'd seen on a screen.

"Personally," she heard the woman say, "I try not to watch it. It's never good, is it?"

Maggie shook her head in agreement. A glimmer of hope sprouted inside. If his wife dismissed Arthur's observations so easily, she probably didn't need to worry. Who else would he tell? He'd barely uttered a word in her presence. It was unlikely he'd turn voluble now. Besides, what was the point of worrying before she knew what news report they'd seen? It could be anything. And hadn't Arthur thought she was his daughter earlier? That's how confused he was. She had to relax. Or she'd drive herself crazy. But she wouldn't really be able to relax until she'd seen the report. And how was she going to do that on the train?

"Are you coming for dinner, dear?"

"What?"

"We could go together. Give you some company."

"Oh. No. I ate earlier. Before I got on the train." Maggie smiled. "But you should go. They'll be waiting for you if you have a reservation."

The woman's face fell, as if she were the one who wanted company. She gave a hopeful smile. "No doubt we'll see you again later."

No. No. No! As the couple headed off Maggie was tempted to immediately lock the door, close the curtains and hide away. But nobody had come for her ticket yet. Where were they? Why was it taking so long?

She jumped up, peered out the door. A guard stood at the end of the corridor nearest the dining car, checking the couple's tickets. He stepped aside and let the couple squeeze past him.

"Everyone seems in a hurry for their dinner tonight." He made his way toward her, checking each roomette on the way.

He examined her ticket, gave her a quick glance. She sensed a hesitation. Had he seen the news report too? As soon as he'd zapped her ticket she stepped back inside and started to close the door.

"Enjoy the trip, Ma'am."

She hesitated. Suddenly had an idea. "Is there Wi-Fi on the train?"

"Wi-Fi? No, Ma'am. I'm sorry, there's not."

"Really?"

Was that possible? The way the internet providers talked it was everywhere nowadays. So much for her idea of checking the news online. Twenty-four hours. She was going to have to wait at least twenty-four hours before she could find out what story Arthur had seen. So much for any hope of being able to relax on the journey. She'd be a bundle of nerves until she knew for certain. She should have asked what channel they'd seen it on, whether it was a local or nationally breaking story. Her disappearance wouldn't garner the latter, not this early on, surely. But to ask might only raise suspicions too.

She slid the door shut, the loud click as she swung the lever to lock the door bringing a frisson of relief. She pulled the curtain across the door and fussed with the Velcro bindings until she was satisfied no one could peek inside. She flopped back into her seat.

At last, alone.

Chapter 21 – Friday overnight

She should have bought some wine. A couple of glasses might have allowed her an hour or two of sleep. Instead she tossed and turned, the rocking motion of the train a distraction rather than a lull. She'd been pleasantly surprised at how comfortable the bed was, but despite a deep exhaustion her mind refused to shut down. Lynchburg, Greensboro, Charlotte, she registered each stop. Peered out the window as the train pulled to a halt. Watched the alighting passengers straggle off the train, dazed and disorientated, some to be welcomed by tight embraces, others left to head for the short row of available taxis, the drivers hopeful the train would deliver them some customers.

It seemed so lonely and sad, each well-lit station a tiny inhabited oasis surrounded by dark, empty streets save for the occasional glow from a distant window. As a line of people filed out of one of the waiting rooms, beckoned by the train conductor, she wondered where they were going that brought them onto the train at such an ungodly hour. Were their journeys missions of duty, desire or hope? She doubted anyone else was traveling for the sake of it.

Most of the passengers were directed toward the coach cars. A solitary man wheeled a weekend case in the direction of the sleeping cars, his brisk pace a sharp contrast to the others. She watched him interact with the attendant, heard a muffled laugh before he disappeared from view.

Moments later heavy footsteps in the corridor paused outside her room. She tensed, staring at the door as if she expected it to open. Let out a deep breath when the door of the compartment opposite slammed shut. She closed her eyes. Pleaded for oblivion.

At five o'clock she gave up. Opened the picture window drapes fully and gazed out at the view. A haze muted the dense green forest which lined the tracks, a forbidding fortress whose walls swooped and dipped with the terrain. So many trees, hours and hours of them, untouched by human intervention, unseen in parts except by passengers on this route. She'd been traveling less than twelve hours and was already struck by the sheer enormity of the country. She had another fourteen or more before arriving in New Orleans.

She sat on the bed, hugging her knees to her chest and watching the scenery roll by. New Orleans and then what? After she'd bought the rail ticket she'd managed to find somewhere to stay, a private hotel in the Garden District, only a few minutes taxi ride from the station. Because she hadn't wanted to pay by credit card the owner had been reluctant to take her booking but told her it was likely she'd have rooms available anyway.

She planned on staying for two nights. It didn't sound like the kind of place she'd be comfortable wandering around on her own. She'd read too many articles about how New Orleans ranked as one of the most dangerous cities in terms of crime, but after twenty-four hours on a train she couldn't imagine getting straight onto another one, if indeed that was an option.

Of course, she could always get off earlier. She didn't have to go to New Orleans. She switched on the overhead light, reached for the train schedule, all without having to get off the bed—there was something to be said for small living spaces—and checked out her options.

The train slowed. Maggie peered out the window. Clemson. She'd never heard of it. Another look at the schedule told her she was in South Carolina. The next stop would be in Georgia. She'd already put a decent distance between herself and Daniel.

She heard the door opposite open, as it had at the two previous stops. Maybe the guy was a smoker, desperate to indulge a craving. Some of the stops had been long enough for people to "step off the train" as the conductor announced over the intercom. Somehow she doubted this one would be.

There was no other sound from the corridor, any footsteps or voices. But there hadn't been earlier either, just a gentle click of the door being closed again as the train moved on. Someone else who couldn't sleep?

She studied the timetable again as the train picked up speed. Apart from Atlanta and Birmingham, more towns she'd never heard of. She tossed the leaflet aside. What was she thinking? She'd paid for the whole journey, she couldn't afford to waste money. Not when she'd have to get back on this route at some point.

If only she could get off for a few minutes, to catch the news on television or check out the internet for this breaking story. See if she really had anything to worry about yet. If only the train had Wi-Fi or had one of its extended stops somewhere she could go into the station and buy a newspaper—assuming stations sold newspapers anymore. Though why wouldn't they when it was impossible to get a daily fix of news on the internet? The wonder of modern technology, sometimes it made her want to scream. She couldn't fault the convenience—where would she be on this trip without being able to check schedules and hotels anonymously?—but sometimes she longed for the old-fashioned ways when news dripped into the public's conscience one news show or newspaper report at a time, stories gaining prominence as interest or intrigue propelled a growing swell of public gossip organically rather than going viral at the touch of a few keys.

Still, it did mean once she could get online she'd easily be able to track what was going on with regard to her own situation and also with Daniel and the company.

She frowned. What if there was no mention of her disappearance? What if her story didn't merit much attention? After all she wasn't a celebrity. And what if Daniel spun some story? Said she'd gone away for a few days. Eventually the truth would come out when she didn't reappear, but that could be days or weeks even. He could invent a family emergency requiring her long-term presence, or claim she'd gone to visit Craig. Until the police got involved there'd be no reason for anyone to doubt Daniel's explanations. He was the solid husband and father, the likeable neighbor, the respected businessman.

She sniffed. The bastard. How could he have put the family at risk like this? And for what? What did he get out of it that made it worthwhile? The money he earned might be good, but not the kind of sums to encourage criminal behavior or risking everything he'd spent his whole life working for.

Unless…

Unless he was stashing other money away without her knowledge, in addition to the cash in his office. A secret account, overseas perhaps. But why? They had a good enough life. Yes, who wouldn't like a little extra? But they were hardly desperate for it. Not that desperate.

What did it mean that he had money she didn't know about or, at least, wasn't supposed to know about? That he planned some future without her? Or that he believed she was so ignorant about their finances she wouldn't realize they were living way beyond their means? He'd always saved for their retirement, assured her they'd be comfortable. Was this his insurance policy?

She sank her face into her knees. She hated the uncertainty, not knowing where she stood. There'd be no peace until she did know. And yet she had another twelve hours left. Another twelve hours of going over scenario after scenario.

If she could only go back to sleep. Sleep the day away. She snorted. That was a joke. Maybe in New Orleans she'd pick up some sleeping tablets. She was sure there was stuff you could buy over the counter. Or a big bottle of wine. If it didn't knock her out for a few hours at least the hangover would make thinking of any kind too damn difficult.

She leapt off the bed. She couldn't afford to think like that. She needed her wits about her at all times, no matter how enticing the alternative might sound. And sitting here alone all day brooding would not help. It was only six-thirty, hard to imagine others would be flocking to the dining car this early. She'd go and enjoy a proper breakfast, get out of this room for a while away from her self-imposed solitude.

And who knew, maybe someone in the dining car would have a newspaper.

Chapter 22 – Saturday morning

"Good morning, dear."

Maggie flinched. She forced her instinctive grimace into a smile as she turned toward the voice. Why, oh why, did they have to pick this early to go for breakfast? There'd be no getting away from them now. Before she could speak the door opposite her compartment slid open and the man she'd seen get on the train during the night stepped out, glancing first at her and then back at Arthur and his wife.

"Good morning." His cheery tone belied the bleary look in his eyes. "I guess we're all headed for breakfast."

Maggie muttered "Good morning" back and led the way down the corridor wondering whether she should have a last minute change of heart about eating breakfast. She paused as she entered the dining car. Her luck was in. Two tables were full. A third had one space, the other occupants already tucking into their meals. She headed purposefully toward it. After all, the attendant had emphasized the community seating, but before she could reach it the attendant appeared from the rear of the car, did a quick head count of the group and gestured them toward an empty table on the opposite side of the aisle.

Maggie reluctantly slid into the seat beside the window. Arthur waited patiently for his wife to maneuver herself in opposite, leaving the younger guy, who introduced himself as Neil, to sit next to her.

"Nice to meet you. I'm Edith," the woman said. She nodded toward her husband. "And that's Arthur."

Neil acknowledged the other man with a nod before glancing at Maggie.

"Abigail." She rushed the name out as if she said it fast enough it wouldn't be a lie.

"Did you sleep well, dear?" Edith asked.

The endearment was beginning to grate on Maggie's nerves.

"We were both asleep by ten, weren't we, Arthur? Must be the rocking motion of the train, but we both slept like babies, better than we do at home, isn't that right, Arthur?"

Arthur merely stared at Maggie, his furrowed brow evidence of his inward search for some connection. She prayed the night's sleep had wiped out any memories of the news report even as she wondered whether Neil could shed any light on exactly what the report entailed. But how could she bring the subject up in casual conversation? And without getting Arthur excited? It was just too dangerous.

"Where you all headed?" Neil turned toward her as he spoke, but fortunately Edith jumped in with her story first and Maggie was content to let her prattle on about her destination and their time in Washington. The good night's sleep had elevated their day out with their daughter from nice to wonderful, at least in Edith's eyes. Arthur let his wife do the talking.

Suddenly there was a pause. She realized the others were looking at her as if they expected her to contribute to the conversation. She had no idea what had been asked of her.

Neil gave her a knowing smile, as if amused by her predicament. He seemed to delight in making her wait, but finally repeated his question—why was she was going to New Orleans?

"I've always wanted to visit the city." She shrugged. "Now seemed like a good time."

"You're visiting on your own?"

"No, no." Maggie feared he might offer his services as a companion. "I have friends there. I'll be meeting up with them."

"I thought you said you were going to see family," Edith chipped in.

Maggie hesitated. Had she said she was going to see family? She couldn't remember. And would Edith also remember she'd originally said she was going to Florida? Because she was sure she had said that, though maybe not to Edith. She faked a smile. "No, I'm visiting friends."

Before Edith could point out any other potential inconsistencies in her story, Maggie turned to Neil.

"What about you?"

"Business."

"Okay, folks. What can I get you?" The waitress glanced at each of them in turn, raised her eyebrows when she got to Maggie.

Maggie shriveled inside from the scrutiny until she realized the waitress was merely waiting for her order. She stammered out her request, asking for a full breakfast because it was the first item on the menu. The waitress worked through a long list of options: eggs fried or scrambled, sausage or bacon, toast or croissant, Maggie parroting back the first option each time without any consideration for her actual preferences. When did ordering a meal become so complicated? And why hadn't she picked the continental choice? It had been years since she'd last eaten a cooked breakfast, cereal and fruit being her usual fare.

"What business are you in?" she asked Neil as the waitress left with their orders. She hoped he'd be the type who liked to talk about himself, who with a little prompting would fill the time it took to eat with his stories, barely noticing he wasn't giving anyone else a chance to speak.

"Computer consultancy."

"Oh." Her knowledge of computers amounted to using a laptop for e-mail and social media. "That must be fascinating," she added lamely.

"It's a job. It pays the bills."

Maggie suppressed a sigh. His tone of voice suggested he didn't want to talk about it.

"How about you?"

"Me?" She laughed, although she wasn't sure why. Creating a fake identity was harder than she'd imagined. Just changing your name didn't do it. She should have created a whole history, learned it by heart so it would trip easily off the tongue. Making it up in the spur of the moment was a recipe for disaster. But it was too late to think of that now, so best to stick as near to the truth as possible, at least for today.

"I'm a stay-at-home mom."

Neil's face cracked into a huge grin. "But you're not staying at home at the moment. What's this, a mother's escape?"

"Escape. No!" Was it that obvious she was fleeing? "My son's grown up. Off at college."

The lie came easily. Now she just had to remember it.

"Hey, no offense." The guy raised his hands in surrender. Maggie noticed he wasn't wearing a wedding ring. "Twenty odd years of raising a kid and you deserve a break."

"What about your daughter?" Edith asked.

Daughter? What daughter? Had she made up a daughter? She didn't think so. But just to be on the safe side, perhaps she should.

"Oh, she's flown the nest too. I'm an empty-nester now."

"You don't look old enough," Neil said.

She blushed. Then blushed even more, embarrassed by her reaction to what was surely just a polite comment.

Luckily Edith jumped back into the conversation with her views that a woman's place was in the home when she had children and how most of society's evils could be traced back to women wanting to go out to work instead. She made no mention that her own daughter fell into the selfish category which she readily assigned all working women, making Maggie rethink the mother-daughter interaction she'd witnessed the previous day. Her daughter-in-law in New Orleans obviously epitomized the perfect mother in Edith's eyes, and Maggie guessed Hannah didn't take too kindly to being usurped in her mother's affection no matter how much her mother might pretend to strangers that she was proud of her daughter's accomplishments.

"What about you, Arthur?" Neil managed to interject as Edith took a pause for breath. "Where did you work?"

Arthur looked slightly stunned by the question. He glanced at his wife, a need for reassurance obvious in his expression.

"He has his good days and his bad days, I'm afraid." Edith smiled tenderly at him. "Today's one of the not so good. It's being away from home. It confuses him. He has his routine at home. It keeps him focused."

A cloud of sadness flitted across her face.

"It can be hard at times. Knowing what he was like. Seeing him come to this. He was always so sharp, never missed a trick. One of the reasons he was so good at his job. Thirty-five years, longest serving officer in our town. Knew everyone and everyone knew him. Respected him too. Even some of the ones he had to arrest."

Maggie didn't hear the rest. An ex-police officer? One who had good days and bad days? But who yesterday thought she resembled someone he'd seen on a news report. What if yesterday was a good day? What if his old instincts had kicked in, enabling him to recognize the similarities between a photo on television and the person in front of him?

She hoped today was a really bad day. That the synapses in the brain weren't working properly. Or yesterday's news report had already been forgotten. After all, hadn't Edith reminded Arthur that they'd met her yesterday in the station? Edith obviously doubted his capacity to remember and she should know. So why was Arthur staring at her now? His faint smile, was it a smile of achievement, a moment of clarity?

The waitress returned with their food and the conversation stopped while toast was buttered and coffee sweetened. Maggie hoped it stayed that way. Her latest plan, eat fast and get away. And at least Arthur had his plate to focus on rather than her face.

She managed to eat without having to say anything else. As soon as she finished, she excused herself from the table and the invitations to join Edith and Arthur in the observation car. Neil took the opportunity to leave too even though he'd only eaten half his breakfast.

He stood, let her out of her seat, and followed her back to the sleeping car. As she opened her door, he exhaled heavily. "She sure knows how to talk."

Maggie smiled. "I think she's lonely. Her husband probably isn't the best of company. It can't be easy. Just when you think your children are finally grown, suddenly your spouse needs a caretaker."

The guy shuddered. "Scary, right? I bet when they were our age they had no idea what lay ahead. You assume you have this whole future ahead and suddenly it's gone."

Maggie couldn't respond. If only he knew. If only he knew it wasn't just an age thing, it could happen to anyone at anytime. The best of plans, poof! Disintegrated at the sound of a few mere words.

"Are you okay?" His concern suggested her expression had given away her thoughts. "I hope I didn't say anything to upset you."

"No, no." She stepped into her roomette. "It's fine, really. It was nice meeting you."

She closed the door before he could say anything else. He stood outside, his own expression one of surprise at her abruptness. She yanked the drape across the window, blocking him from view and waited. She heard footsteps but not the sound of another door closing. He might have left, or not bothered closing his door. Why would he, unless he too had something to hide?

She imagined, for a moment, inviting him in. Blurting out her story, using a stranger as a sounding board. Oh, the relief of having someone to talk with. And he gave the impression of being genuine, caring, and nice. But the same could be said of Daniel on first meeting. And look where genuine, caring and nice had got her. If she couldn't trust Daniel, she couldn't, didn't dare trust anyone else. Ever again.

She sank into a seat and hid her face in her hands.

Chapter 23 – Saturday

Atlanta, Birmingham, rivers, mountains, industry, farmland. The scenery slid past in a blur as the train continued south. At the approach to each station Maggie briefly considered the merits of getting off early, away from Edith, Arthur and Neil. At various times they'd knocked on her door, checking whether she was going to lunch, whether she needed anything from the café or if she wanted some company to while the time away.

What did they not understand by the door being closed? If she wanted to be social she would have left it open with the drapes drawn back so everyone passing could see in and stop for a chat on their wanderings along the corridor. Why did people have to be so friendly? She just wanted them to leave her alone.

She'd snapped at Neil the last time he'd appeared at her door. Judging by the number of trips he'd made to the cafe he was either bored by the lengthy journey or lonely. She guessed he hadn't come across any other fellow solo travelers or he would have left her alone. She felt a twinge of guilt. There'd been no need to be rude. It was only thanks to his quick reaction that she'd avoided jamming the fingers of his right hand in the door as she slammed it shut. Any slower and she might have been the target of a lawsuit, an untimely end to any hope of anonymity. Still, he hadn't bothered her since. He'd probably written her off as a crazy woman to be avoided at all costs. Good.

The train slowed to a halt. A sign outside the window proclaimed they were in Picayune, wherever that was. With nothing else to do, she checked the route guide. Mississippi, just north of the Louisiana border. Which meant only one more state to cross. But still another two hours of the journey left. She groaned. She felt as if she'd been sitting on this train forever.

Two more hours, add another hour to get to the hotel and set up her laptop and maybe, just maybe, she'd finally be able to find out whether her disappearance had generated any news.

She leaned back in her seat as the train pulled out of the station and watched people on the platform waving. Some with those big smiles meant to mask the desire to cry. She'd worn a similar smile when she'd waved Craig off at the airport the previous year. Tears of love and the pain of separation. The separation had been hard for her to bear because although she knew he'd be back in a year she also knew that from then on it would not be for long. Home would be a pit stop between adventures. Craig had an adventurous spirit. She'd be lucky if he ever lived within commuting distance.

Friends told her it was time to reclaim her life, rekindle her relationship with Daniel with romantic dinners and weekends away. Ha! Daniel's new job had put an end to those ideas. Besides, Daniel couldn't understand why they needed to put any more effort into their relationship. They loved each other. They were happy. There was no need to rekindle when the flame had never gone out.

She scoffed. He'd actually said that. Then he'd quickly added, of course, when his work situation had settled down they'd take more trips together.

What could she say? She'd thought he was only doing what was best for the family. The job could make the difference in how comfortable their retirement was. But she didn't want a more comfortable retirement if it came at the price of other people's suffering. And Daniel should know that. So what did it say about their relationship that he was willing to fool her with deviousness? Granted, he hadn't actually lied to her. Everything he'd told her about the job was true. It was all the information he'd left out that astonished her. He was living a lie whether he admitted it or not.

And now he'd forced her to live a lie. Against her will and with no promise of a comfortable retirement.

Rage bubbled up inside. How dare he? How could he? What had turned him into such a monster that he'd happily trade in others' misery to make his living? Young women, possibly young men too, desperate to improve their lot, offered the promise of a better life only to end up enslaved in a world of sex and drugs.

Young people, many their son's age. Did he ever think about that? How would he feel if it were Craig who fell into the trap?

Or if he were one of the parents whose child mysteriously disappeared abroad?

The mere thought made her sick. Made her want to contact Craig immediately and make sure he was okay. Even though she knew he was. Although whether he'd be alright when he found out what his father was involved in she couldn't imagine. Or that his mother had disappeared. Somehow she'd have to contact him. Let him know at least one of his parents could still be relied on. He'd just have to get used to the fact she was living under a different name.

But what about her sister? And her friends? Her doctor, her dentist, the familiar faces at the post office, the supermarket and the library, everyone who in some way influenced or added to her life. Made it comfortable, safe and predictable. She liked predictable. It was reassuring. She'd built her lifestyle around predictable.

Who could have predicted this? There was no comfort and safety now.

How could he do this to her?

The anger rippled through her body in tremors. She clenched her teeth, fighting against the temptation to scream out her frustration. If Daniel stood before her now, she'd slap him.

Slap him again and again. Give him no chance to defend himself. Hit him until his cheeks flamed red and his eyes watered and… and what? Did she think he'd get down on his knees and beg forgiveness? Tell her this was all a terrible mistake and everything would be alright now. They could put it behind them, forget it ever happened.

Ha! As if. Forget that the man she loved believed it was okay to trade in human lives. That he had been willing to associate with the worst kind of criminal, ones with no sense of compassion or decency for their fellow men. Those who saw others less fortunate as a means for them to live the high life.

Did Daniel have any clue as to how much he had betrayed her? Forget the slaps. If he was with her now, she'd want to strangle him. Murderous thoughts, the seeds planted in her garden of do-no-harm by her lying, perverted, sick, disgusting husband.

The tears came fast and furious; her sobs muffled whimpers as she struggled to keep the noise down. She wanted to roar at her naiveté, roar at her helplessness.

She'd never been so alone before and, no matter how brave a face she put on, she wasn't sure she could cope with being alone now.

Chapter 24 – Saturday evening

The taxi turned from a bustling main street onto an ill-lit side road of empty lots interspersed with dilapidated buildings.

Maggie fought back a wave of panic. She eyed the taxi driver. A foreigner, judging by the few words of broken English he'd muttered as she got into the car, but from where, she had no idea. Had she made a mistake? Should she have waited for another cab? But he'd been in line at the official taxi rank. That had to mean something.

Should she say something? Let him know she was onto him? A little late now, when the only thing she knew for sure was that she was in New Orleans.

The taxi made a left turn, this time onto a street lined with residences, some elegant, some in need of loving care, but each one behind high wrought-iron fences with locked gates.

"We here." The driver pulled the car up outside one of the better kept properties.

"This can't be it."

The three story building showed no sign of being a hotel.

No sign of life. No welcome sign or any sign apart from the house number on the wall near the door. The number was right, but this surely had to be the wrong street.

The driver glanced over his shoulder, pointed at the meter.

She gaped at him. He expected her to get out? In the middle of nowhere, on a street all but deserted of traffic?

The driver pointed again, this time toward the gate. "Ring bell."

And summon who? Suppose there was no one home? Then she'd be stuck in a strange street in the dark with no idea which way she should go—a recipe for disaster.

"Nice hotel." The driver seemed to sense her reluctance. He gave her a reassuring smile, revealing he was short on teeth, and added, "Ring bell. Someone come."

He pointed at the meter again. The fare had nudged up another quarter.

She pulled a twenty dollar bill from her pocket, glad she could cover the cost without resorting to her wallet. A safety tip she'd read online somewhere. Don't flaunt your wealth or someone might try to relieve you of it. She'd never before lived anywhere where she'd had to worry about such precautions. Something else to consider now.

The driver retrieved her suitcase from the trunk and made to get back into the car.

"Wait." She couldn't bear the thought of him driving off, leaving her alone. She pressed the bell. "Can you wait until someone comes?"

She pressed the bell again.

The driver didn't answer, merely slid into his seat and closed the door. But he didn't start the engine.

She tried the bell again. There was no way of telling whether it worked.

A door in the building to the left of the house opened and a woman sauntered down from the wide porch, a broad smile on her face.

"Mrs. Thornton, you made it." She unlocked the gate. "Welcome."

Maggie heard the taxi pull away, the loud click of the gate as it was closed behind her, the woman's admonishments to keep the outer gate locked at all times, and allowed herself to relax if only a fraction.

As she followed the woman toward the second building she noticed the fenced area enclosed three similar properties. Inside, the first room off the hallway had been converted into an office. Uncarpeted and furnished with only a registration counter, it was a spartan space devoid of any welcoming ambience. The woman more than made up for it with a constant stream of chatter and advice as she completed the registration formalities, barely letting Maggie get a word in.

Finally, she led her back outside and down a narrow paved alley into a rear patio overhung with foliage and dotted with ornate metal tables and chairs.

"Watch your step," she said as she unlocked a side door and beckoned for her to enter.

Maggie half expected to find herself in a kitchen. Instead she entered a lobby furnished only with a huge side table above which a gilt-framed mirror reflected back a barely recognizable haggard traveler.

To her surprise the internal door opened not onto a corridor but into an enormous bedroom about twice the size of her previous hotel room. The high ceilings and heavy drapes at the window made her feel as if she'd stepped back in time, an illusion fortified by the shabby but solid mahogany furnishings.

"Breakfast is served next door between six and nine. If you need anything the office is open until eleven." The receptionist handed the key over. "Charles Street is one block over. There are plenty of restaurants there if you need dinner, but please be careful walking around on your own, especially after dark."

Maggie had already decided that her hunger pangs would have to be satisfied by the remainder of the snacks in her bag. The train journey had emotionally exhausted her. She couldn't face the prospect of venturing out alone.

She double checked the door lock after the woman left. The internal door also had a chain. She secured it. Stood in the middle of the room and listened. Blissful silence, broken only by the rhythmic click of the wobbling overhead fan and the occasional chirp of nocturnal insects.

She drew the drapes, blocking out the encroaching night and, by default, the outside world. New Orleans, the last place anyone would imagine she was. New Orleans, touted as one of the most dangerous cities in America but, for tonight at least, offering her a much needed sense of security. How ironic was that?

Chapter 25 – Saturday evening

The internet connection was surprisingly fast. Within seconds Maggie had the search results for Maggie Cumberland. The number of them shocked her. She'd expected one or two but the name cropped up in every snippet on the first page, the source links crediting The New York Times and the local Journal News, plus television stations from News 12 to the local affiliates of the major broadcasting channels.

She swallowed hard. It was over forty-eight hours since she'd left home. Less in terms of how long anyone would know she'd disappeared. She'd deliberately picked a day when she had no commitments. Mila wouldn't give her absence a second thought. She'd assume Maggie had gone to the shelter and out to lunch with friends. It would have been evening before Daniel discovered she wasn't there. She could imagine his panic. It was totally out of character for her not to be there when he got back from work.

Her hands shook as she clicked on The New York Times link. Might as well start with the big one.

The page loaded. She frowned.

Company directors arrested in police swoop, the headline read.

She scanned the first paragraph of the article, her eyes widening as she took in the implications. The police had finally acted on her information.

Two evenings earlier police had pulled over a Mastersons Distribution truck. The driver had protested, he wasn't speeding, but the police weren't interested in how fast he'd been going. They had a search warrant and wanted to see the cargo. The driver's claim that he only had the manifest but no key was disregarded. It took only minutes for one of the officers to gain access. The container was packed full, a wall of medium sized boxes marked fragile all that could be seen. Antique furniture headed for Chicago according to the manifest.

Police removed enough boxes to allow them to squeeze through to the rear of the container. Three rows back they found a wire-mesh partition dividing the space in two. Beyond it, there weren't boxes, but bodies. Six drugged young women sprawled unconscious on a thin mattress on the floor.

The truck had been impounded, the driver arrested, although the report quoted an unnamed officer's statement that judging by the expression on the driver's face when they found the women he had no idea his cargo wasn't what it should be.

As dawn broke the following morning, teams of officers descended on the homes of the three Mastersons' directors before they had a chance to learn their latest cargo had been intercepted. Also included in the swoop was the Chief Financial Officer, Daniel Cumberland, who was believed to have direct knowledge about the company's illegal activities.

Maggie stopped reading. That would have given the neighbors something to talk about. No matter how discreet the police were in arriving to arrest Daniel, once they had him there would be no need for stealth. The early morning joggers and commuters could hardly fail to notice the police presence at the Cumberland house. No trees or wall separated it from public view, only the driveway and an expanse of grass.

Would they have sent one car or two to pick Daniel up?

She imagined two. After all, they couldn't be certain how many others were in the house at the time. They presumably expected to find her there. And would they search the house looking for incriminating evidence?

She shuddered at the thought of strangers' hands touching her possessions, rifling through drawers and closets, invading her privacy. Though, since she'd be unlikely to ever use them again, did it really matter?

She continued reading. The more she read the more she trembled. The Mastersons trio and their alleged activities were the focus of the lengthy report. It wasn't until the final paragraph that she found a reference to herself.

Police were concerned, she read, to learn the whereabouts of Daniel Cumberland's wife Maggie who, her husband claimed, hadn't been seen since the previous morning.

Ha! They had every right to be concerned. Without her input the arrests would probably never have happened. Judging from the report this wasn't some local crime ring but a complicated organization with tentacles reaching into many cities not only in the US but also abroad.

If she'd known the full extent of their activities she would have been too terrified to go to the police. But she had. And how had they responded?

"Go home and act normal."

When they didn't find her at the house, she hoped Detective Abbot had the decency to feel guilty.

She clicked through a few more articles. They all said much the same, her disappearance often reported as an afterthought. Good. It meant everyone was focused on the crime rather than her. Her photograph had yet to appear. For now she was a name without a face, not even a written description.

She froze.

Except Arthur had seen someone on television, someone he thought was her. She clicked on the News 12 link, drummed her fingers against the battered desk as if that might speed up the loading process. The familiar logo filled the screen before segueing away to show the regular news anchor sitting at a desk. "Our top story," she said, causing another tremor to ripple through Maggie as she heard the same story but this time told with the emphasis on the local resident involved, Daniel.

She stared transfixed at the screen as the anchor switched "live to the field for more details."

A female reporter excitedly relayed how police had turned up early that morning to arrest Daniel Cumberland for his alleged part in a major human trafficking ring. She gestured behind her and the camera panned in until Maggie's home filled the screen. Two police cars stood in the driveway. A uniformed officer stood guard at the doorstep. The front door was ajar.

Was Daniel still inside the house?

Opposite the driveway a group of onlookers had gathered, neighbors no doubt, curious to find out what tragedy had befallen the Cumberlands. One or two of the faces looked familiar, but nobody Maggie could put a name to.

A mugshot of Daniel appeared on one half of the screen. On a weekend, the tousled hair and unshaven chin were a familiar sight, but as this had been taken on a weekday they offered proof that he'd been roused from his bed unexpectedly. Maggie liked to joke how much sexier he looked rather than in the clean-shaven, slicked-down hair mode he presented to the working world. He'd laugh and tell her he saved his sexy side only for her.

Well, thanks to the internet a few million others were being offered a peek too. Though more likely, based on the accompanying tight-lipped mouth and blank stare, they'd see just another criminal.

Maggie frowned. The blank stare niggled at her. Shouldn't he be distraught, worried? If not over the arrest, surely over her disappearance. In fact, he should be downright frantic. His arrest would mean he wouldn't be able to search for her, leave no stone unturned. Wasn't that what someone who loved you was supposed to do? Where was the outrage, the grief?

She didn't care if he'd just woken up. What was he doing even sleeping, knowing she was missing? He should have been scouring the streets, contacting their friends. Sleep should have been the last thing on his mind. It would have been for her if the roles were reversed. And yet there he was, wife missing, arrested for a heinous crime, and looking as calm as if he were having his passport photo taken. She wanted to scream at the ridiculousness of it all.

The photo disappeared. The scene reverted to the reporter outside the house. A well-dressed middle-aged woman stood at her side.

"Residents are shocked by the events of the morning." The reporter pointed her microphone at the woman. "Mrs. Jackson, I understand you've lived in the neighborhood for over twenty years."

"Almost thirty." Mrs. Jackson corrected her in a tone which demanded congratulation. None were forthcoming so she continued. "And there's never been anything quite like this before. This is a nice neighborhood. The people are nice. This family has lived here for a long time and they seemed such a nice family."

Maggie peered at the screen. Who was this woman, this Mrs. Jackson? She couldn't remember ever seeing her before. How would she know whether they were a nice family or not?

"Do you know the Cumberlands personally?" the reporter asked.

"Oh, yes. Especially the wife. Such a nice lady."

Maggie scoffed. "So what's my first name?"

"It's so very sad. You think you know your neighbors, but you don't really. You don't know what goes on behind closed doors, do you?"

"Because you don't know us at all," Maggie yelled at the screen. "Who are you?"

"Have you seen Maggie Cumberland recently?"

Maggie groaned. Now she'd never know whether Mrs. Jackson really did know her first name.

"Actually, I haven't seen Maggie for a week or two." Mrs. Jackson hesitated. "But that's not unusual. We're all busy people."

The reporter faced the camera. "Local police have started a separate investigation into the whereabouts of Maggie Cumberland. According to her husband, he came home to an empty house last night and has no idea where his wife is."

Beside her, Mrs. Jackson's jaw dropped open. This was one tidbit she obviously hadn't heard.

The reporter continued. "Although under normal circumstances the police say they would wait forty-eight hours before beginning an investigation they are obviously concerned there may be a link between Mrs. Cumberland's disappearance and today's arrests."

Maggie whimpered. Felt the blood rush from her head.

No! The reporter couldn't insinuate that. The police would never have suggested it. Not in a way that made it sound as if Maggie had something to do with the arrests. That would be like shining a huge spotlight on her for the world to see. The tabloids would have a field day—the woman who turned in her husband and took down a major crime ring in the process. She could end up with a price on her head.

This was exactly why she had disappeared.

She sank her face into her hands. Had she made a terrible mistake? Should she have stayed? Done a Mrs. Jackson and claimed you could never really know the people you love and live with. Well, that part was true anyway in her case.

She glanced back at the screen. Her image smiled back at her. A photo taken about a year earlier, at a friend's wedding. Thankfully, portraying the familiar Maggie Cumberland look: smart clothes, impeccably styled hair and immaculate make-up. If this was the image Arthur had seen she couldn't fathom how he'd made the connection, even if he was a retired detective.

A number appeared under the photograph. Police were asking anyone who might have seen her to call.

The news snippet ended. Maggie worked her way through several more, different reporters on the scene, but each telling the same story. The neighborhood must have been overrun with news vans and eager reporters. Mrs. Jackson managed to pop up on other stations too. The woman was definitely determined to get her fifteen minutes of fame out of the scandal.

Maggie slumped back in the chair, weary of reading the same story over and over again. If she read another ten, no doubt they'd be the same. The reports she'd read had been from the previous day. The arrest had been made, Daniel taken into custody. There was no one home to pester. The reporters must have moved on to another story.

Really?

That didn't sound right. A major trafficking ring bust and it generated only a morning's worth of news? What about the victims, weren't their stories worth telling? And what about her? Why wasn't there anything more recent? If police were concerned yesterday morning surely they should be even more concerned now.

She got up and paced the room. A gamut of emotions fought for attention. Mostly guilt over being the one to cause Daniel's arrest even if he did deserve it, and fear of the consequences of her actions. Vulnerability from having no one to turn to, and sheer sadness at the glimpse of the home she might never be able to go back to again.

She was a fool. Why had she fled? What difference did it make whether she was in New York or New Orleans? She was always going to feel as if she was looking over her shoulder.

At least if she'd stayed the police might have offered some kind of protection after the arrest. But then she'd also have to deal with the stigma of being the wife of a criminal, one who ratted on her husband. She didn't think she could cope with that. What if the old saying was true, that you never knew who your real friends were until you needed them in a time of crisis? And what if she discovered she didn't have any, just a bunch of fair-weather friends?

She tried to imagine herself on the other side of the situation. Say it was one of her friends who'd found themselves in this mess. How would she react? She liked to think she'd do anything she could to help, offer a shoulder to cry on, be a sounding board for ideas of how to move forward, help out with the kids if need be, provide a few home-cooked meals, the usual stand-by-your-friend stuff. As she'd done for a couple of friends who'd suffered in the recession. Friends who'd found others less compassionate, as if their problems might be contagious by close contact. It had certainly made her see some of her other acquaintances in a different light, but they were still in her circle while the less fortunate ones had moved away, the promises to keep in touch mere words, backed by no intention. The thought of being the next target of gossip and derision made her shudder.

Fear and shame. One alone she could probably cope with, but both together, and without Daniel's support, she doubted it. That's why she'd fled.

She stopped pacing. It didn't make sense that the story had broken yesterday morning and vanished by this morning. Such a huge and horrific story, there had to be follow-up reports, though maybe not involving her. She cleared the browser and typed in Mastersons Distribution.

She was right. The story had gone viral on the major newspaper and television sites, most of them updated within the last hour or so. She started from the top, worked down the first page of links.

The reports all told the same story. The directors and Daniel had already appeared in court. The directors were charged with human trafficking. The prosecutor cited them as a flight risk and bail was refused. Daniel was charged with money laundering and granted bail, but according to the post had not been able to come up with the money so was still in jail.

Maggie reread the section twice. It didn't make sense. Granted it was a hefty sum, but Daniel could surely have pulled the money together, so why hadn't he?

Her sense of guilt increased. Had he put her disappearance together with his arrest and assumed she'd return if he was still in jail? Did he realize she was responsible for putting him in jail in the first place?

There was no further mention of her, but if the police were putting pressure on him as to her whereabouts he might think this was the best way to get her to return. Assuming she could. So he'd wait until he heard she was back and then get himself released. And then what?

If he knew of her involvement why would he want to be in the same house as her? And if he didn't, why would he assume she'd be willing to stand by him? He knew only too well her opinions on any kind of abuse.

She yawned, stretched her arms up over her head and leaned back to release the tension in her shoulders. The bedside alarm clock showed it was almost three hours since she'd started her search and if she was honest, the last two hadn't produced any new insights. But she'd had to read each report and watch each clip, afraid the one she skipped would be the one she needed to read.

She glanced around the large room. Imagined Daniel in a tiny cell somewhere. Pictured their house dark and empty.

If she hadn't fled would they both have now been sitting in their cozy family room? Daniel explaining his involvement in a way she could understand? Reassuring her that her life had not been turned upside down as she imagined by his outrageous actions? Convincing her it had been a horrible mistake. That no one in the company knew those girls were in the container. Someone had tampered with their cargo, perhaps a competitor who wanted to muscle in on the business and had no scruples as to how they did it. Or a crime ring who'd taken advantage of a weakness they'd found in Mastersons' delivery process.

She pictured him sitting close, stroking her hand as he stared into her eyes and gently mocked the idea that he or any of the three Mastersons brothers would be involved in anything so heinous.

And, oh, how she'd want to believe him, would willingly have believed him because, after all, he was her loving husband who only wanted to do right by his family. A guy who would never hurt a hair on anybody's head, never dream of making money from another's suffering.

And she'd look into those beguiling brown eyes that begged to be trusted and she'd wonder how she'd ever fallen for this stranger whom she'd lived with for the last twenty-two years. This pathological liar who had no idea he could come up with the most imaginative excuses possible and she wouldn't believe a word. Because she'd been there, heard him talk of shipments and numbers of girls and where they came from and where they were going and finally, in a calm voice as if he were reporting the weather, talk of wire transfers and bank accounts.

He had no idea she'd been standing in the hallway, frozen rigid as she listened to his words. Or that she'd snuck out of the house while he was still talking.

Looking back, she didn't know how she'd done it, how she'd managed to drive to the club, even stopping at a pharmacy on the way to pick up some tennis balls. She'd apologized profusely to her opponent Sue for being late and proceeded to play the worst game of tennis of her life, giving Sue, who languished at the bottom of the club league, an easy win. Even Sue couldn't quite believe it, asking her if she was coming down with the horrendous flu going around.

To preempt any further prying by Sue, she'd agreed she might be. Sue was a kind-hearted soul who could be trusted not to spill secrets, but was akin to a bloodhound on the trail if she could sense one in the making. She lived alone, her husband dead and the children grown, and being a confidant for others apparently compensated for the lack of excitement in her own life. Maggie was surprised she hadn't popped up in one of the television reports. Maybe that was too much excitement for her.

What she'd give to be able to talk to Sue now.

She yawned again, hoped this apparent tiredness would translate into a few decent hours' sleep. She shut down the computer, stripped down to her underwear and slid between the sheets of the king-sized bed. Her case lay unopened on the rack. She hadn't had a shower for two days, but who was there to care?

She closed her eyes. Prayed for oblivion.

Chapter 26 – Sunday morning

Maggie woke to the sound of loud laughter outside her window. She groaned at the lack of consideration shown by the night owls, rolled onto her side to peer at the clock and jolted upright. It was after ten. The heavy drapes had kept the room in a constant state of darkness and sheer exhaustion had finally defeated her restless mind.

She'd missed breakfast but it was a small price to pay for the improvement in her frame of mind. She made some coffee while she waited for her laptop to boot up and settled back against the pillows to see what news, if any, had developed overnight.

Additional arrests had been made in connection with Mastersons Distribution in several major cities and two more shipments of women had been intercepted, some of the victims barely old enough to be classed as adult.

The mere thought of what those girls might have experienced turned Maggie's stomach. How could one human be so cruel to another? The clientele might think they were paying good money to have their needs satisfied, but did they ever stop to think, really think, about the women providing the service beyond whether she was attractive in whatever way turned them on? Did they ever stop to think whether the woman was really a willing participant? How could they let their selfish needs blind themselves to the reality of the horror of the women's lives? How did they justify financing such a horrendous business? Did they realize that while they might think they were just paying for sex they were also lining the pockets of the perpetrators of major crimes? Take away the demand and the business would dry up.

It sounded so simple, but Maggie knew it wasn't. Prostitutes had plied their trade throughout history and were likely to continue into the future. She'd heard some European countries had legalized it in an attempt to stamp down on the seedier side of the business, give the women some protection without having to resort to pimps, and perhaps as a way to stamp out sex-trafficking, but Maggie suspected it wouldn't make much difference. Fearing for your life and not having anywhere to turn was a powerful antidote to telling the truth to some bureaucratic inspector. Putting on a false façade was how the traffickers caught their prey in the first place, how difficult would it be to use another to satisfy or circumvent the law?

She let the anger at what she read roil through her. She didn't normally pay much attention to politics, but her work with the abused women's shelter had made her sensitive to any form of mistreatment of women. That was why she'd decided to go to the police with what she'd overheard, despite the potential ramifications for herself and her family. The abused women at the shelter were told they needed to be strong and unafraid if they were going to create a new future for themselves. How could she expect any less of herself in her attempt to help them?

The news reports focused mainly on the owners of the company. Daniel's name was barely mentioned. She figured that meant he was still in jail and his involvement was considered less newsworthy by the national press than that of the company owners.

She switched over to a local news site. Sure enough, Daniel had hit the headlines there. The report did little more than recount the previous day's news though they'd managed to find a photo of him that wasn't a mug shot. It depicted his work day image, smart and serious. A thin smile played on his lips, a smile that conjured up reliability and trustworthiness with a dash of charm.

She marveled at how easily he'd fooled people, especially her. Day after day to live a lie, it had to take a toll but, as she searched her memory, she couldn't think of any instances where he'd let his façade down.

Her friends had all joked she had a perfect husband. Well, perfect was obviously an exaggeration. He had his flaws like everyone, his non-existent domestic skills for one. And despite being able to recall the date and detail of his sports teams' victories and defeats going back to when he was a boy, she still had to drop hints about forthcoming wedding anniversaries and birthdays.

So, no, not perfect. But was there such a thing? And compared to some of the flaws among her circle of friends— violent tempers, gambling, alcoholism and infidelity—she'd had nothing to complain about.

Until now.

A knock at the outer door startled her. She peered out the window but couldn't see who was there. She kept quiet hoping whoever it was would go away.

Another knock was followed by the rattle of the door handle.

She slammed her laptop shut, unlocked the inner door and came face to face with a young Latina woman carrying a bucket of cleaning supplies.

"Sorry, Ma'am." The woman backed away. "I thought the room empty."

Maggie sighed with relief.

"I come back later," the maid mumbled. "So sorry, Ma'am."

She dashed out the door before Maggie could say anything.

Maggie shrugged, bemused by the woman's reaction until it dawned on her she was dressed only in yesterday's t-shirt which she had pulled on when she'd first got out of bed. Based on its crumpled state the girl probably took her loud sigh for exasperation at having been woken and assumed she would be reprimanded.

Maggie made a mental note to try and find the woman later, under the pretext of letting her know she was going out and reassuring her it hadn't been a problem. But first she needed to finish reading the report.

This reporter had managed to get hold of the next door neighbors. Both couples expressed their shock at the news, declaring that Daniel had seemed such a nice guy, always ready with a friendly greeting although on the whole the family kept pretty much to themselves.

She scoffed. The neighbors on both sides were fairly recent arrivals. Youngish couples. One had no children, left home early in the morning and returned late at night most days, although obviously not on this day by the sounds of it, while the other couple, Jessica and Jim, had pre-school children and a nanny and had politely rebuffed Maggie's attempts to make their acquaintance beyond knowing their names. This had puzzled her. She might be past her child rearing stage while they were only at the beginning, but she doubted there was more than ten years' age difference between them. She'd only been twenty-four when Craig was born. She guessed Jessica was already in her mid-thirties.

Finally, at the last paragraph, she found what she was looking for. Police were still trying to contact Maggie Cumberland. Concerns were growing as to her whereabouts and a full inquiry had been launched into her disappearance.

Maggie double-checked the time of the report. It had been filed late the previous evening. The investigation should have started, so why no mention?

She clicked back onto the browser. Typed in Maggie Cumberland. Drummed her fingers on the desk as she waited, the anticipation of what she might find making her tremble.

She scrolled through the search results. She wanted a video report not a written one. Found the local news channel and sat back to watch. It was the same reporter as the day before. She appeared to be standing in exactly the same spot—had she been there the whole time? Waiting for the next piece of breaking news?

"With no sign of Daniel Cumberland's wife Maggie since

Thursday," the reporter said, "and amidst growing concerns, police launched an investigation this morning to find the missing woman."

She gestured toward the house. Crime scene tape encircled the property. Several cars, some unmarked, lined the street outside. If crowds had gathered again they were being kept out of sight.

"Police returned to the house for a second time in the hope of finding some indication of where Mrs. Cumberland has gone. They stress at this point this is not a criminal investigation, but given the timing of her disappearance the day before her husband's arrest, they are concerned for her safety.

"According to neighbors, Mrs. Cumberland was last seen leaving the house with her husband last Saturday evening. If anyone has any further information regarding her movements since then they are asked to please call the hotline shown on the screen. The police are also looking for Mrs. Cumberland's car. According to her husband, her silver-colored Honda Pilot was in the driveway when he left for work that morning, but gone by the time he returned that evening."

The video switched back to the anchor in the studio. He repeated the request for information and moved onto another story. The clip froze.

Maggie leaned her head back against the pillows. She could end this now with one phone call. Let everyone know she was safe, but that would mean she would have to give away her location. Or would she? The police would want proof that she was Maggie Cumberland, presumably visible proof, but if she told them her concerns maybe they'd agree not to divulge where she was. Quietly announce she'd been found and close down that part of the investigation. But what if they refused? Demanded she return home? Suppose they assumed she'd fled because she too was involved in the crime rather than solely an innocent informant? She could end up with both the police and Mastersons' cohorts after her.

She assumed the police would focus their search close to home to start with. The story would remain a local one and that's what she wanted. Not to go through every hour of every day afraid someone might recognize her from a news shot. Or at least no more afraid than she already was.

She sank her face into her hands. She'd come up with this plan in a moment of desperation and let the intricate attention required to put it into action subsume her thoughts beyond anything but getting away.

Call in or not? Neither offered a winning solution. But if she didn't call in, would that be a crime? A waste of police resources, not to mention the emotional effect on those she knew.

She, who had never had a speeding ticket, never even been stopped for speeding. Never done anything really to raise people's eyebrows. She was a mother, a housewife. She'd briefly been a secretary. Nothing in her life had prepared her for this kind of situation.

She replayed the video, fast-forwarding to the hotline number, grabbed the room phone and started punching in the digits. Her finger hovered over the last one.

It was the right thing to do. For everyone. Except maybe herself.

It was the right thing to do.

She double-checked the numbers against those on the screen. One call. That's all it would take. And she could go back to being Maggie Cumberland. Risky, but she'd have people on her side. Not like now, all alone.

She checked the numbers again.

Alone, but invisible.

She hung up the phone.

Chapter 27 – Sunday morning

The sights and sounds of Bourbon Street assailed Maggie's senses. Bars and restaurants lined the narrow street. Music and chatter from the outdoor seating on the second level verandahs drifted down to the passersby below. Crowds thronged the street, in places spilling off the sidewalk into the road. A horse-drawn carriage added the staccato drumbeat of hooves to the melee.

Interspersed between the dining and the drinking establishments, a multitude of gift shops offered identical souvenirs at identical prices. Desperate to have something to take her mind off her dilemma, Maggie wandered into each. She examined the mugs and the dish cloths, the magnets and the spoon rests, despite being aware she currently had no use for any of them.

She hesitated over a mouse mat depicting an illuminated night scene of the street, debating whether it would be a useful gift for Craig. She put it back. She wouldn't be able to give it to him, not for the foreseeable future anyway. The thought made her want to cry.

She grabbed a dish cloth for herself instead—it was bound

to come in useful at some point—and headed for the cash desk. Halfway there she changed her mind. Decided to get the mat. Somehow she would let Craig know she was okay. She'd no idea when, or how he would react to the news, but she couldn't block his existence out of her life forever. It wasn't possible. One day she'd see him again, of that she was determined.

"Are you okay, Ma'am?"

Maggie blinked and focused on the woman behind the counter.

"Yes." She blinked again. "Just something irritating my eyes."

She waved it off as if it happened all the time and busied herself digging in her purse for some money. Money she shouldn't be spending on non-essentials, but old habits were hard to break, especially this one, and the assistant was giving her strange looks to start with. It was too late to back out of the purchase now.

She managed a polite smile as the assistant handed over the bag and change. She made to leave, let out an involuntary gasp and froze.

"Ma'am, are you sure you're okay?"

Maggie shook her head, blinked again, and stared at the window. There was no one there. Or at least no one who resembled the guy from the train to Washington. And yet she could have sworn she saw him peering in from the other side of the glass.

She hurried out of the shop. If he'd been there at all he'd disappeared so quickly he could only have gone in one direction. She dodged through the crowd, trying to pick out any man who appeared to be on his own. A blue shirt, she was sure she'd seen a blue shirt, but the glimpse was so brief maybe she'd imagined it.

There were no blue shirts in sight or men on their own as far as she could tell. Forced to stop for traffic at a cross street, she reconsidered.

He'd said he was going to Florida. She must have imagined him. He couldn't possibly have got there and then made his way to New Orleans in such a short time. Not by train. She knew from the schedules there wasn't a route between Florida and New Orleans anymore, not since Hurricane Katrina.

She followed the crowd across the road. Decided she had let all the stress from the decisions and the doubts get to her. Let her fears take over her mind. There may well have been someone looking through the glass at that very moment, they may have been wearing a blue shirt, may have had the same coloring, and her imagination had taken those few facts and created them into someone who couldn't possibly be there.

The crowd stopped again to let a group of people exit from a gate out of a narrow alley. Maggie looked through as she passed, saw an outdoor restaurant with tables along both sides, and noticed the couple at the table nearest the gate get up to leave.

Still shaken by her experience she decided she needed a drink. And given it was mid-afternoon some food wouldn't go amiss either. She caught the hostess' attention, pointed toward the empty table, but the hostess led her to where the alley opened into a pretty courtyard with a covered patio off to one side. Most tables were full, families, friends and colleagues enjoying a late lunch.

The table chosen for her was in the far corner of the covered area. She had to squeeze through the narrow gaps between other patrons' chairs to get there. It had the benefit of being out of the oppressive afternoon sun, but made her feel she was being hidden away due to her solo status. It irked her, made her feel like a second class citizen, an outsider looking in.

The table next to her was littered with enormous empty glasses, the six occupants' loud voices, unintelligible sentences and raucous laughter over inane comments obvious signs of the effect of imbibing the contents.

Maggie smiled. Watching the interaction between the four girls and two guys took her back. She'd been like that once, hard as it was to believe. Carefree, before life's responsibilities set in. Reckless. Well, not really reckless. Her personality type tended toward the safe and acceptable, but she could have been reckless, the opportunity was there. She'd just never taken it.

As one of the girls shrieked at something one of the guys whispered in her ear, a pang of loneliness engulfed Maggie, not helped by the amount of time it took for a waiter to pay her any attention.

She considered the menu. On a whim, decided against a salad and ordered refried beans and rice. They sounded suitably southern and now was as good a time as any to make some new choices as Abigail. The waiter asked if she wanted a drink. She shook her head. Water would be fine. As he made to leave, she suddenly stopped him.

"I'd like one of those." She pointed at a large drink on the next table.

"A Hurricane?"

"Yes, a Hurricane." She had no idea what was in it, but if it made her forget her problems for a few hours it would be worth it. A Hurricane. She liked the sound of it. Blow away her worries and her cares. Totally irresponsible. Totally. But she needed some release.

The drink worked its magic. She took her time. Let the alcohol numb her mind into a false sense of serenity. She wolfed down the food and then, because she didn't want to leave her new found sanctuary, ordered dessert.

While she ate and drank she people-watched. Tried to guess the relationships between dining partners, whether they were happy or sad or angry. She'd never really stopped to look at other people's body language before and she was surprised by how much they gave away. She saw spats and petulance, and hands caressing hands across the table. She saw mothers and fathers enjoying the company of their kids and others weary from constant whines and sibling squabbles. She saw fathers aloof from the family dynamic and children desperately trying to engage distracted parents.

She wanted to interfere. Point out the obvious. Simply by the change of a few words or a look, hurt and discord could be replaced with affection and harmony.

She chuckled out loud. Noticed the puzzled glances from those at the surrounding tables.

She ordered another drink.

There was something to be said about being an outsider. The other diners probably took her for a crazy lady, sad and alone, having to laugh at her own jokes. Little did they know she was undergoing an epiphany. In her solitude she could see what others couldn't. See how easy it was to solve others' problems.

Maybe it was a gift. After all, she was the one her circle of acquaintances tended to turn to when they needed someone to confide in. They knew she'd be discreet. Their secrets would be safe with her. She'd listened to woes about husbands, children, in-laws, parents, even pets! Sometimes the solution could be glaringly obvious. She'd offer her counsel, careful not to offend or appear superior. They'd thank her, leave full of good intentions, only to return at a later date with the same woes and excuses as to why her ways wouldn't work for them.

She took a large gulp of her drink.

Some people seemed to prefer to live in misery.

She took another gulp.

Words were fine, but had to be followed by action. No matter how much a problem was chewed over, it wouldn't be solved unless someone followed through on their words. Politicians were a perfect example. They talked and talked and talked. But what good did it do? It was just talk. And the problems stayed the same from one year to another, one government to the next.

She swiveled the glass between her fingers. Who was she trying to fool? It wasn't a gift. The answers were obvious. The problem lay with the consequences of those answers and the demands involved in putting them into action. They often required courage, fortitude and hardship, an unattractive choice when compared to the sense of security and familiarity of deep-rooted habits. Which was why it was always easier to see the solution to another's problems. The judgment was painless, the hardships someone else's to bear.

She emptied her glass. What would those friends she'd counseled over the years suggest she do in this situation? And would she pay any more attention to their advice than they did to hers? Somehow she doubted it. The way and the will to solve a problem had to come from one source.

She studied the empty glass. She hadn't needed to flee. She could have stayed and faced the consequences. Lived a life of lies and fear of retribution if those lies should ever be revealed. But she didn't have the courage. Or she thought she didn't.

And so she'd fled. And to what?

To a life of lies and the fear of retribution if those lies were discovered.

Chapter 28 – Sunday evening

Maggie woke with a thumping headache and only a vague recollection of retracing her steps back to the streetcar and eventually the hotel. The red digits on the alarm clock showed it was just after ten, whether morning or evening, she had no clue.

She lay on her back waiting for the pain in her head to recede. She'd assumed those two drinks would be mostly ice and soda, obviously an incorrect assumption and, under the circumstances, a dangerous one. With no one to look out for her she needed her wits about her at all times.

Her deep-seated sense of loneliness intensified. There was no one to care whether she was sober or drunk, happy or sad. She'd never been in this position before. First there'd been her parents and her sister, then her roommates, and then Daniel and Craig, always someone to help pass the time or to hold her hand in new situations.

She'd both envied and pitied her sister's self-sufficiency while not understanding why Jane insisted on it. She'd laughed off Jane's claims that no woman should need a man to feel complete, or children for that matter. What was wrong with following a tradition that had endured for so many years? Besides, being married and having children didn't preclude being self-sufficient, did it? Jane had agreed, said for many it didn't, but her tone of voice made it clear she didn't consider Maggie among that group.

Jane, of course, was. She'd know exactly what to do. She wouldn't be lying in bed, nursing a hangover and feeling sorry for herself. She'd be out there carving out an exciting life, as she had in each of the towns and cities she'd visited. She could plant herself anywhere and take root.

Maggie winced at the analogy. She meanwhile was akin to a hot house plant. She'd wither away without care and attention.

Dare she call Jane? Swear her to secrecy and ask her advice? Jane wouldn't rat on her. Not when she heard the full story. And the mere knowledge there was one person out there, on her side, would be such a relief.

Except she'd be asking, no forcing, Jane to be complicit in her lies, to keep secrets from her own husband and friends, spreading the deceit, all for Maggie's benefit. And if Jane felt the need to confide in someone else, the tentacles of secrecy would span out, slowly but insidiously until one day they reached someone they shouldn't. And she'd only have herself to blame. If she couldn't keep a secret, how could she expect anyone else to?

She eased herself out of bed and padded over to the window. Beyond the drapes a single old-fashioned street light illuminated the patio. So it was evening, not morning, which gave her plenty of time to sleep off the headache before she decided on her next move, assuming she could get back to sleep.

First though, she needed to check for any updates on the search.

Her car had been found almost immediately after the bulletin about it had gone out. One of the evening shelf-stackers at the supermarket had noticed it as he finished his shift. Thought it was weird because he was sure it was the same car he'd parked next to when he'd arrived several hours earlier. Staff had a separate parking area they were supposed to use, but he generally parked wherever he liked. "It wasn't as if the lot was overfull at night," he was quoted as saying. But he didn't think too much of it until he heard the news bulletin the following morning. The article reported the student was "pretty stoked to think he'd helped in the investigation and hoped the lady driver would be found safe and well."

Maggie hated to disappoint someone who had her wellbeing at heart, but in this case she hoped he would be, at least as far as her being found was concerned. Would the student follow the story now, a story which he might normally have skipped over, eager to see how it played out after his contribution?

Police had examined the car inside and out, but refused to admit whether they'd found any evidence, saying only that the investigation was ongoing. Their ambiguity puzzled her. Her fingerprints would be all over, as would Daniel's, and no doubt they'd both left other signs of their presence inside. Hairs, DNA, whatever it was the forensic guys searched for—but as it was a family car surely that wouldn't be much help to the police?

Or would it? If there were no signs of other people in the car would the police deduce either she or Daniel had to have driven the car to the supermarket? So no evidence could still be evidence—a point worth remembering for the future, a warning against becoming overconfident in her decisions and actions.

A thin smile played on her lips as the report continued. Her purse, complete with wallet, credit cards and driver's license had been found in the trunk of the car, this disturbing find suggesting she hadn't abandoned her car of her own accord.

The reporter insinuated the local police had interviewed Daniel in jail as part of their investigation, wanting to know his movements since he'd left home on Thursday morning until his arrest the following day.

Maggie's smile widened. As she'd guessed, they were looking at him first, a complete waste of their time, but useful to her if it kept them from looking elsewhere.

The report didn't specify how Daniel had responded but she knew exactly how he'd passed his day. He'd told her not to bother with dinner. He had a day of high-level management meetings and at Mastersons Distribution those meetings always including a catered lunch served in the executive dining room located on the top floor of their offices overlooking the Hudson River. No platter of sandwiches from the local deli for the Mastersons. Lunch was a multi-course event prepared on the premises by freelance chefs and lingered over for hours while they finished off several bottles of fine wine.

She'd always been skeptical about Daniel's claims that they still managed to get a lot of work done at these meetings. Had visions of the previous weekend's golf figuring high on the agenda. Now she wondered whether the conversations over the steaks or salmon centered on where the next shipment of girls was going to come from and where they would send them.

She hoped they'd enjoyed Thursday's meal. Hopefully, the last decent meal they'd have for many years. Too bad the caterers hadn't poisoned them all.

She wished she could have been a fly on the wall for the interview. To hear what lies he spun, the excuses he made. Or his struggle to convince the detectives that he knew nothing about his wife's disappearance.

There was no suggestion the police considered him a suspect, but there was also no outright denial. He must have realized the police were likely to zero in on him, especially in the absence of any compelling evidence to the contrary. Which would worry him most, the justified arrest for money-laundering or the false suspicion of being involved in his wife's disappearance? Whichever, it was fairly certain he wouldn't be sleeping well either.

Good. He deserved every miserable minute of his existence.

She switched off the computer.

If she told herself that often enough she might just begin to believe it, be able to drown out the automatic rush of concern and worry for the man she once loved.

Chapter 29 – Monday morning

The next morning Maggie was first into breakfast, having already been awake for over two hours. The pain of the headache had receded but left her heavy headed and slow.

Her morning search for updates on the investigation revealed nothing new. She'd been surprised by the paucity of them. Was the story already slipping from people's minds? Of course, with Daniel in jail, there was no opportunity for a tearful conference where he pleaded for his wife's safe return in front of the media. That would have garnered another day or so of interest in the case. Instead the reporters had merely stated that the case was ongoing.

She should be pleased. The less publicity the less chance of being recognized. But it also meant the less she knew about what was going on. She needed to know whether the Mastersons had any idea she might have been the one to bring them down. She'd assumed her disappearance would have hit the news well before the arrests. The unfortunate coincidence in timing of the two events surely suggested some connection.

Would Mastersons have initiated a separate search for her? The problem was she'd never know. They wouldn't go public with such a search, but they may well have connections who could keep them up to date with the police investigation.

Given she'd changed her name, used only cash and stopped using her social media accounts, there was no trail either paper or digital for police or the Mastersons to follow. The police, no doubt, would be searching through all her accounts looking for any clue to her whereabouts. The thought of them reading her personal e-mails, looking at her posts on Facebook, disturbed her more than the idea of them going through her closets. She had debated deleting some of the e-mails and posts before she left but, after deleting a few, realized such a premeditated action could be taken as evidence she'd fled. Besides, her e-mails were hardly interesting; they'd probably bore the officers who had to go through them to tears.

She'd taken every precaution she could think of. So why did she still feel so nervous?

The six other tables in the tiny breakfast room were now all full. She heard snippets of conversations. One couple waylaid the hostess filling their coffee cups with tales of the previous day's adventures while other groups excitedly planned their activities for the day ahead.

She listened enviously. She had no plans for the day, for the week, for the year. She really was rootless. She needed a plan but had no idea where to start. As it was, she'd discovered her choices were limited if she'd wanted to leave New Orleans that day.

The trains to Los Angeles only operated three days a week, meaning she either had to travel that day or wait until Wednesday. The alternatives were to retrace her steps or head toward Chicago, neither of which appealed. She liked the idea of keeping as much distance between herself and New York as possible so wanted to stay in the south. And, besides, she didn't feel ready to get back on a train yet so when she'd confirmed she could extend her stay at the hotel by an extra two nights it seemed the easiest option.

"Mind if we join you?" A skinny young woman clad in skimpy shorts and a lacy tank pulled out a chair and sat down without waiting for a response. Her partner—a spotty-faced youth in need not only of a hair cut but also a hair wash—waited for Maggie to give a perceptible nod before following suit.

Maggie watched as they silently wolfed down the contents of their laden plates, pastries, rolls, bananas, yogurts, the food disappearing as if they were fortifying themselves for a siege.

The woman noticed Maggie staring. Her cheeks flushed pink as she offered a mea culpa smile.

Embarrassed, Maggie glanced away, fighting back the instinctive motherly urge to ask them when they'd last eaten. Somehow she sensed it might be their only meal of the day, an assumption confirmed when the girl got up to restock her plate and, with a furtive glance around on her return, slipped two rolls and two apples into her bag.

"That's lunch sorted. Got to watch the cash." Her glare challenged Maggie to object, or rat them out in some way.

Maggie just nodded, silenced by the sudden realization that far from being outraged by such actions she needed to learn from them. She hadn't had to worry about where the next meal would come from, always assumed there would be plenty, but the moment she'd walked out of the house she'd left that lifestyle behind. Sure, she probably had much more money on her than these youngsters, but if she didn't start adopting a frugal mindset, the funds would soon run out and, until she found some kind of job, she had no way of replenishing it.

She beckoned the waitress over, asked for a refill of coffee. The couple left before Maggie had a chance to glean any more cost-saving tricks, a relief really when she considered how embarrassed she would be to ask, even if they were complete strangers. And what if they were curious about the story behind her fall from financial stability? Better to go to a bookstore, find a guide to traveling on a budget. See what other tips she could find there.

She smiled. No doubt she could find the information on her laptop, but a trip to a bookstore or, better, a library sounded like a plan for the morning, something concrete to do. She took her empty plate over to the buffet counter, selected a banana, a roll and some sliced cheese. Back at the table she discreetly slipped the banana into her bag. She buttered the roll, added the cheese and cut the sandwich into two unequal pieces. She ate the smaller piece before quickly wrapping the remainder in a napkin and stuffing it in her bag while no one was looking.

She sipped her coffee while she waited for her heartbeat to stop racing, for the warm flush to leave her cheeks. She'd make a lousy criminal, had no coping strategies for guilt. As a child she'd never got away with much, her parents able to tell in an instant if she'd been up to mischief. Unlike Jane, whose ability to hide her feelings allowed her to convince others of the veracity of outrageous statements before chortling with glee at having suckered the listener once again.

As she made to leave, an elderly gentleman blocked her path. He inspected the contents of the fruit basket, finally selected an apple and proceeded to toss it in the air as he left the breakfast room, seemingly not a care in the world.

Maggie sighed. Why couldn't she be like that?

Chapter 30 – Tuesday morning

Maggie gazed out across the murky gray waters of the Mississippi. A vaguely familiar tune played over the loudspeakers as the paddle steamer churned its way along the river, the lively beat tempting her to go inside and watch the live jazz band. But then she'd be foregoing the opportunity to see the real New Orleans, the city away from the hustle and bustle of the touristy French Quarter or the sedate Garden District which she'd half-heartedly explored the previous day.

And what a difference it was. Huge cargo ships lined the docks, towered over by the tall metal structures used for loading and unloading. An enormous complex, which she'd guessed had been abandoned, turned out to be a functioning sugar refinery, its sooty buildings and grime-encrusted windows an ugly blight on the landscape matched only by the monstrous oil refinery nearby.

She settled back in her chair by the upper deck railings. Listened as the narrator explained how some of the buildings they were currently passing in the ninth district were still awaiting repair after Hurricane Katrina.

"How dreadful, to be uprooted from your home in that way."

Maggie turned toward the speaker, an English woman judging by the sound of her voice.

"It's hard to imagine having to leave your home and possessions behind and not know whether you will ever return or whether they'll still be there if you do." The woman shuddered. "Nature can be so cruel, don't you think?"

Maggie winced. Not just nature.

"Oh, I'm sorry." Concern creased the woman's forehead. "I hope I haven't upset you."

Maggie shook her head while she tried to regain her composure.

"So silly of me. Just because I'm a visitor, I shouldn't assume everyone else is too. Were you affected by the storm?"

Maggie managed a smile. "No. It's okay. I'm a visitor too. And I was thinking the exact same thing."

"It's a fascinating city, isn't it? Full of contradictions." The woman didn't give her a chance to reply. "Where are you from?"

Maggie hesitated. What harm could there be in talking to a tourist, an English tourist at that. She'd hardly be likely to pay attention to the news, not unless it had a global impact. Besides, she needed to talk to someone, to abate the growing sense of isolation.

"New York. What about you?"

"Richmond, Surrey. Though it seems an age since I was there."

"Really?"

"Yes. I've been traveling... Oh, it must be about six weeks now. I started in Boston. Made my way, slowly I might add, down to New Orleans."

"Wow. That's some trip." Good. The more the woman talked the less talking she would have to do.

The woman laughed. "That's not the half of it. I'm not finished yet. I've got another six weeks to go. I'm heading west tomorrow."

"Are you enjoying it?" Maggie asked, barely able to tone

down her incredulity. Twelve weeks! She'd been away less than a week and already she wished she could go home.

The woman's eyes lit up with enthusiasm. "It's been fantastic. There's so much to see and do. In fact, originally, I thought by now I'd be on the West Coast, had a rough schedule and everything, but now I'm simply taking each day as it comes, moving on when I've had enough."

"You're traveling alone?"

The woman gave a throaty laugh tinged with resignation.

"Yes. My husband died two years ago. We'd always planned to do this trip once he retired, but fate had other plans. Sadly, he didn't make it to retirement. He had six months to go when he dropped dead. Huge heart attack."

"I'm so sorry."

The woman sighed. "It was quite a shock, but in some ways it wasn't. He was a lot older than me, and he'd had some health issues in the last couple of years. He should have retired early. He could have afforded to, but he had his plan and he was determined to stick to it."

She scoffed softly.

"I think he thought he was immortal. The idea he might not get to fulfill his plans never entered his head." She paused. "Though really, what's the point in living any other way? Who wants to sit around and wait for death?"

Maggie had no idea what to say in response. She'd always planned her life around other people, not herself. Fortunately, the woman kept talking.

"For the first year I was rather a mess, totally adrift, but eventually I realized he wouldn't want me to mourn forever. Our kids are grown and I had been really looking forward to this trip too, so I decided, what the hell, I'd do it anyway."

"But on your own. How brave."

"Oh, my dear, I'm no stranger to traveling on my own, or at least dealing with strange places. My husband's job sent us all over the world and while he worked I had to handle the day-to-day stuff pretty much on my own. New places, new routines, new schools for the kids, new friends, you have to be a self-starter or you'll be crushed. It's definitely not for everyone." The woman laughed. "Sorry, I'm prattling on as usual. But what about you? Are you with your family?"

Maggie hesitated again. Decision time. How much to lie? She admired this woman, her capacity to cope, but at the same time felt irritated by her, by the traits she displayed that Maggie knew she personally lacked. Traits which, if she possessed them, would make this journey so much easier. How to follow a story of strength with one of weakness?

"I'm on my own too." She cringed inwardly at the unintended apologetic tone in her voice. That wasn't who she wanted to be.

She coughed. Started over.

"My husband and I have recently separated. After twenty-two years. Our only child, my son, has already left home so I felt I needed to do something, to get away, try and sort out what I want to do now." She shrugged, gave a half smile. So far she hadn't lied. "So here I am."

"Why New Orleans?"

"It has a train station."

The woman gave her a quizzical look. "So do lots of other cities."

"I'm not staying here for any length of time. Just passing through like you." Maggie grimaced. "Except I don't have a definite plan. I'm traveling on a whim really."

"Good for you."

Maggie heard only encouragement in the woman's tone, no hint of derision or superiority. "To be honest this is the first time I've traveled alone. Some days I wonder what was I thinking?"

She paused.

"I'm not sure I was even thinking, more like reacting, but I needed to put some distance between us. Unlike you, we'd lived in the same community all our married life. It's hard if you separate because everything is connected to your married life, everyone you know, all your favorite places, and they're all tainted by association."

"You didn't have any close female friends?"

"Yes, but…"

What was she doing? Too much information. She'd opened the floodgates and if she wasn't careful wouldn't be able to close them.

"They only know me as a wife and mother. It's how I was defined. I didn't work outside the home after my son was born, well, except to volunteer. When he left it was as if he took half my identity with him, but most of my friends were at the same stage, so we had a common purpose. How to fill our lives now our children didn't need us anymore. But they've still got husbands, loyal, trustworthy husbands."

"You think."

Maggie frowned. "Sorry?"

"You think they have loyal, trustworthy husbands. You don't know for sure. Few people are totally open about the state of their marriages. Or at least not until the marriage goes wrong. It's always puzzled me, this idea of the perfect marriage. Why do we pretend it exists? Maybe if we didn't more marriages would last. People wouldn't feel they had to live up to some unobtainable standard."

The woman spoke as if from experience. Maggie wondered what kind of disloyalty her husband had displayed, but didn't like to probe. Whatever it was, this woman had chosen to stand by her husband to the end. Who could say whether it was an admirable quality or not? It surely depended on the problem. Personally, she hadn't known any woman who'd stayed with her husband after finding out he'd had an affair, Fortunately not a situation she'd had to confront, but that greatest of marital crimes paled in comparison to Daniel's breach of trust.

As the narrator informed them they were approaching the district of Algiers with its famous clock tower, the woman stood up and started taking photos.

She was attractive in a no-nonsense way. A short spiky haircut framed a fresh, relatively unlined complexion. A touch of eye-liner and mascara the only obvious signs of make-up. At first glance Maggie had assumed the woman was younger than her, but she'd said she had grown up kids so unless she'd started ridiculously young, that couldn't be right.

Was it the haircut? Would a shorter style take years off her appearance? Maybe she should consider it. Her hair hadn't been short since she was a toddler so the change could come in useful in helping her avoid recognition.

Suddenly, the woman aimed the camera at her.

She raised her hands in front of her face, but feared she might have been too slow.

"Please don't. I hate having my photograph taken. I always end up making a stupid face."

The woman fiddled with her camera, held it out for Maggie to see. "Don't be silly, there's nothing wrong with the picture."

There wasn't, except Maggie didn't want any photos of herself on anybody's camera. It was an unnecessary risk. Though how could she ask for it to be removed without appearing churlish?

"I'm sorry, I should have asked first." Despite her apology the woman made no attempt to delete the picture. "My memory's not great, so I'm creating a photo journal of my trip to help me remember who I've met where. Otherwise over time they'll start to blur into one another. I've met so many people while traveling. It's true what they say about Americans being friendly, isn't it?"

She stuck out her hand. "I'm Rebecca by the way.

"Abigail."

Rebecca repeated Abigail's name as they shook hands, her attempt to commit the name to memory providing welcome confirmation to Maggie that she'd used the right one. One of the reasons for avoiding others was the fear she'd blurt out her real name by mistake.

"Why don't I take a photo of you?" Maggie reached out for the camera. Maybe she could accidentally delete the earlier photo. She examined the various options on the back as Rebecca readied herself. So much for that plan. The camera was totally different from any she'd used before. It took her several minutes to work out how to take a single photo.

Rebecca insisted she take several. As she handed the camera back an elderly gentleman offered to take a photo of both of them. Before Maggie could turn him down Rebecca had pressed the camera into his hands and beckoned Maggie over to the railing.

Two middle-aged women on a boat. Who would look twice? It was harmless enough and easier to agree than to protest.

She forced a grin as the man said, "Say cheese."

She only hoped Rebecca wasn't the type to plaster her photos all over social media.

Chapter 31 – Tuesday evening/Wed morning

Maggie slapped her laptop shut, leapt up off the bed and started pacing. It wasn't possible. It had to be a fluke, a sheer coincidence. Over one hundred sightings had been phoned in since the police had asked for assistance in tracing her. She'd been spotted all over the country, even in Mexico and New Zealand. New Zealand! How did anyone in New Zealand even know about the police alert? So they had to be false leads, probably phoned in by people who had nothing better to do. Nothing to worry about, right? Except, one report mentioned a sighting in Washington, another New Orleans. How much of a coincidence was that? No mention of exactly where or when so there was no way to figure out if they were genuine. The police were following up on all leads. What did that mean? Were the police in New Orleans actively looking for her? Surely not. Why would they expend manpower on one missing woman from New York?

She froze.

Arthur. Washington. New Orleans.

She swallowed hard. Had the retired detective called in his

concerns? And if so, would the police be more likely to pay attention to one of their own, even if he was getting on in years? She searched her memory for whether there had been any mention of exactly where in New York Edith and Arthur came from. She didn't think so, she'd been careful to avoid specifics, afraid of letting something slip in response.

And if it was Arthur, what else might he have told them? That she was going by the name Abigail, not Maggie? That she'd ditched the smart clothes, opting instead for a more casual look?

She wanted to scream with frustration. This could not be happening. She caught a glimpse of herself in the full length mirror on the closet door. What a fool she'd been to think a change of clothes and a different hairstyle would conceal her identity. She should have dyed her hair, had it chopped off or worn a wig. And instead of going bare-faced, she should have gone the other way. Piled on the make-up, created a whole new look.

It was still a possibility, except it would mean she'd have to scrap her newly-made plans. After the river cruise Rebecca had asked if she wanted to go for a coffee. She knew of a place close to the river. They could sit outside and enjoy live jazz. Maggie jumped at the chance to put off being alone again. Rebecca liked to talk and Maggie discovered that if she got her started on a tale about her overseas adventures she would hold forth on the subject, barely noticing Maggie contributed little to the conversation.

As she listened, Maggie felt a twinge of regret. It sounded so exciting, so glamorous. She'd wiped tears of laughter from her eyes at Rebecca's account of dealing with Chinese-speaking plumbers through mime about a broken toilet. How easy her life had been by comparison, easy but mundane. Rebecca spoke a smattering of several languages, most learned out of necessity. English was all Maggie had ever needed. She wouldn't have dreamed of going anywhere where she might not be understood, anywhere where everyday life would provide a challenge. Which is why she felt so adrift now. Settling for easy had made her soft.

When Rebecca mentioned she was going to check out the French Market Maggie asked if she could tag along, a suggestion which seemed to delight Rebecca. By the time she'd returned to her hotel, they'd taken in the market, visited a nearby jazz museum and had dinner on Bourbon Street.

Over dinner Rebecca asked what her plans were for the rest of her stay in New Orleans. Maggie explained she was leaving the following day, heading west, being deliberately vague about exactly where as she still hadn't decided.

Rebecca's eyes lit up with excitement. She too was leaving the next morning, headed to San Antonio. She'd always wanted to see the Alamo and she'd heard the city itself was worth a visit. Why didn't Abigail come with her? Or at the very least leave on the same train as her? It would be so nice to have company on the fifteen hour journey.

Maggie promised only that she would think about it. She'd considered San Antonio as a possibility but discounted it when she discovered the train arrived there at two in the morning. The idea of arriving in a strange city so late with no accommodation booked terrified her. She wasn't about to admit it to Rebecca, the woman would probably laugh at her, but if Rebecca was with her she'd feel more comfortable.

They parted, agreeing to meet in the station the following morning. Whatever Maggie's decision, they would both be leaving on the same train.

Union Station was quiet when Maggie arrived a full hour before the train departure. She was relieved to see there was no line at the ticket window. She wanted to buy her ticket out of sight of Rebecca. She didn't want her to see she was paying cash, it might raise awkward questions.

She scanned the concourse, eyeing the other travelers. None looked like police officers. Scarcely reassuring—if they were plain-clothed she'd have no way of knowing. She'd woken in the middle of the night, panic-stricken by the realization that if Arthur had been the informant, the police would have good reason to check out the trains, especially the ones leaving New Orleans.

She approached the counter with trepidation. Despite paying cash the clerk would still want some identification. What chance he'd been tipped off to be on the look-out for anyone called Abigail? It was a risk she'd have to take. Staying in New Orleans was no longer an option either.

"I'd like a ticket to San Antonio, please. For today."

The clerk barely looked at her. He tapped on a keyboard, his eyes focused on a screen. "Some identification, please."

Close to hyper-ventilating, Maggie handed her license over. She watched the clerk's eyes for the slightest flicker of recognition as he studied the details. He flashed a smile at her as he began to type again. It seemed to take him an interminable amount of time. She wanted to tell him to hurry, but had no reason to do so.

"Abigail!"

Maggie pushed her money across the counter before turning to Rebecca.

"I'm so pleased to see you." Rebecca threw her arms around her as if they were life-long friends. "I was afraid you might change your mind overnight."

"No, no. I'm so looking forward to this." Maggie stepped out of the embrace and quickly took her ticket and change from the bemused clerk.

"San Antonio for you too?" he asked Rebecca.

"I already have my ticket, thanks."

He smiled. "Enjoy your trip, ladies."

Maggie smiled back. Ladies. Not one lady traveling alone, which is what the authorities would be looking for, but two middle-aged ladies traveling together. Who could be suspicious of two ladies, even if one of them was called Abigail?

Her smile broadened. Meeting Rebecca might just turn out to be a life saver.

Chapter 32 – Wednesday morning

No sooner had they settled in their seats after the train left the station than Rebecca insisted they moved to the observation car. Maggie tried to argue against it—they had a perfectly acceptable view where they were—but Rebecca was determined. Maggie decided to humor her. She'd go for a few minutes and then find an excuse to return to her seat.

They had to walk through three cars to get there. Rebecca hurried ahead, but Maggie had to clutch the back of each seat as she passed in an effort to maintain her balance against the sway of the train. Only a few seats were occupied which gave her hope the observation car would already be full.

Some passengers were already fully reclined, fast asleep, obviously with no interest in the passing scenery or too tired to care. She stumbled over the extended leg of one such passenger, barely managing to stay upright. She turned to apologize and to suggest perhaps he should keep his legs out of the aisle only to find her accidental kick in the shins hadn't disturbed the culprit.

Thank goodness. Because when she did a double take, the

sleeping man reminded her of Neil. She'd have to see his eyes to be sure, and this guy definitely had more facial hair, and, yes, she was totally paranoid at the moment, but she'd be willing to bet on it. So much so, that she raced along the rest of the car, hit the release on the sliding doors between the compartments as if her life depended on it, and nearly collided into Rebecca who'd stopped to wait for her.

"Are you alright? You look shook up?"

Maggie exhaled hard. "Some idiot back there tripped me up. Nearly ended up flat on my face. Some people are so inconsiderate."

Rebecca grinned. "You're talking about the guy whose foot was sticking out in the aisle? He was asleep. Probably had no idea he was in danger of tripping anyone up. It must be tough, traveling when you're tall. Nowhere to fit the legs. Did you get a look at him, though? He was kinda cute."

"Kinda cute?" Maggie gaped at Rebecca in disbelief. "I think you've been in America too long. Kinda cute? He's got to be about our age."

Rebecca shrugged. "So what? Is there an age limit on cute? I hope not. I like the expression. Has more emotion than, "I say, that chap is rather good looking"."

Maggie burst into laughter at the prim English tone Rebecca mimicked. It wasn't particularly funny, but it gave her time to decide whether to be up front about knowing Neil.

"I didn't pay any attention. Too busy trying to remain upright."

Rebecca's apparent disappointment made Maggie wonder whether there was an ulterior motive behind the other woman's trip. She'd said her husband had died two years ago. Maybe she was on the hunt for a replacement. Which could be a plus as she probably wouldn't want anyone tagging along if there was a suitable male on the horizon. Probably would be happy to be left alone in the observation car.

The observation car was half empty. As Rebecca made a beeline for a group of four vacant seats in the middle of the coach, Maggie immediately dropped into one of two chairs near to the door and called after her, "This will do."

Rebecca made a face but didn't object. They sat in silence, concentrating on the passing scenery as the Louisiana landscape switched from industrial to rural. Miles and miles of flat land, some cultivated, some water-logged, stretching as far as the eye could see with only the occasional small cluster of trees to break up the skyline. The bayou, maybe? A place Maggie had heard of but never imagined she'd see. Such a contrast to the densely forested hills of the previous train journey. Heavy, threatening clouds added to the sense of isolation.

She shivered. She couldn't imagine living somewhere like this. It bore no resemblance to the America she knew. The vast open spaces unnerved her. To her, Northern Westchester where she lived was rural and quiet, but she didn't have to go far to be in a city. Here she assumed a person could drive for miles and not meet another soul.

Though perhaps this was the kind of place she should be looking for? Surely the locals would have little concern for news about a missing woman from New York. Though how would she explain her presence in a place with few attractions to an outsider? Especially for any length of time? Besides, in reality, a day or two in a place like this would drive her crazy. If she couldn't interact too closely with people for fear of being spotted, she needed to be places with libraries, museums or simply busy streets.

Rebecca pulled out her camera, took one shot after another. Maggie couldn't see the point. The scenery didn't change much, but at least it meant Rebecca didn't want to talk.

How long before Neil, assuming it was him, woke up? Decided to come and enjoy the view or get a coffee from the downstairs cafe? She couldn't rule out the possibility he'd been the one who saw the appeal for information regarding Maggie Cumberland, picked up on the similarities in appearance and remembered how eager she'd been to brush off attempts at being friendly. Maybe even if he wasn't sure, he was the type of guy who'd phone in his suspicions anyway. Like Arthur, he'd only be able to tell them she'd been on the train to New Orleans. He had no way of knowing where she'd stayed or how long she'd stayed.

The moment she'd stepped off the train the trail had gone dead. Or so she'd assumed. So she had to make sure he didn't notice she was back on the train.

There was a simple way to ensure that. Her regular seat was two cars back from Neil's. With the observation car, the cafe and the dining car towards the front of the train, he'd have no obvious reason to walk back down the train. If she could get back to her seat unnoticed and stay there, all should be well. Except how to explain to Rebecca why she'd rather sit back there all day rather than enjoy the panoramic views on offer?

She yawned loud enough to catch Rebecca's attention. Yawned again, exaggerating the gesture, and then let out a tired sigh.

"I didn't sleep well last night. Not sure why. And the motion of the train is making me sleepy." She yawned again. Laughed. "I think I'll go back to our seats and have a nap."

Rebecca started to stand up.

Maggie panicked. If Neil was awake and spotted her she didn't want Rebecca present. There was no need for the woman to know they knew each other. Especially following Rebecca's cute remark. She might insist they sit together for the rest of the journey. How awkward would that be? And supposing it was Neil who'd tipped off the police, what if he called again and told them exactly what train she was on? The police could be waiting for her when she got off.

She sucked in her breath. Or would they get on the train at the first available stop? Trap her like a fox in a snare, with no chance to run.

"No, you stay here. No point in your coming back too."

Rebecca seemed hesitant. Maggie couldn't understand why. It wasn't as if they were the best of buddies, had to stick with each other all the time.

"Can you wait a few minutes?" Rebecca asked. "Let me go and get a coffee while you save my seat."

"Of course." Relief washed over Maggie. She hadn't noticed the lounge car had filled up so quickly. There were barely any free seats available.

Rebecca dug her wallet out from her bag. "Can I get you anything?" She dropped the bag onto the seat.

"No, thanks."

Maggie settled back into her seat. Let her mind drift. Her morning search of the news sites had turned up nothing new, only a few rehashed reports of the previous days' events. Until the trial, the whole story would hopefully slip from the public's mind. How long would it take for the story of her disappearance to do likewise? The police couldn't go on looking forever. Eventually they'd move on to other more imminent matters, her case just another unsolved mystery.

It would be left to her family to keep the pressure on the authorities, to keep the story in the public eye. Daniel couldn't. Not from behind bars, and if the newspapers were to believed, he faced serious jail time. That left Craig and Jane.

Did Craig even know yet? Who would have told him? She liked the idea he might be ignorant of what had happened. He'd always had an independent streak. To date, if they received an e-mail a month saying he was well, they were grateful. And in the time he'd been away Maggie's e-mails had also become less frequent so it could be a while before the lack of communication concerned him.

Jane was the immediate problem. She wouldn't let the matter rest, not without a body and a conviction. She'd assume something untoward had happened. Would never believe her sister would have the gumption to disappear of her own free will. Luckily being on the other side of the country and pregnant, Jane wouldn't likely be leaping on a plane to make her case locally. Still she was surprised there'd been no mention of Jane so far, no comments from a heartbroken sister. Surely she must know. Or was it possible Jane had missed the national headlines about the Mastersons' and Daniel's arrests? Not seen the numerous mentions about the missing wife?

"Penny for them."

Maggie glanced around to see Rebecca standing beside her, an amused expression on her face.

"Wherever you were, I don't think it was here." Rebecca

put a coffee and a croissant down on the table.

"Second breakfast. If I keep this up I'll need to go on a diet after this trip." She shrugged. "But what can you do? I love food so much. And sitting on a train offers so much time to eat."

As she eased herself through the narrow gap between the seats, she hoisted her bag up off her chair. One handle slipped from her grasp, the bag tipped to one side, and several items spilled out.

Maggie bent to retrieve them. Almost bumped heads with Rebecca who brusquely swept the items out of her reach.

"I've got this." Rebecca sounded flustered.

"Okay." The ferocity of Rebecca's action took Maggie aback. She watched her dump the handful of items, including a spectacle case, a passport and a packet of tissues, back into her bag, pushing them forcefully down out of sight.

"Lucky your camera didn't fall out," Maggie said as she caught Rebecca eyeing her. The look lasted only a second but seemed full of suspicion. Did Rebecca think she'd gone through her bag while she was away?

Rebecca didn't respond.

Maggie stood up. "Enjoy the view. I'll see you later."

As she walked away, Rebecca called after her, "Are you going to go for lunch later in the dining car?"

"No, I need to watch my money until I get myself sorted out. I brought mine from the hotel."

"Let me treat you."

Maggie thought of the roll and cheese she'd taken from the breakfast buffet. It was a tempting offer but too risky. What if Neil showed up?

"That's very nice of you, but no thanks. Besides, I don't usually eat a big meal at lunchtime."

"Maybe dinner?"

Maggie forced a grin. "Let's decide later." Once she'd had time to think of another excuse, Maggie added mentally as she left the car. Or ideally, once she'd proven Neil was a figment of her imagination and the sleeping man looked nothing like him.

As the door of the observation car slid shut behind her, she checked back to ensure Rebecca wasn't looking in her direction and then peered through the window of the next door, looking for the guy who'd tripped her. He was easy to spot. His leg still jutted out into the aisle and, from the way his upper body lolled to the side, she assumed he wasn't awake.

She entered, fighting back the urge to sprint. If she walked slowly toward him it would give her plenty of time to confirm she'd made a mistake.

Logic told her it couldn't be Neil. It was too big a coincidence. And from this distance she could see why she might have been confused.

The sleeping man was similarly built, had the same hair color as far as she could remember, a similar cut too. Only the facial hair was different, but the few days since she'd last seen him could account for that. She wanted so desperately to believe it wasn't Neil, but gut instinct told her it was.

She was two seats away from him when he stirred. He stretched, his leg protruding even further into the aisle. Suddenly, as if he sensed someone there, he opened his eyes, pulled his leg back and mumbled, "Sorry."

Maggie made to pass him at full speed.

"Abigail?" An element of doubt tinged his call.

She ignored the voice. Reached out to open the door.

"Abigail." He sounded more confident now.

She had a choice. She could acknowledge him, keep the chat brief and then head back to her seat and stay out of his sight for the rest of the journey or she could risk him following her back, either now or later. Memories of how persistent he'd been on the previous train came to mind.

She turned back, plastered what she hoped was a puzzled expression on her face.

He stood in the aisle, grinning at her. "Abigail, I thought it was you."

She squinted at him as if she had no idea who he was.

He laughed. "We met on the train. To New Orleans. Remember? Neil?

"Oh, hi." She blushed. Hopefully he'd take it as a sign of

embarrassment at her failure to recognize him and not for what it was: the discomfort of lying.

"Where you headed?"

"Out west."

He laughed again. "I hope so, seeing it's the direction the train is going in."

Maggie's blush intensified.

Neil grimaced. "Sorry, I wasn't trying to embarrass you."

She waved off his apology. She wanted to know where he was going but not at the cost of revealing her destination.

"Nice seeing you again." She turned away, hoping he'd take the hint.

"Hey, would you be interested in going for a coffee."

She sighed. What was it with him and coffee?

"Just had one. Now I need to get back to my seat."

He didn't hide his disappointment. Should she tell him that if he went to the lounge car he'd find a woman who'd labeled him cute? Rebecca would have coffee with him. She'd probably even have lunch or dinner with him.

She held her tongue. Hit the door release instead.

As the door opened she stepped through. She expected Neil to say something else, but the door closed before he had a chance. She continued on, not daring to look back, but sure he was watching.

Staying anonymous was harder than she'd imagined. Maybe it had been a mistake to travel by train. By car there'd be no chance of bumping into anyone en route. But a car rental was out of the question without a credit card. True, she could probably buy a cheap car for cash, but with what she knew about cars, it was a guaranteed recipe for being ripped off.

Back in her seat, she huddled up against the window in an attempt to make herself as invisible as possible. She wished she had a blanket to throw over her head. She had a towel, but decided that would definitely look weird.

Every time someone walked past she flinched, sure it would be Neil coming to search for her. Had he been the one to call in the sighting? His first question had been where was she headed, no obvious surprise at the coincidence of them meeting again or no polite enquiries about her visit to New Orleans.

Could he even now be calling back the hotline, updating them on her whereabouts? She closed her eyes, prayed the cell phone service on the train was spotty or better still non-existent.

Maybe she should have gone for coffee with him. It would have been a chance to glean if he had any suspicions. But it would have meant she'd have to introduce him to Rebecca.

She opened her eyes as the motion of the train changed. They were pulling into a station, New Iberia, Louisiana. She scanned the people on the platform as the train rolled past, looking for anyone official. She paid particular attention to two guys who didn't have any luggage. It raised her suspicions because everyone else did. She only relaxed when each in turn greeted someone getting off the train. She was safe for another few miles.

Or maybe now was the time to get off. Neither Rebecca or Neil would realize for a while. She wasn't beholden to them in any way. Besides only Rebecca knew she had a ticket for San Antonio. And the ticket collector. Would Rebecca panic when she came back and found the seat empty? Would she call the guard, create a fuss, insist on telling the police. Or would she realize that Abigail had taken her suitcase and so must be okay? Write her off as a weird encounter on her grand trip.

She frowned. Something about Rebecca unsettled her, which was strange because yesterday there'd been no reason for concern. The previous evening, traveling together had seemed like a great idea. Now she wasn't so sure. Was it purely that she'd lied to Rebecca about knowing Neil? That was insignificant, could easily be explained away. She sensed her concern was something bigger.

Nothing had happened that morning to raise the alarm though. They'd waited on line for the train for about half an hour, admiring the colorful murals and posters in the station waiting area, discussing their likes and dislikes in music, especially jazz. There'd been little conversation between them since they got on the train so apart from Rebecca's insistence they go to the lounge car there wasn't anything to pinpoint there either. True, she'd been rather shocked by Rebecca's outburst over the bag, but she didn't know the woman well enough to know whether it was out of character. Maybe she just had a short fuse.

A very short fuse.

And people with short fuses tended to be unpredictable. The need to tiptoe around them in order to prevent setting them off was a valid reason to avoid them altogether in her view. It was too much trouble, not knowing where the next explosion might come from. A character trait destined to create unpopularity. She knew of a few people who suffered from it. They tended to be bitter and mean personalities. But Rebecca had come across as sweet and caring. It was wrong of her to ascribe such a characteristic to her. But something had raised an alarm, a sub-conscious alarm, a feeling all was not as it seemed. And under the circumstances that was cause for alarm indeed.

Chapter 33 – Wednesday afternoon

The train pulled out of the station. Maggie pressed the side of her face against the window and stared blindly at the passing scenery. Too late now. She was stuck until the next station and there was no guarantee she'd be on her own then.

This was all too complicated. She thought it would be much easier to be invisible, but it required a willingness to ignore others, to survive in a cocoon of isolation, self-made in her case, and that was a skill set she'd never had to learn. She needed company. But company came with the threat of exposure if she couldn't keep her story straight and so far she'd said the first thing that came to mind, assuming it didn't matter, the people she spoke to were passing strangers, unlikely to be seen again. But only a few days out and look how wrong she'd been. Edith and Arthur, Neil, she could barely remember what she'd told them. That wouldn't do. She needed a solid story, one that with repetition over time would come as naturally to her as the real one.

She scoffed quietly. How many people got a chance to make up their past? She could be anyone she wanted to be. Within reason. Her back story had to justify her future actions. The story she'd spun Rebecca made a lot of sense, gave her the perfect excuse to be nomadic. A newly separated woman trying to work out what she should do with the rest of her life. And if she emphasized the newly separated aspect most people would be sympathetic but not want to pry too much for fear of upsetting her. Still, she should have a reason ready as to why she'd separated.

An unfaithful husband?

She couldn't imagine Daniel being unfaithful.

Abusive?

No. She'd heard too many heartbreaking stories of abuse at the shelter. She couldn't create a fake one. It wouldn't be right.

An addiction? An obsession? She scoffed again. How about a tendency to be economical with the truth? Certainly no lie. Ironically too close to the truth to tell without breaking down and, while she wanted sympathy, it was too dangerous a road to go down.

Best to stick to the mundane. Two people growing apart, their children the only common ground, and when the children were grown, what was left? A common situation. Nothing elaborate, nothing dramatic. A livable lie, even if it was so far from the truth in her case.

She'd told Rebecca she only had one son, a truth she'd have to stick with. And she didn't see any reason why she should change any details about him. She'd mention him only if asked.

The more she thought about it, the more she realized how little she needed to change about her past except for the reason for leaving her marriage, and also where she came from. The latter was easily solved. She'd grown up in Poughkeepsie, had been a frequent visitor there until a year earlier when she and Jane finally sold the family home. She knew the place well and, best of all, it matched the address on Abigail Thornton's driver's license.

Hide in plain sight. She wasn't sure whether that was just the name of an old movie or part of a philosophical quote, but it struck her as apt. She'd made the decision when she left home, there could be no going back, but nor could she hide in fear for the rest of her life. The quicker she built a new life, the less chance of being discovered by friend or foe.

She closed her eyes. Listened to the hum of the train as it sped her toward her new reality. Felt the beginnings of a smile. For the first time since this nightmare began she felt confident she could carry off her plan. Maybe she would have lunch with Rebecca after all.

She dozed off. Woke to find Rebecca sitting beside her.

"At last, I thought you were going to sleep forever." Rebecca grinned.

As Maggie looked at her watch, she added, "Only joking, I've only been here ten minutes." Her grin widened. "Guess who I've been talking to."

Maggie groaned inwardly. Decided lunch wasn't such a great idea. "Your cute guy?"

Rebecca nodded triumphantly. "And he's not just cute to look at. He's interesting too."

Maggie didn't reply. She was too busy silently bemoaning her luck. Bad enough that Neil was on the train, but that of all the guys on the train Rebecca should zoom in on him was totally unnecessary and unfair. Was it too much to ask for just one break?

"So, are you coming?"

"What?" Maggie hadn't heard a word Rebecca had said.

"For lunch. Are you coming?"

Maggie checked her watch again. Eleven-thirty. "Isn't it a little early?"

"No. The dining car's open. And I'm hungry."

Hungry? Hadn't she had two breakfasts?

"Why don't you ask that guy if he wants to go to lunch?"

"Oh, I have." Rebecca winked at her. "I told him we'd meet him on the way back."

"We?"

"Of course. I told him I had a traveling companion."

"I told you I'd brought a sandwich for lunch."

"Oh, come on. You've struck out on your own. You can't hide away. You need to meet people, make new friends."

"Well, I was thinking of friends that would last longer than a train journey."

Rebecca stood up. "Friendships can start in the most unusual of places." She looked pointedly at Maggie. "Are you coming?"

Maggie made to refuse, but reconsidered. There were more than twelve hours of the journey left. She didn't want to get off the train early, so she could either try to hide from Neil for the remainder of the time or she could take control of the situation and get the inevitable over now and maybe, just maybe, enjoy the rest of the journey.

Chapter 34 – Wednesday afternoon

Neil was waiting for them in the observation car, sitting in the seat formerly occupied by Maggie. The broad smile he offered Rebecca as she approached widened as he spotted Maggie behind her.

"It's you." He leapt up. "Well, what do you know? We meet again."

Maggie cringed at the familiarity. She glanced over at Rebecca to explain, but Rebecca didn't look at all surprised.

"Soon as I mentioned your name, he said he might already have met you." Rebecca said. "How's that for coincidence?"

Maggie hesitated. She didn't detect any barbs in Rebecca's voice, but why hadn't Rebecca mentioned it earlier? She could have casually dropped it into the conversation. Was it a trap? Had she been waiting for her to admit she already knew Neil?

"Didn't think it was likely there were two Abigails on the train," Neil said.

Maggie forced a laugh.

"You're probably right. So many shorten it to Abby nowadays." She laughed again. "I'm sorry I'm so bad with names.

What's yours again?"

"Neil."

"Neil." Maggie repeated it as if trying to commit it to memory.

"Nice to see you again," she added because she couldn't think of what else to say and had just remembered he'd reminded her of his name when they spoke earlier. He was going to think she was a total idiot.

"Shall we go for lunch?" She gestured toward the dining car, willing Rebecca to take charge, but Rebecca appeared lost in thought. Maybe wishing she'd left Maggie out of the invitation, enjoyed Neil's company alone.

They stood in uneasy silence as they waited to be seated. Maggie let Rebecca sit by the window and slid in beside her while Neil took the seat opposite Rebecca. She'd already decided she'd only speak if spoken to. She didn't want to get in Rebecca's way. She wondered what else the pair had said about her, other than her name. Though maybe it was egotistical to think they would have said anything more.

As she listened to them she admired their ability to indulge in easy banter after knowing each other for such a short time. She always felt uncomfortable talking to strangers, felt both the need to impress and the uneasiness of knowing she likely wouldn't. Mostly she let Daniel do the talking. Come to think of it, it was a long time since she'd made a friend or even spoken to a stranger except in a shop or restaurant.

Rebecca laughed, more of a snort really, not a particularly attractive sound. Maggie glanced across at Neil to gauge his reaction. He raised his eyebrows as if to say, "What was that?" but there was a twinkling in them so she guessed no harm had been done.

"Rebecca tells me you're heading to San Antonio."

Did she now?

Maggie nodded. "Heard it's a nice city. So I thought why not."

"Wow. The empty nester goes rogue. A trip to New Orleans. Then on to San Antonio. Where will be next? Doesn't your husband mind?"

Maggie frowned. She was aware of Rebecca shaking her head as if to warn him not to go there. His expression suggested he was joking, but Maggie wondered if he was also digging. Could he have been the one to call in the sighting?

She took a deep breath. Now was as good a time as any to put forward her story. Convince him she was who she said she was and not who he might think she was.

"My husband doesn't mind. Probably doesn't care." She paused to give her comment time to sink in. "We're actually separated."

She paused again, pursed her lips in a slight pout hoping it made her look wistful.

"Once my son left home, there didn't seem much point in staying together. I had no idea what I wanted to do so I decided to travel for a while."

"I'm sorry. I didn't mean to pry."

"You didn't. And these things happen. To be honest, when we were at breakfast with Edith and Arthur, I decided not to bring it up unless I had to. She was such a character, so set in her ways. I didn't want to risk sparking a lecture on the sanctity of marriage."

Neil laughed. "She sure could talk. And you're right, I'm sure she would have had something to say about the state of marriage today."

"Are you married?" Rebecca's question surprised Maggie. Rebecca should surely have got that one out of the way as soon as possible.

"Was. Not now." Neil picked up his fork. Twiddled it in his fingers, the sparkle in his eyes fading.

"Spent too much time on the job and not enough with my wife. At least, that's what she said." He put the fork down. "And she was right. I liked the idea someone was waiting for me at the end of the day. That was enough for me. Can't say I blame her for wanting more. And she found it. Fortunately, there weren't any kids to complicate the picture."

He grimaced apologetically at Maggie. "How's your son taking the break-up?"

"He hasn't said much. He's not been at home since the split so maybe it hasn't really sunk in yet."

"What about your daughter?"

Daughter? She couldn't have a daughter. She distinctly remembered telling Rebecca she only had a son. She could hardly add one into the mix now. Except, stupidly, she had on the previous train journey and, of course, Mr. Perfect Memory over there had to remember that tidbit.

"Are you folks ready to order?"

Maggie pretended to study the menu, grateful for the waitress' interruption. Chicken, burger, steak, pasta or salad? What to have? Her appetite didn't help, it had deserted her. Could she use the break to ignore the question? Start the conversation off on another track?

She heard Rebecca order the salad.

Or she could settle this once and for all and have a constant story going forward.

Neil ordered the steak.

Besides, Rebecca might be curious enough to bring the subject back up anyway.

"Chicken, please." She handed the menu back to the waitress. Gave Neil a guilty look.

"Another lie, I'm afraid. I actually don't have a daughter. But when Edith said she thought I'd told her I had, I didn't want to get into it, so I decided to say she was an adult and leave it at that. I think Edith had enough to deal with. It can't be easy dealing with someone who's deteriorating mentally, especially when it's your husband."

"I wouldn't be so quick to write him off," Neil said. "I had lunch with them too. Granted it might have been one of his better moments as Edith liked to call them, but he seemed to be on the ball. Telling me about his job and some of the characters he'd come across. Poor guy, sounded as if he didn't want to retire when he did. Edith reckoned he follows the local crime news stories even now. And apparently, he's not beyond calling in to his pals still left on the force with his ideas—though she said as the years go by fewer of them are willing to take his calls."

Maggie sighed. It had to be Arthur who'd phoned in to the hotline to say he'd seen a Maggie Cumberland lookalike on the train to New Orleans. Which meant she no longer had to worry about Neil being the source—admittedly a ridiculous idea anyway, one fueled by allowing her overactive imagination to run riot.

Neil had been to San Antonio before, several times. Considered himself quite the expert on what they should see and do. He reeled off a multitude of facts about the Alamo, telling Rebecca that many of the men involved in its defense were from Europe, especially Britain. Maggie was not especially interested in history, but couldn't think of a way to change the subject. She picked at her chicken, resisting Rebecca's attempts to draw her into the conversation.

She perked up when she heard Rebecca ask Neil how long he planned to be in San Antonio.

Neil blotted his mouth with his napkin. Said he wasn't sure, it depended on the job, it may be for a day or two, could be longer. It also depended on where he was going next and the train schedule.

"Why don't you fly?" Maggie asked. "Wouldn't it be quicker? More efficient?"

Neil dabbed at his mouth again. "I don't like flying."

Maggie almost choked on a piece of chicken. "You have a job requiring you to travel around the country and you don't like flying? How do you even get such a job? Doesn't your employer mind it takes so long for you to get from one place to another? It seems such a waste of time."

Neil chuckled. "Not at all, I can work on the train."

An image of him sprawled asleep came to mind. And the time he'd spent chatting with Rebecca earlier and, now, having lunch with them. If this was a typical journey, she didn't see much work getting done.

Neil must have read her mind because he added, "And I work for myself."

Maggie blushed, her mind drawing a blank on how to respond. Rebecca came to her rescue.

"What exactly do you do?"

Maggie was surprised Rebecca hadn't already discussed the topic with him. Wasn't it one of the first subjects that strangers usually touched on? Had Rebecca spent the whole time earlier talking about herself? It wasn't necessarily the best way to make an impression on someone.

"Consultancy." He paused. "Computer consultancy."

Maggie remembered his earlier answer. Remembered how he'd brushed the subject off. How he'd said, "It's a job," as if he didn't much care for it. She was tempted to ask why he worked for himself if he didn't much care for the work he did.

"I have an idea," Neil said. "Why don't we go to the Alamo together tomorrow morning?"

"Don't you have to work?" Maggie asked.

"Not in the morning."

Rebecca didn't respond. Maggie hesitated. Would Rebecca want her to refuse, make up some commitment so she could go with Neil alone? After all, it wasn't as if they were committed traveling companions.

"I'm not sure."

"Sounds a great idea. We don't have any plans yet for our stay, do we, Abigail?" Rebecca gave her an encouraging smile. "It'll be nice to have someone who knows something about the subject to show us around. Don't you think?"

Rebecca's response confused Maggie, but at least the woman couldn't argue Maggie hadn't given her ample opportunity to get Neil alone.

She forced a grin. "Sounds great to me too."

At least that was not a total lie.

Chapter 35 – Thursday early morning

Alone at last.

Maggie engaged the deadbolt on the hotel room door and leaned back against it, weak from the release of tension. For the next few hours there was no need to pretend.

Not that she begrudged Rebecca and Neil's company. It had helped while away the hours spent traversing endlessly similar Texan scenery. And she'd been grateful for their presence on arrival at their destination after midnight, someone to share the unfamiliar journey through the well-lit but deserted streets of downtown San Antonio. When Rebecca and Neil discovered they were both booked into the same hotel, they insisted she should stay there too, Rebecca even offering to share a room with Abigail if the hotel was full or too expensive for her budget.

Maggie had no intention of hotel-hunting alone in the middle of the night in a strange city, but she'd declined Rebecca's offer despite her concern about the cost. How could she explain the need to search the internet for news from her hometown at one o'clock in the morning? As each hour of the journey passed, the lack of access to the news had increased her anxiety. She needed to know the Mastersons were still behind bars, whether Daniel had come to his senses and got out on bail—no matter what he'd done, it still pained her to think of him sitting in jail needlessly—and what progress, if any, the police had made in the search for the missing wife.

No news on that front was good news, but only if she knew there was no news. What if she'd forgotten some vital point, discovered police were closing in. Guilt and fear made terrible traveling companions, distracting her to the point where she used any excuse she could think of to spend as much time as possible back in her seat alone as the day wore on.

Barely glancing at her surroundings, she made a beeline for the full-size desk and booted up her laptop, her nerves trembling at the anticipation of what she might find when she opened the bookmarked sites.

She started with the local news. They had more reason to keep the story going until a more interesting one came to light, and there was less likelihood of that.

She gasped as she read the first headline. Daniel had been declared a person of interest in her disappearance. Despite knowing this might happen, the reality of it shocked her. What evidence could they possibly have to link him to her absence? Did they think he'd driven her car to some random supermarket and left it there? She doubted Daniel even knew of the existence of the supermarket.

She clicked on the full article link.

Gasped again.

The report stated that a search of her home had turned up compelling evidence as to her disappearance. But that was ridiculous! What evidence? She hadn't left any. And apart from her purse, which she'd left in the car, she hadn't taken anything that could be missed except for the outfit she'd been wearing.

She searched quickly through other similar stories hoping to find more detail as to the nature of the compelling evidence, but found only one which said police had removed several items from the home including both their laptops.

Good luck with that, she thought. She hadn't used her

176

laptop for anything in connection with her departure. And Daniel's computer would prove a dead-end.

Wouldn't it?

She pushed back from the desk, her musings taking her to places she didn't want to go. If there was anything on Daniel's computer to implicate him it would suggest he had been plotting to get rid of her, but for what reason? He didn't know she'd overheard him or that she knew about the money, and he'd been in jail since Friday so any incriminating information would have to predate the call.

She shuddered violently. This made no sense, no sense at all. The reports had to be wrong. The police had to be wrong. Daniel wouldn't want to harm her. It was one thing to hate Daniel for what he'd done, but she couldn't bear to think of him being accused of something he hadn't done. But what could she do?

Apart from the obvious. Give herself up. Call the police and say, "here I am." But how exactly would that play out without putting her firmly in the middle of the whole Mastersons investigation? She could hardly claim she'd merely taken a trip at the exact time as the investigation blew up. A trip she'd forgotten to mention to her husband. A trip during which she'd left her car miles from home in a supermarket parking lot. Why would she do that?

She wouldn't, unless she'd gone crazy. Crazy enough to leave her purse behind too, but sane enough to have someone else's ID on her and a huge wad of cash which she'd taken from her husband's stash of ill-gotten gains.

Not that she knew anything about them being ill-gotten gains. Maybe all husbands had envelopes stuffed full of money squirreled away at home in case of... of what? Emergencies, pandemics, bank collapses. A disaster readiness fund, together with the other essentials of water, canned foods, flashlights and batteries, and medicine that she'd read they should have at hand in case a cataclysmic event should occur.

Did Daniel know the money had gone? If so, he'd have to know she'd taken it. There was no other possibility. Mila was the only other person with access to the house and it was hardly likely

Mila was aware it was there given she herself had only just discovered its existence. But if Daniel didn't know it had gone, how would he explain the envelopes full of banknote size strips of newspaper the police would undoubtedly find in their search?

She smiled. One conversation she'd enjoy being a fly on the wall for.

That one piece of ingenuity made her proud. Showed she wasn't totally helpless. As she removed the money she'd realized she couldn't put the empty envelopes back. Daniel would know immediately by the lack of bulk that the money had gone. So she'd patiently cut up old newspaper, made up bundles similar in size to the ones she'd removed and bookended each stack with a genuine note to add authenticity.

Confronted with this odd evidence would Daniel claim it proved his wife had engineered her own disappearance? He'd have to explain why the money was there in the first place, but would the police believe him? Or might they assume it was a ploy to persuade them he had nothing to do with her going missing? After all, if he had been involved he would know the first place the police would search would be the home. So why not plant some false evidence?

Maggie rubbed her eyes. These conjectures and assumptions weren't helping. She needed to sleep. There were too many angles to get her tired mind around. And to try would only make her crazy. She needed to concentrate on what she knew for certain. She was alive and therefore, without a body, the police could suspect Daniel all they wanted but never convict. Besides, any guilt she felt over the angst she might cause him paled in comparison to the angst he'd caused her. Let him suffer. He deserved it.

Chapter 36 – Thursday morning

A ringing telephone saved Maggie from the grasp of a shadowy group of men who'd cornered her in a dead-end alley. She jerked awake, confused by the unfamiliar surroundings and the sudden shift in circumstances. It took her a moment to remember she was in a hotel in San Antonio, far from the clutches of any menacing strangers. She rolled over in the king-sized bed which the hotel directory claimed would offer its occupants the perfect night sleep and bemoaned the fact it didn't also offer a nightmare-free option. She'd be willing to pay extra for that comfort.

"Hi." Rebecca's cheerful voice made Maggie wish she hadn't answered the phone. "I hope I didn't wake you."

"No." Maggie tried to make it sound like she meant it.

"Good. We were about to go out for breakfast and wondered whether you wanted to come along too."

We? Maggie heaved herself into a sitting position.

"We" sounded rather intimate. Had something happened during the night or what was left of it by the time they checked in? But how? She'd seen them both check in separately, knew their three rooms were on different floors. She'd been the first to get out of the elevator, her late booking netting her a room without a view on a lower floor. She wondered who'd made the first move.

"We?" The question slipped out.

"Neil and I."

"Are you sure you want me to come along?"

"What?"

Before Maggie could reply Rebecca guffawed.

"Abigail, really! I'll have you know I've had a solid six hours' sleep."

Maggie automatically checked the bedside clock. Eight-thirty. Plenty of time to get some nocturnal activity in and still get six hours sleep. Maybe that was the reason the sleep was so solid. Still, if Rebecca wanted to be coy that was up to her.

"When are you going?"

"Ten, fifteen minutes. There's a café across the street. We thought we'd go straight from there to the Alamo."

"We" again. Was that a subtle hint Rebecca wanted to be alone with Neil, had only extended the invitation to assuage any guilt she might feel at excluding Maggie? If so, she was in luck, ten or fifteen minutes wasn't near long enough to check out the news channels.

"You go ahead. I'm not hungry. I'll join you later, say, forty-five minutes?"

"No hurry."

Maggie smiled. No doubt Rebecca was smiling too.

"When you come out of the hotel, turn right and you'll see the cafe on the corner opposite. Don't forget to bring your sunscreen. It's going to be a hot one today."

Rebecca hung up giving Maggie no time to reply. A fleeting pang of envy engulfed her. She wished she had someone to cuddle, someone to tell her everything would be alright. From her conversation with him, Neil struck her as being the strong, reliable type. He'd probably know what she should do.

She sighed. Except that's exactly how she'd viewed Daniel. She had to face it, she couldn't trust anyone. She was the only one who could get herself through this. Hoping for a savior was a complete waste of time.

She resisted the temptation to go online until she'd taken a quick shower and dressed. Rebecca may have said there was no hurry but she probably didn't mean for her to take as long as she wanted. It was too easy to get caught up in needing to read one more report or watch one more news clip. She wanted to be ready to dash out the door as soon as she finished. As a precaution she set the alarm. She'd allow half an hour and no longer.

There'd been no further developments overnight but a slew of articles rehashed the facts and theories so far. Various so-called experts were quoted.

One put great emphasis on how brutal and far-reaching trafficking organizations could be, reeling off a list of horrific crimes which could be traced back to similar outfits. A sense of dread filled Maggie as she read, but she couldn't stop. Associates, informers, innocent bystanders, the business was a multi-million dollar operation making anyone who put a foot wrong or spoke too loosely a liability that needed to be erased. Even family members weren't beyond reach.

Another expert conjectured that Mrs. Cumberland may well have been the innocent victim of her husband's illegal activity, maybe her disappearance had been a warning to him to toe the company line, a warning superseded by the police swoop. He added if that was the case, Daniel Cumberland was probably living in fear for his life, whether he was in jail or not.

Maggie snorted. Read the article again. He made a valid point given he couldn't know her disappearance hadn't been a warning. Daniel had been involved as fully as the rest of them.

She froze.

She didn't know that for sure. What if Daniel had taken the job in good faith and only gradually discovered what was going on? At a point when it was too late to back away, when he was deemed to know too much? Maybe he'd been threatened so he couldn't leave. They'd threatened harm would come to him or his family.

Her eyes widened. Maybe they'd threatened to harm her. Maybe Daniel had only been trying to protect her and she'd gone and put his life in danger.

Her breath caught in her throat.

Was that the reason he'd refused bail? Had he pleaded to be put in protective custody? Told the authorities he would help them if they would keep him safe?

The lump in her throat grew bigger. Thank goodness she hadn't eaten breakfast, she felt sick to her stomach. How had she not considered that possibility before? Why had she immediately assumed he was guilty?

She leapt up. Paced back and forth as if movement might somehow help ease the terror. What had she done? What had she done?

She gripped the back of the chair, hung her head in shame. She had to go back. Prove to the police that Daniel had no part in her disappearance, that for whatever reasons they thought he was involved, they were wrong. If they believed he had something to do with her disappearance, they would be skeptical about any claims he'd been coerced by the Mastersons into being involved in the trafficking because why would he hurt his own wife?

She closed her eyes to stop the tears of frustration. He must think she was dead, murdered on the orders of the Mastersons, snatched from home or somewhere along the route of her daily errands. That would explain the car, the purse, the reason her personal belongings were still in place.

She had to go back. No matter how scary the possibility of having a huge target on her back from the moment she arrived home. Or if Daniel stayed in jail, how she'd be all alone.

But if he decided to make bail, to be with her, they'd both be targets. What good would that do?

Could she call in? Tell them facts only Maggie Cumberland would know. Information they could check with Daniel, or Jane or Craig.

Craig. She groaned. How she hoped he was still ignorant of what had happened. A slim hope. More likely, he could already be back in the US or, at least, on his way.

She frowned.

But if he was, surely there'd have been some mention of him in the reports. The only child, father in prison, mother missing presumed murdered. The press would be hounding him constantly for his story. And yet she was sure she hadn't seen a single mention of a son. Was that weird? Or a case of Daniel not wanting to attract attention to any other family members? She tried to remember whether he'd been mentioned by any of the reporters or neighbors in the live reports from outside the house.

She jumped at the sound of the alarm. She needed more time to think.

Go. Call. Stay. Go. Call. Stay.

Rebecca and Neil were waiting for her.

Go. Call. Stay.

And what about the compelling evidence the police had found? What the hell was that about? A glaring contradiction to her newfound theory of Daniel's innocence. What if she was latching on to the slightest glimmer of hope that she was wrong about him? And did Daniel's innocence or guilt make any difference since the Mastersons were certainly guilty and almost just as certainly would suspect her vanishing had something to do with their arrest?

She let out a strangled scream. She had to stop these circular thoughts.

She jumped again as the phone rang.

"Abigail." Neil sounded surprised she'd answered the phone. "Are you coming?"

"Rebecca said there was no rush."

"No, but I was hoping we'd get there before lunchtime."

Maggie hesitated. "Actually, I don't think I want to go. You two go on without me."

"What? You're in San Antonio and you're not going to see the Alamo. That's crazy."

Was it? Why? Okay, it was a historic site famed for a gun battle, but she'd only heard about it through the movies. She couldn't remember learning about it at school, not that she'd paid much attention to history.

"I've got a headache. I don't think being out in the sun will help."

She heard Neil relate her excuses to Rebecca. She didn't catch Rebecca's response.

"Sorry to hear that." Neil sounded it, making Maggie's guilt ratchet up another notch. "Is there anything we can get for you?"

Maggie heard Rebecca again in the background.

"Rebecca's suggesting we wait until this afternoon, give you a chance to get over your headache."

Stop being so nice, Maggie wanted to tell him. She didn't want compassion. She was already on the verge of tears. She needed some solid advice, of the kind she couldn't discuss with him.

"Please, I don't want to ruin your plans."

"You're not. There are plenty of other things we can do this morning. How about we say we'll meet in the lobby at two? Should give you time for a rest and hopefully to shift the headache."

Or time to think of another excuse. Maggie agreed, mainly to get rid of him. She insisted she had plenty of painkillers so there was no need for them to disturb her, and ended the call before he could come up with any further suggestions.

Now what?

The room, or studio as the hotel directory referred to it, came with the usual standard furniture plus a kitchen unit with a sink, refrigerator and microwave. Every necessity for someone who wanted to hide away from the world, except the fridge was empty and the cabinets held only dishes. She wondered how far away the nearest supermarket was.

But she didn't need food if she was going to leave. Besides, she couldn't stay and hide in her room while Rebecca and Neil were there. They wouldn't let her. And part of her didn't want them to.

She lay back on the bed. Recalled the days when the toughest decision was what to make for dinner or what to wear to a special event. She wanted those days back.

Chapter 37 – Thursday afternoon

By midday Maggie had given up on the idea of going back home, at least for a day or two. The situation was too complicated. She couldn't decide whether her return would solve problems or create even greater ones. It might remove some suspicion from Daniel, but it wouldn't affect the reason he'd been arrested in the first place. Jail could be the safest place for him. If he had voluntarily been involved in that awful business, he belonged there. And if somehow his involvement had been coerced, the suggestion he might have got rid of his wife would surely signal his loyalty to the Mastersons cause.

For all she knew, they may have made threats against her, but they knew they had nothing to do with this latest development. Whatever doubts they might have had about her role on first hearing the police were looking for her would be assuaged by the news Daniel was suspected of killing her. She only hoped the lack of a body wouldn't raise any questions. Hopefully, they'd think Daniel had been thorough, the missing body a sign of a job well done.

Exhausted, she sprawled on the unmade bed and rubbed at her forehead. She really did have a headache now, the result of no food, copious amounts of black coffee and a morning spent flicking from one screen to another on her laptop, desperate for the details she'd somehow missed that would provide the answer to her problems. She'd known they weren't there, but refused to accept it.

She had two hours until she was due to meet the others. She'd go to the Alamo with them. She had nothing else to do now she'd decided to stay. And their company might take her mind off everything else. Probably wishful thinking, but hiding away, bemoaning her situation wasn't going to change it. Keep busy, that's what she needed to do, but without housework or her voluntary job to occupy the hours, that could be a challenge.

She sat up.

A challenge? Yes. Impossible? No.

And the best way to face a challenge was to make a start on surmounting it, however small. She didn't have to wait for the others to get out and start exploring. She'd managed in New Orleans before she met Rebecca, she could surely handle San Antonio in the daytime.

That belief faltered as she stepped out of the hotel lobby into a baking heat. Her newly purchased wardrobe of jeans and T-shirts were totally unsuited to the climate. She scanned the street looking for signs of a clothing store but, with the exception of a drugstore and the cafe Rebecca had mentioned, there didn't appear to be any retail outlets in sight.

To her left, the road crossed a bridge. At the far end she noticed a gap in the stone balustrade, through which a steady stream of people passed, their casual dress suggesting they too were tourists. They had to be headed to something worth seeing so she decided to start there.

Stone steps led down to a path by a narrow river. Faced with a choice of which direction to walk in, she followed a family group whose confident stride suggested they knew where they were going. The trees and low-rise buildings along the walk provided welcome shade, but Maggie made a mental note to add a cap to her shopping list. Not only would it keep the sun off her head, but it would also act as another form of disguise. She never wore a cap at home or any hat if she could help it. She hated the way they messed her hair up.

She stopped in her tracks, a slow smile spreading across her face. If the police believed Daniel was responsible for her disappearance, they'd be searching for a body not a person. Likewise the Mastersons would think the problem of Maggie Cumberland was solved. No need to hunt her down.

She wanted to laugh out loud at the absurdity of it.

If she was dead in their eyes, she'd no longer have to worry about anyone following her. Or spotting her. The police would stop asking for information and, on the slight chance anyone did call in a possible sighting, they'd dismiss it as a crank call.

Yes, yes, yes! She wanted to pump her fists with relief, yell at the top of her voice. But there were too many people around so she made do with her usual more modest reaction of a huge exhale and a broad grin.

She was free. Providing she could keep up the pretence of being Abigail Thornton instead of Maggie Cumberland she was safe. No need to look over her shoulder or be wary of people she met. No need to think of a cap as a disguise.

She strolled on, her head held high, her shoulders relaxed, taking in the sights and sounds. A flat-bottomed tour boat passed by. Two small children waved enthusiastically at the walkers. Maggie grinned and waved back, aware that ten minutes earlier she would not have even noticed them.

Chapter 38 - Thursday afternoon

Maggie stopped at an information board displaying a map of the area. It wouldn't do to get lost, not when she was supposed to be recuperating in her room. She discovered she was in the Riverwalk Area, a downtown island created by a tributary of the San Antonio River. Making a mental note of where she'd joined the path running around the island, she figured she had enough time to complete the circuit so she strolled on. Restaurants and bars lined the riverside, their tables and chairs spilling out onto the walkway, colorful planters blending with the profusion of vibrant greenery to create a bustling but charming scenario.

She checked out the eateries as she passed, their presence reminding her she'd skipped breakfast. She bypassed the more formal restaurants, she only wanted a snack, but the tables outside the more casual places were already beginning to fill up. After the long train journey the previous day and the morning in the hotel she wanted to be outside. Besides, she could entertain herself by watching the passersby.

She was practically back at her starting point when she

found a British pub with a raised covered terrace overlooking a bend in the river. Perfect. A rear table offered both ample shade and an adequate view. She ordered a coffee and fish and chips and settled back in her chair to watch the world go by to the tune of classic rock hits.

She could almost fool herself she was on vacation. The muscles in her back relaxed and expanded, her headache was gone. She closed her eyes for a moment. If only she could retain this sensation. Then, just maybe, she could cope with anything.

She opened her eyes at the sound of her food being set down on the table. She gave the young waitress a huge smile. She'd give her a big tip too when she left.

She wolfed the food down and sat back sated, lingering over her coffee. Another tour boat emerged from the bend and glided slowly past, the Texan drawl of the narrator bringing a smile to her face. Texas. She, Maggie Cumberland, was in Texas. Who would have thought it likely? Texas today, who knew where tomorrow? The stay-at-home Maggie transformed into the globe-trotting, or at least America-trotting, Abigail. A few days ago she would have laughed at the idea: Maggie Thornton, with only one suitcase of clothes to her name, no home, no family, no friends, no country club.

The smile disappeared. The momentary confident fantasy replaced by practical panic. Who was she trying to kid? Maggie Thornton was dead by all accounts. She no longer existed. She couldn't expect a funeral. No body, no funeral. Maybe she'd merit a memorial service. She deserved one at the very least. Assigned to eternity by all who knew her, but whatever they did, the ghost of her past would never be laid to rest, it would dog her footsteps and haunt her for the rest of her days.

She blinked, scared by the roller-coaster of emotion, hurtling within seconds from the heights of unjustified confidence to the depths of realistic despair, looping the loops so fast she could only hang on with grim determination, praying for the ride to please, please end.

She blinked again, aware of being on the verge of a meltdown. She forced herself to focus on her surroundings, the people strolling by, the lyrics of a Simon and Garfunkel song, whose title escaped her, and the aroma of freshly cooked fish from the platters being served at the adjacent table.

A middle-aged couple sauntered past, hand in hand, talking and laughing. Maggie watched enviously as they stopped to read the menu at the next restaurant and then continued on weaving their way through the establishment's tables lining the curve of the bend. As they squeezed past a table for two which had been extended to allow for three, she stifled a gasp.

Rebecca and Neil. And a second man.

She slithered down in her seat. Could they see her? The stranger had his back to her, but Rebecca and Neil were facing the bar. If she had been sitting on the outer row of tables she probably would have been visible but hopefully the patrons at those tables shielded her from view.

She straightened up. What was she thinking? Worrying about whether they'd seen her. So what? She was free to do what she liked, she had no obligation to them. She could stroll over, explain the headache had gone and she'd come out for a quick explore before meeting them. Join them. Save them the trip back to the hotel.

She attracted the attention of her waitress, asked for the check. She wondered who the third person was. Another friend acquired on their travels. If only she could be so easily sociable. Would the threesome going to the Alamo turn out to be a foursome? She hoped Rebecca didn't get any ideas about trying to match her up with someone. Life was complicated enough.

The stranger stood up. Rebecca said something to him and then grinned broadly.

Maggie held her breath, willed him to leave, to turn down whatever offer Rebecca might be making if it involved her.

The man stepped back.

Maggie let the breath out.

He turned in her direction.

She almost choked.

Either her eyes were playing tricks on her or else it was the man from the train, the one going to Washington and Florida. The man she thought she'd seen in New Orleans.

But that was impossible.

He strode along the walkway, dodging the sauntering tourists coming in the opposite direction and bounded up the steps to the street, two at a time.

Maggie looked back at Neil and Rebecca. Rebecca had a wine glass in her hand. Neil had turned in his chair as if to attract a waiter's attention.

Any thought of going over to them disappeared. Maggie stood up, dropped twenty dollars onto the table and left without waiting for the waitress to return.

She'd persuaded herself meeting up with Neil again was a coincidence, might have been able to convince herself likewise about another sighting of the Washington guy if she'd seen him on his own, but for him and Neil to be in the same city, and talking together, that wasn't a coincidence. Couldn't have been. That was something else altogether. She had no idea what, but until she did she'd have to tread cautiously.

Chapter 39 – Thursday afternoon

She hurried back to the hotel. She peered through the lobby door for any sign of the other man. Given her luck so far, she half expected to discover he was staying at the same hotel. Satisfied he wasn't in sight, she raced across to an open elevator and punched the button for the fourth floor several times, willing the doors to close. Her room was as she'd left it, the bed unmade, but she'd spotted the housekeeping cart down the corridor so she put out the do-not-disturb sign and double-locked the door.

She paced the room. What should she do now? The easiest solution, plead off the afternoon trip, claim the headache still persisted. Then when Rebecca and Neil had gone, she could check out of the hotel, find another or, better yet, get out of San Antonio completely.

She checked the Amtrak schedules. The gods were against her. The train out was not until seven the next morning. The Texas Eagle headed to Chicago. She didn't want to go to Chicago. Wouldn't feel safe on her own. If she had someone like Rebecca with her it would make all the difference. She'd still be nervous but she'd go.

Rebecca.

A soft moan escaped her lips.

Rebecca had to be an innocent party to whatever was going on. She'd inadvertently got mixed up in a situation which, if Maggie's suspicions were correct, could prove deadly. If Neil and the other guy were tracking her, they had to be working for the Mastersons. Why else would they be doing it? And, if their orders were to get rid of her, it wasn't hard to imagine that Rebecca's well-being would be of little concern if she got in the way.

She had to warn Rebecca. But how, without revealing her true identity or coming across as a crazy woman? Rebecca obviously liked Neil. Would she be willing to believe Maggie's theories? Be willing to accept Neil's attentions toward her may have been purely to get closer to her new friend? That for her own safety she should get as far away as possible from both Maggie and Neil? And the other guy, whoever he was.

The two men must have been following her in New Orleans, taking turns to keep her under surveillance. She'd been correct in thinking she'd seen the first guy there. It hadn't been a figment of her imagination. They, whoever they were, were onto her and had been since the moment she left New York.

She shuddered. So how was she still alive? Was it merely luck? Somehow her actions had failed to provide the perfect opportunity. All the time she'd wandered alone in Washington. Alone, save for the other tourists. And in New Orleans, unbeknown to her, those rowdy crowds of drinkers and sightseers may well have saved her life.

But for what?

So that the first moment she found herself on a quiet street or in a deserted square, she'd be snatched away or possibly killed on the spot? An unfortunate victim of a random mugging. And with her fake identity, no one might realize who the victim was. Ironically, adopting a new identity worked in Mastersons' favor. Unless the authorities discovered she'd changed identity, there'd be no link between the Mastersons and Abigail Thornton.

And worse, if they'd been following her since New York,

they'd know the police were on the wrong trail, because they'd know she was still alive.

A rap on the door interrupted her thoughts.

Couldn't housekeeping see she'd asked not to be disturbed?

The rapping increased in volume. Followed shortly by Rebecca's voice. "Abigail. Abigail."

Maggie groaned. Now what should she do? She couldn't ignore the knocking. Rebecca might get concerned by her lack of response and call management, and what explanation could she give?

She rushed into the bathroom. Called out, "Just a minute," and flushed the toilet. She grabbed a hand towel on her way out, pretended to be drying her hands as she opened the door.

Rebecca let out a huge relieved sigh. "Are you okay? We were worried. It's past two."

There was no sign of Neil. Maggie motioned for Rebecca to come inside. This was her opportunity to come clean with her, warn her away.

Rebecca eyed the unmade bed. "How's the head?"

"Still there." It wouldn't do to get rid of the headache completely. She might still need it. "How was your morning?"

"Wonderful." Rebecca perched on the edge of the bed. "Exhausting though. I went down to the river. There's a walkway there, really pretty."

Maggie resisted the temptation to say she knew.

"The main section is busy, lots of tourists." Rebecca laughed. "Can hardly complain seeing I'm one too. But if you follow the path south you soon lose the crowds. There's a historic district, King William, full of grand old houses. Some are are open to the public so I took a tour of one of them."

She kicked off her shoes, wiggled her feet.

"And then of course, I had to walk back. It seemed a lot further than I'd realized on the way out. And it was a lot hotter too."

Maggie let her chatter on. She couldn't decide how to broach the subject of Neil without revealing her true identity and some sixth sense warned her against doing that, at least for the time being. She still couldn't be a hundred percent sure she could trust Rebecca, no matter how much she might want to.

"Then I met Neil for lunch."

The mention of Neil refocused Maggie's attention.

"You met for lunch?" Maggie tried to keep her tone casual. "He didn't go on the walk with you?"

"No. After we spoke to you, he said he wanted to do some work, clear his afternoon for the trip to the Alamo."

Maggie frowned. Had she been mistaken about Neil? If he was following her, what other work would he have? Unless it was an excuse to stay at the hotel, stay close to her, check that she didn't try to take off. But he'd still been willing to go to lunch with Rebecca.

"What time did you go for lunch?"

"About one. Why?"

Maggie shrugged. "Just wondering."

One o'clock. Plenty of time for Neil to see her leave the hotel and head down to the river. He'd have seen she didn't have her case with her so he would be fairly confident she wasn't going far. Did that mean it was no coincidence they'd ended up at the restaurant near to the one she was in? He could have watched her go into the bar, staked out a table with a view of it and told Rebecca to meet him there.

"Actually, I was down by the river too. I felt better so decided to go for a stroll, see if some fresh air helped."

Maggie watched for Rebecca's reaction.

"You could have joined us."

"I didn't know where you were."

"You should have called me." Rebecca expression changed to one of concern. "You have eaten, haven't you? You didn't have breakfast."

"Yes, I found a British bar down by the river. Had lunch. Fish and chips."

"I think I saw the place you mean when I was out earlier. Sign with a bulldog on it out front." As Maggie nodded, Rebecca continued. "Neil suggested we eat there, but as I pointed out, I have plenty opportunity to eat English food. I wanted to try the local delicacies, so he suggested the place next door. Shame, we must have just missed each other. Wait until Neil hears. He'll be disappointed."

Maggie doubted it. "Why would he be disappointed? He had your company."

She hoped her comment would spur Rebecca to mention their other lunch guest.

"I think he likes you," Rebecca said.

"What?"

"Neil. I think he likes you." Rebecca grinned. "He keeps mentioning your name."

"In what way?"

"Sorry?"

"Why does he keep mentioning my name?" The words came out more strident than Maggie intended.

Rebecca looked bewildered. "I told you, I think he likes you."

No, he doesn't, Maggie wanted to scream. He's trying to lull us into a false sense of security, find out how much you know about me and figure out how much of a threat you are. Or use you to get to me.

She had to think of some way of getting both herself and Rebecca away from him.

"I don't like him." At Rebecca's stunned response, she added, "There's something about him I don't trust. The way he's latched onto us. It's creepy."

"He's just looking for some company, that's all." Rebecca shook her head as if she couldn't believe Maggie's comment. "You didn't talk to him as much as I did. His job takes him all over the country. He's not married. It must be a lonely existence. Who can blame him for wanting the company of an attractive woman?"

It took Maggie a moment to realize Rebecca meant her. She didn't feel attractive. Hadn't the moment she'd changed her appearance. Another reason why she didn't trust Neil, he'd say anything to get to her.

Rebecca slid her feet back into her shoes. "Please come with us. It'll be more fun if you do." She pushed her bottom lip out in a fake pout. "I want you to come."

"I thought you liked Neil."

"I do, but..." She laughed. "Oh, you mean that kind of like? Whatever made you think that?"

"On the train, you said you thought he was cute. Remember?"

"Oh." Rebecca dismissed the comment with a wave of her hand. "I appreciate seeing a good-looking guy."

"But you spend most of the day talking to him."

"You were there too, most of the time." Rebecca paused. "Is that why you kept disappearing back to your seat? Because you thought I wanted to be alone with him?"

Maggie wanted to say no, to tell the truth, but instead offered Rebecca a sheepish grin.

"Believe me, no interest at all in that sense. He's just fun to be around for now. We'll probably leave San Antonio and never see each other again. It's all part of the travel experience. New places, new people. And then move on." Rebecca shrugged. "Except now, we'll probably add each other to our Facebook friends."

Rebecca's disavowal gave Maggie hope. If she could get her away from San Antonio Rebecca would be out of harm's way. Now she'd need a valid excuse as to why she had to go elsewhere. But she couldn't decide where elsewhere was until she found out exactly where Rebecca was planning to go.

"So are you coming?" Rebecca sounded impatient. "Neil is waiting for us."

Maggie hesitated. She felt trapped. Not only did she have Rebecca to worry about, but also the second guy. If she told Rebecca she was going to stay behind, she might be rid of Neil for a few hours but wouldn't have a clue where the other guy was. He and Neil could be taking turns to follow her, to put her off her guard with Neil. Or she could be growing more paranoid by the hour.

Rebecca made a show of looking at her watch.

"Okay, okay. I'll come." Maggie grabbed her sunglasses and room key card off the table.

She'd go. She'd make a point of talking about where they were each headed, except she'd hold back until the other two had made their choices. Wherever Rebecca picked, she'd choose somewhere else or say she'd decided to stay in San Antonio, whatever it took to make Neil realize Rebecca would soon be out of the picture, that if he bided his time he'd only have to deal with Maggie.

She gulped. That would still leave her with the problem of Neil. And what if he tried to be vague about where he was going or when?

She sighed loudly.

"You sure you're okay?" Rebecca asked.

Maggie merely nodded. Not at all okay, she wanted to say. And neither are you.

Chapter 40 – Thursday afternoon

The trip to the Alamo passed in a blur. Maggie stuck close to Rebecca, followed her from one information board to another. She read the words, tried to match Rebecca's awe as the history of the place was unveiled, but moved on from each none the wiser, her mind refusing to consider anything other than her predicament. After a while she just wanted to be done with the place, get down to what really mattered.

Rebecca wanted to read every word, look at every picture, every panorama. She lapped up all the additional facts Neil had to offer. The guy proved to be a font of knowledge about the subject, a font which Maggie wished she could turn off. Her attempts to hurry them along failed miserably.

As he launched into yet another detailed analysis of some particular aspect of the siege, Maggie switched from listening to watching him. His enthusiasm for his subject shone through, his manner relaxed and easy-going, not exactly how she'd imagined a hit man. He laughed a lot, and judging by the laughter lines around his eyes, this was no mere performance for her benefit.

She forced her face through a series of expressions, mirroring Rebecca's reactions, letting Rebecca ask all the questions. She uttered the occasional "wow" and "fascinating" so they'd think she was paying attention. She could only hope they were appropriate responses. Neither called her out on them so she guessed she'd got away with it.

Could this man, with his boyish grin despite being well into his forties, really be dangerous? It was hard to imagine. What kind of killer would he be? She eyed him over. He didn't appear to be armed. His outfit of jeans and a polo shirt provided few hiding places for a weapon unless he had a small gun or knife tucked away in an ankle holster.

She couldn't discern any noticeable bulges around his calves but, as she didn't know what she should be looking for, that wasn't too reassuring. Besides, maybe he didn't need a weapon. She glanced at his hands, slender with long fingers, his gestures fluid and strong. She imagined those hands on her neck. Tried to suppress a shudder at the thought.

Neil paused, his grin replaced by concern. "You okay?"

Maggie allowed the shudder out. "Just thinking what it must have been like, knowing you were likely to die, stuck out here, miles from your family."

She could feel tears welling in the corner of her eyes.

She turned away. "I need to find a bathroom."

Neil pointed across the courtyard. "Next to the gift shop."

"You two keep going. I'll catch you up," she said as she walked away.

A line of teenagers dressed in pale blue shirts snaked back from the entrance to the women's restroom. Maggie took her place at the end. Just her luck. A few minutes earlier and she would have beaten them to it. At this rate, Neil and Rebecca would be finished with the exhibits before she was done.

She could just see them from her vantage point, standing outside one of the compound buildings. Rebecca glanced over, waved at her and pointed toward the door, letting her know they were going in.

Maggie waved back but Rebecca had already gone inside.

Neil followed.

Maggie tensed. This could be her chance to get away unnoticed. Neil wouldn't see her leave, and as for the other guy, he'd hopefully have no reason to be following her, believing she was with Neil.

She strode toward the exit, took a moment to glance back and ensure Neil hadn't suddenly reappeared, and hurried out onto the street. The hotel was only a short walk from the Alamo. By the time she got to her room the others would just be beginning to wonder what was keeping her.

Rebecca would have no reason to think she would leave and Neil would be hard pushed to tell her why he thought she might. Hopefully, they'd waste time searching for her at the site. Time enough to grab her bags and get out of the hotel. There had to be a bus station in town. She'd go there. Get the first bus out, regardless of where it was going. Worry about the next move later.

A tour coach stood outside the hotel entrance, the passengers blocking the sidewalk as they retrieved their luggage from a growing pile at the side of the bus. Maggie dodged between them, aware every second counted.

Inside a tour operator tried to persuade the recent arrivals to form orderly lines at the reception desk, keep the access clear. She flashed an apologetic grimace at Maggie, her eye roll a silent request for understanding. Maggie ignored it, concentrated on finding a path through the jungle of bodies and bags. She'd almost made it to the relative quiet of the elevator area when she spotted the other guy, sitting on a sofa directly opposite the elevator doors, reading a newspaper or pretending to.

She spun around, collided with an elderly couple behind her. She mumbled an apology and pushed past through the throng back onto the street.

Had he seen her? She didn't think so, but to be sure she ducked into the doorway of the adjacent building and peered back out in the direction of the hotel. The crowd on the sidewalk had thinned out. She could see people going into the lobby, but no one came out.

She swallowed hard, struggled to get her breath under

control, to calm the pounding in her chest. She had to face the truth. She hadn't let her imagination run away with her as she'd secretly hoped. Neil and this guy were connected somehow, which meant they had to be on the same side, the wrong side.

What was she supposed to do? She needed to get back to her room, collect her belongings. She could live without the clothes, but she'd left the bulk of her money in the room. Without it, she couldn't go anywhere. And now Neil would realize she was onto him. For all she knew he may have already been in touch with his pal, warned him to be on the lookout for her.

She watched as the last of the tour party filed into the hotel. Too bad she couldn't tag on with them. Get lost in the crowd.

She hesitated. Maybe she could. But she'd have to act fast. She hurried back to the hotel entrance. The tour guide had managed to coral the group into an L-shaped line creating a wall of humanity between the front and back of the lobby. In consideration of the other guests a narrow pathway had been left uncluttered. Using the line as a shield Maggie joined the end and cautiously peered around the woman in front of her until the sofas came in sight.

The guy was still there. Still reading the newspaper. As a family walked toward the elevator he appeared to pay no notice, not even when the elevator doors opened and several people stepped out. He presumably knew she was out so wouldn't be expecting to see her come out of the elevator, but it still struck her as shoddy surveillance. Which suited her perfectly.

When a large multi-generation family group left the reception desk with their keys, she hurried over to catch up with them as they made their way to the elevator. Every light on the floor indicators inched ever upward, all heading for the same upper floors. She prayed for one of them to start its descent.

A teenage girl eyed her curiously, before leaning back and whispering something in an older man's ear. The man dismissed the comment with a shrug without even looking at Maggie.

The ding announcing the elevator's arrival sounded overly loud. Maggie peered nervously across at the sofas afraid it might have distracted her tracker from his paper, causing him to look up.

He kept on reading.

She inched her way to the front of the group as the doors opened, made sure someone had stepped in behind her before facing front. Now she could only see the top of the guy's head over the open newspaper. A picture of carnage in some war-torn city occupied the prime spot under the New York Times banner. Beneath the fold another smaller photo, this one of a smiling woman, caught Maggie's eye.

The doors slid shut, the swish concealing her sharp intake of breath.

Why was she on the front page of the New York Times?

Chapter 41 – Thursday afternoon

Back in her room, Maggie resisted the temptation to open her laptop and waste valuable time checking out the story in the Times. She didn't understand how she'd missed it earlier, but first things first. Her most important task was to get away. The story would still be the same whenever she got to it and, since it was unlikely to be true, irrelevant anyhow.

She threw the previous day's clothes into her barely unpacked suitcase, cleared her toiletries out of the bathroom and double-checked all the drawers in the room despite knowing she hadn't put anything in them. As an afterthought she took the miniature toiletries provided by the hotel. She wasn't used to being cost-conscious but now every penny saved mattered.

She checked through her backpack, quickly making sure each wad of money she'd secreted away in the various pockets was still in place. There was too much to carry in the money belt she wore on her waist and she couldn't be sure she would always be able to keep an eye on her suitcase, so the backpack seemed the logical place to keep it. God forbid she should lose it. Then she really would be stuck.

Within fifteen minutes she was ready to go. She felt guilty about not checking out officially, but she'd paid in full on arrival for two nights so they could hardly complain. She also felt bad about leaving Rebecca so suddenly. She considered leaving a message claiming some family emergency demanded her return to New York, but decided saying nothing was safer. Neil would see straight through any excuse.

She opened the door quietly, checked there was no sign of anyone in the hallway in either direction. Better not to have any witnesses to her departure. She hurried down the corridor, by-passed the elevator for the stairs, grateful that her suitcase was relatively light and her room was only on the fourth floor.

She made it to the ground floor unnoticed. Through the glass panel on the stairwell door she could see the rear of the lobby. To her right the last of the tour party waited for the elevators, the reception area now deserted of guests. To her left was a side entrance, her intended destination, but to reach it she had to walk several yards in view of the guy on the sofa, a seemingly impossible task.

If only someone would go up and talk to him, distract him for a moment or two, she'd take her chance, but she could hardly wait in the stairwell for that to happen.

Suddenly, the guy dropped his newspaper to one side, pulled a phone from his shirt pocket and studied the screen. He scowled and surveyed the lobby, his movements hinting of panic.

Maggie jumped back out of sight. Had he received a message from Neil saying she was missing?

She risked another peek through the window. His attention was back on his phone, but he neither spoke nor appeared to text. Whatever he was reading or watching caused the furrows on his forehead to deepen. At the ding of the elevator he grabbed the newspaper again, opened it up in front of his face so he was hidden from view but from her vantage point she could tell he could still see who exited. He appeared disappointed until another elevator announced its imminent arrival.

She grimaced as a bellboy blocked her view with a cart

laden with suitcases and boxes and a carefully wrapped wedding dress hanging from one end.

Suddenly, she saw her chance. She snuck out of the stairwell beside the cart, her back slightly hunched so hopefully she couldn't be seen over the top of the bags. The bellboy had his back to her, she didn't think he'd noticed her, but still she held her breath until they were through the automatic doors and onto the street.

A white limousine stood at the curb, the driver loading the trunk with the contents from a similar cart, his efforts hampered by the shrill instructions to "be careful with that" and "no, not that one there," from a scowling woman who Maggie assumed was the bride.

Two taxis had lined up behind the limousine. Maggie dashed over to the first, opened the rear door and was about to haul her case inside when the driver leaned over.

"Sorry, lady." He gestured at the car in front. "We're on a call out."

He held out a business card. "Another car should be along soon. Or you can call and order one."

Maggie wanted to yell at him. Instead she ignored the card and slammed the door shut. With a quick check that no one had followed her out of the hotel, she set off walking, verging on running, to the end of the block. Only after she'd crossed the road and made it halfway down a side street did she slow down.

She glanced over her shoulder. Still no sign of anyone following. She'd done it. She'd got away, outwitted them. They'd have no idea where she'd gone. How could they? She had no idea where she was going.

She continued on for a few more blocks. She should have taken the card. Not a single taxi passed by, full or empty. She had no clue whether she was headed toward the bus station or away from it. She should have looked at the map before she left the hotel.

She should have given more consideration to this stupid plan. Shouldn't have got friendly with Rebecca and Neil. Should have trusted her first instincts about him. Should, should, should, so many damned shoulds. But how was she supposed to know? She wasn't cut out for this. She wanted to be back at home, deciding whether to go to Pilates or yoga, not worrying about how to stay alive and invisible.

She came to a T-junction. Should she go right or left? The grand building opposite looked vaguely familiar. It took a moment to realize why. Neil had pointed it out to them earlier. The Court House and Post Office, a magnificent edifice only a short walk from the Alamo, possibly a short walk from where Neil and Rebecca were.

She hastily retraced her steps to the previous intersection. She needed to put as much distance as possible between her and the Alamo. She asked an elderly lady for directions to the bus station but got only a look of incomprehension and a smile for her efforts. She tried a businessman who told her he didn't think there was one, but he'd never needed to go anywhere by bus so he could be wrong. Old people, young people, no one seemed to know the way. Finally, she asked a couple of backpackers who said she was walking in the wrong direction, gave her painstaking detail as to how to get to the station only to warn her they didn't think there were any long-distance trains at that time of day. Oh, she wanted the bus station, did she? They had no idea where that was.

Close to despair, she spotted a motel on the corner up ahead. They would surely know where the bus station was. The blast of cold air as she opened the door made her shiver.

The woman behind the desk gave her a welcoming smile. "It's hot out there, isn't it?"

Maggie nodded. Far too hot to be rushing around. Her t-shirt, heavy with sweat, clung to her like a damp rag. Compared to the receptionist, calm and collected in a navy dress, she felt a mess. She needed to get some lighter clothes, a sundress or two, maybe a pair of shorts.

"You have a reservation?"

"No, actually," Maggie grimaced, embarrassment flushing her cheeks. "I'm trying to find out where the bus station is, if there is such a thing in San Antonio."

The women grinned. "There is, and it's not too far away."

She peeled a page off a pad of visitor's maps and circled an intersection with her pen.

"This is where you are now. The bus station is here." She marked a cross several blocks to the west and one block south and linked the two points with a line. "No more than a few minutes' walk."

Maggie studied the map. The previous hotel was only a short distance away from the bus station too. She'd wasted so much time and got hot and bothered in the process for nothing.

"Where are you headed?" the receptionist asked.

Maggie gaped at her, at a loss what to say. "I'm not sure," she finally muttered, aware that, even if she had known, her paranoia was now so great she didn't think she'd tell this woman.

The receptionist sighed, startling Maggie. "You're so lucky. I've always wanted to do that."

"Do what?"

"Travel. On a whim." She sighed again. "Not that I ever imagine I'll be able to afford to."

"Who knows, one day you might get the chance." Hopefully under better circumstances than this, Maggie added silently. She wouldn't wish this on anyone.

"You should go to the Grand Canyon." The receptionist blushed. "That is, if you haven't already been. A lot of our visitors have and they all say it's so awesome. You can ride a donkey all the way down to the bottom. Can you imagine? I wouldn't dare. I'd be terrified it slipped and fell. They say it's never happened, but still, as my father always says, there's a first time for everything."

She chuckled. "My mother says I shouldn't listen to him. Life's too short and all that, but then all she's ever done is get married and raised a family."

"Nothing wrong with that."

"I didn't mean there was." The woman looked stricken. "Just, I didn't have a great example to follow, know what I mean? My mother wouldn't dream of traveling by herself, like you."

Hopefully, the receptionist's mother would never have anything to run from. On the surface the actions might appear the same, but there was a world of difference between acting bravely and acting out of fear, the latter propelled purely by necessity rather than desire. Still, it boosted her confidence a notch to think someone thought she was brave. It wasn't a label that most people would include in a list of her attributes. It certainly wasn't one she would use.

The phone rang. The receptionist answered, her voice instantly sounding calm and professional.

Maggie picked up the map, mouthed a thank-you and started to leave as the receptionist told the caller the motel did have rooms available that evening. She hesitated. What would Neil assume when he discovered she'd gone? Surely, he'd think she'd left San Antonio. It was the logical thing to do and exactly what she'd intended to do. So what if she stayed? Hid out for a day or so in this motel? Gave them time to decide there was no point in hanging around San Antonio anymore. They'd probably go to the train station first. Keep a watch out for her leaving on the early morning departure, but when she didn't turn up they'd consider other means of transport. If she could convince them she'd bought a bus ticket they would assume that's where she was headed. It meant wasting money on a ticket she wouldn't use, but it would be worth it if it led them astray.

The receptionist ended her call. Maggie pulled her case back up to the desk.

"Change of plans. Could I have a room please?"

Chapter 42 – Thursday evening

She was dead.

Maggie stared at the screen, her mind frantically trying to comprehend. Her body had been found, stuffed into a battered blue toy chest in a storage locker owned by her husband. The report included a photo of the box. It was the one they'd kept in the garage, used for Craig's outdoor stuff, his bats, balls, and skateboard. Last she knew, they were still in there waiting to be sorted through on Craig's return. Now they were probably in a heap on the floor.

The box was big. As a preteen Craig had occasionally used it as a hiding place for hide-and-seek, even though she told him not to. The lid didn't lock but she still didn't like the idea of him climbing into any kind of box. What if he climbed into one that did lock?

Getting an adult into the box would be a tight fit. She would have said impossible except apparently Daniel had managed it. He'd squashed her in and taken the chest to his storage locker. Or maybe he'd taken the box first and then her body, because getting the box with her body out of the garage, into the car and then out again at the other end on his own would have required a feat of strength way beyond his capabilities. He was an accountant not a body-builder. Besides, he didn't have a storage locker.

And despite what the New York Times article said, she wasn't dead. The story had holes in it so big it was laughable.

Except Maggie Cumberland was dead. The police were no longer concerned for her safety. They had a body, her body according to the report. A woman bludgeoned to death judging by the injuries to the head, although police were waiting for the autopsy results before announcing a definite cause of death.

There was no mention of a weapon, presumably a household object. A frying pan? She winced at the thought of being hit over the head with her cast-iron skillet. Or Craig's baseball bat? They also had one or two ornaments which would do some serious damage to the head too. She guessed it would depend on whether it was a pre-meditated attack or a spur of the moment action. She scoffed. Like the board game Clue. Daniel in the living room with the verdigris lamp. Or Daniel in the kitchen with the meat mallet.

Except Daniel hadn't killed her.

But the news report said he had. Allegedly.

What was going on?

According to the report Daniel was due in court later that day to face murder charges. His appearance would already be over. She opened a new tab, typed in Daniel's name and sure enough, the first few results related to his arraignment. First degree murder. He'd entered a not guilty plea and been refused bail. Now he'd definitely be staying in jail.

She pushed away from the desk and let the chair roll back until it bumped against the bed. She leaned back, stared up at the ceiling, needing to get some distance from the words on the screen, to organize the chaos in her mind.

She wasn't dead.

Daniel didn't kill her.

Two facts which she, and only she, knew for certain. Facts which she could prove in one easy step.

Another certainty—Daniel knew he hadn't killed her. But

without her presence to back him up, proving his innocence would be a struggle.

The police had a body. A body they'd identified as her. But how? Who had identified it? There was no mention in either report. Daniel obviously hadn't identified it. He would have said straight away it wasn't his wife. So who was it? And how did a dead woman end up in their toy box in a storage unit purportedly belonging to him?

She gasped.

Could the woman be one of the trafficking victims?

If the Mastersons did think she was the informant, and why else would they have Neil tracking her, maybe they were trying to set Daniel up as revenge for his wife's betrayal. Got into the house after Daniel's arrest, took the chest and rented a storage locker in his name. Left a rental document at the house for the police to find when they carried out their search, knowing the police would want to search the storage unit too. With Daniel accused of his wife's murder they could quietly take out the real Maggie Cumberland and, as long as they disposed of her body in such a way that it was never found, no one would be any the wiser.

Could they be that callous?

She knew they could. Anyone dealing in human trafficking had to be lacking in morals.

But that still didn't answer the question of how this other body came to be identified as Maggie Cumberland. The women would have to look like her. How likely was that?

She closed her eyes, swallowed hard. The victim had been bludgeoned, maybe rendered unidentifiable facially. A momentary image of a bloodied and bruised face came to mind. She dismissed it quickly. If not the face, what else could be used to identify someone? She had no distinguishing marks, was of medium height, medium build—nothing there to say with certainty a body was Maggie Cumberland.

She recalled some of her favorite detective shows. Tried to remember what ways they had identified victims. Fingerprints were a popular method, but she'd never had hers taken so that would prove a dead end unless her replacement's prints were on record.

And, of course, the victim's clothes and personal possessions, if any, wouldn't link back to her.

She frowned.

Unless…

Unless whoever broke into the house for the box also took some of Maggie's clothes or jewelry. Maybe Daniel had identified her, not by her appearance but by a ring or a necklace. Maybe he'd been asked to identify the body before the police accused him of the murder.

Maggie clutched her midriff as a pain pulsed through her. What had she done? She pictured Daniel standing over the body. Maybe it was the single pearl on a chain he'd given her last Christmas, or the amethyst encrusted M-shaped pendant, a wedding anniversary gift from years ago. He'd recognize them. Believe that the battered woman lying in front of him was his beloved wife. Because Daniel did love her, deep down she knew he did. The years together, the familiarity, hadn't eroded the love between them.

He'd be devastated. Anyone with him at the time must have seen his reaction, realized he couldn't possibly have been responsible for her death. Yet they'd accused him. She wondered when. As soon as he identified the body? Or had they given him time to grieve before hitting him with the double whammy?

She hated him for what he'd done, but he didn't deserve this. There wasn't supposed to be a body, only a suspicion of guilt at most.

She hid her face in her hands. What should she do? For the first time in days she'd managed to get herself to a safe space. She'd checked into the hotel using the middle name on the driver's license so she wouldn't be registered as Abigail, but she'd bought the bus ticket as Abigail and put on quite a performance for the ticket clerk in the hope he'd remember the wacky lady who finally decided to buy a last minute ticket for the bus to Dallas.

She should be celebrating.

Instead she had to decide whether she could justify the grief she'd caused Daniel in order to save her own skin. If she stayed silent, could she live with herself?

Chapter 43 – Friday morning

She decided to sleep on it. One more night wouldn't change anything. And maybe in the morning there'd be a retraction in the paper. The body had been misidentified; the toy chest while identical to the one in the Cumberlands' garage belonged to another Daniel Cumberland as did the storage unit, a man more evil than her husband. And, yes, pigs could fly.

It took the best part of the bottle of wine she'd bought on the way back from the bus station to put her to sleep but fortunately she'd had the sense to get undressed and into bed before she started drinking.

She woke with a start at the sound of multiple voices warning of imminent danger, saying people had been warned to leave. A momentary sense of panic subsided as she realized she was alone. The television was still on, the need to flee related to forest fires in California and not shady goings-on in Texas. She sank back against the mattress. Would she ever truly be able to relax again?

The day stretched out before her, empty of anything but decisions. Should she call the police? Should she return home?

Should she stay hidden away in this motel or should she move on to another town, another fresh start? But where?

She padded across to the window, the wood floor cool beneath her feet. She parted the drapes. Her room overlooked a courtyard dotted with huge planters full of vibrant greenery and exotic flowers unlike anything Maggie had seen before. A swimming pool occupied the center of the courtyard, the early morning sunshine creating a two-tone effect on the water, translucent aqua under the rays' encroaching reach, the shimmer on the surface giving a sense of movement, the duller waters of the shade flat and calm. Either way it looked inviting. It was also deserted.

Silently bemoaning her lack of swimsuit, Maggie brewed a cup of coffee while she dressed. She'd add a swimsuit to her list for when she eventually went shopping. She wasn't a regular swimmer, but enjoyed it when she got the chance. Something about cutting cleanly through the water always brought a peace of mind, even if it didn't last much beyond getting out of the pool. If this were an up-market hotel, the gift shop would probably offer exorbitantly priced swimwear targeted at the forgetful or impulsive, but the motel offered only vending machines for soda and chocolate.

She settled on a lounger in the strip of sunshine, the warmth spreading through her body, a welcome contrast to the air-conditioned room.

She closed her eyes. Smiled. Not bad for a dead person.

She opened her eyes, the smug thought shattering her momentary sense of well-being.

Decisions needed to be made. Decisions which would determine her future. Should she go on living a lie or should she give up this ridiculous idea that she could pretend to be someone she wasn't for the rest of her life and let fate decide her future?

Neither option particularly inspired her. The first was definitely selfish. And she'd never considered herself a selfish person. Always taken pride in how she put others first: her husband, her son, her friends. Go along to get along, in many ways, her motto. Life was so much easier, less anger, less stress, so what if it required a few sacrifices. She'd benefited handsomely for them—nice home, nice family, nice life.

Nothing wrong with nice, right?

Think of all the people worse off than her. She often did when she suffered the occasional gnawing of dissatisfaction that insisted there must be more to life than nice. She'd remind herself of how lucky she was, how hundreds, no, thousands of women would be envious of her life. She had a better life than her parents, a better life than Jane. Jane worried about how they'd meet the bills once the baby was born and how she might have to put the baby in daycare so she could continue working. Maggie couldn't imagine having to put Craig in daycare. She'd been bereft enough when he started kindergarten.

If she'd had other babies it might not have been so bad, but despite how hard they tried, it wasn't to be. It had taken some getting used to. When she got married, she'd envisaged having four or five children. True, probably a pipe-dream. Daniel had said two or three would be quite sufficient, but if she'd had more she was sure he wouldn't have minded. If it made her happy, he'd be happy, wouldn't he?

Maybe if they'd had more children he wouldn't have got mixed up in this terrible business, would have been too busy navigating the turbulence of teen angst and sibling rivalries. And if he'd had a daughter or two, he surely wouldn't contemplate such a horrendous business. If he got involved inadvertently, he'd have gone straight to the authorities. Daniel was that kind of man. Or at least, she'd thought he was.

What had changed him? What dark thoughts had grown within, thoughts he'd needed to keep secret from her, and why? Was it a phase of life? She'd dreaded becoming an empty-nester, even once jokingly suggested they should think about fostering, but Daniel had dismissed the idea out of hand, declaring they should make the most of this stage of life and the freedom it offered. Ha! So much for freedom—him stuck in a jail cell and her on the run.

But imagine living on the run with kids. She wouldn't have been able to do it, no matter how old they were. The kids would kick up a fuss for a start. How to explain why they needed to leave everything they knew, their friends and their father, because of something their father had done. They might not have believed her. Might have thought she was crazy and alerted Daniel to her plans. So much room for error, she wouldn't have dared leave. She'd have had to stay, cope with it another way, even keep silent, for the kids' sake.

Thank God, there was only Craig. Did he know what was going on yet? He'd have to be notified about his mother's death. Mother dead, father in jail accused of murdering her, welcome home son. Would Craig go and visit his father in prison? She imagined he would, if only to find out why his father had behaved as he had. Would Daniel tell him? Would Craig believe him?

A teen girl clad in a skimpy bikini crossed Maggie's line of vision. She threw a towel down on a chair on the opposite side of the sun-deck and sat on the edge of the pool, dipped her feet into the water and shrieked.

"It's coooold."

"Wimp," a male voice said, followed by a splash as the speaker launched himself into the water, sending a spray over the girl who shrieked again before looking apologetically over at Maggie.

The boy surfaced with a huge grin on his face, swam to the side and pulled himself out close to the girl.

"It's fine once you're in," he said.

The girl inched away from him. "So why you shivering?"

The boy reached out for her.

The girl reared back. "Don't you dare."

"Me?" The mischievous expression on the boy's face contradicted his plea of innocence.

The girl stood up, moved several steps back from the edge.

The boy watched her. As she made to lie down on one of the loungers he mumbled something, turned away and kicked up a mini tempest with his feet.

Maggie guessed he was about the same age as Craig. The girl she put at a year or two younger, his sister judging by their similar coloring and distinctive jaw lines. And by the way she suddenly snuck up behind him, slamming her hands against his back, knocking him off balance and into the water with such force that she followed him in.

Maggie held her breath until they resurfaced, spluttering and laughing, the girl treading water to keep warm. The boy took a diving stick from the pocket of his swim shorts and tossed it to the bottom of the pool in the deep end. Immediately they both dove down toward it, the girl reaching it a second before the boy. She pushed off from the bottom, broke the surface with her arm in the air, triumphant. The boy came up beside her, tried to snatch the stick but she tossed it again and they both dove for it.

Craig would have made such a wonderful older brother. He'd often expressed the wish that he'd had siblings, especially a sister. Maggie knew the reality might not match his imagined expectations, but even though she and Jane hadn't been close there had been moments like this one in her youth, made all the more memorable by being shared with a sibling. Though possibly more moments when they were at loggerheads.

She liked to think they'd given Craig a good childhood. She pressed her lips together, fought against the sob building in her throat. Her beautiful son, his whole future in front of him, now saddled with this mess of his parents' making. It wasn't fair.

Whatever she did, she couldn't allow him to think his mother was dead.

Chapter 44 – Friday afternoon

San Antonio library turned out to be a short walk from the motel, another lucky convenience, except the most direct route would take her past the last hotel. She settled for a more circuitous route, keeping off the major thoroughfares. She assumed the guys were off on the wild goose chase after her, but Rebecca might still be in town and had to be avoided at all costs. Though it would be wonderful to be able to talk to someone, get confirmation that what she was about to do was not the stupidest thing imaginable.

She'd never used a public computer before. Had no need thanks to Daniel's obsession with always having the latest technology at home. Judging by the number of people using the library computers, not everyone owned a computer yet. A twinge of guilt needled her as she sat down at the one unused screen. She wanted to send Craig an e-mail from her previous account, but didn't want anyone to be able to trace it back to her new laptop. Although now she was officially dead presumably no one would bother checking the account for activity so nobody would notice the message from the grave. Or if they did, they would think it had to be a hoax. But what if Craig thought it was a hoax too, a spam e-mail to be deleted without opening? She sighed. All she could do was try.

A message on the screen asked her to input her library card number or ask the reference librarian for a guest pass. Great. She'd hoped to get in and out unnoticed. At the reference desk, the librarians were all busy and there were two people waiting for attention. If she got up she might lose her spot.

She waited a few minutes. There was still no one free at the reference desk. She checked out her neighbors, an elderly gentleman reading e-mails and a girl scrolling through apartments for rent. She felt like a snoop. Knew she wouldn't like it if someone else did that to her.

She glanced back at the man. Had he noticed? His gaze was firmly on the screen, whatever he was reading making him smile. She caught a glimpse of a photo of two toddlers—his grandkids? She shook herself, focused back on her screen, her cheeks hot with embarrassment.

She couldn't just sit there. It was obvious she wasn't using the computer. She snuck another glance at the girl on her left, noticed there was a slip of paper with a code on it on her desk. She could just make out the letters and numbers. Was it what she needed? There was no harm in trying. She tapped the code in and pressed enter. An incorrect password message flashed up. She must have made a typo. She tried again with the same result.

She sighed. There was nothing for it. She'd have to go to the desk. The line was even longer now and there was a shabbily dressed guy prowling the computer area, ready to pounce if she left her seat. She decided to give the code one more try.

"It's a capital O not a zero," the girl said to her.

Maggie blushed.

"They should make it more obvious," the girl continued. "I bet it catches a lot of people out. It got me at first."

"I'm sorry," Maggie began. "I didn't mean to—"

The girl offered the paper to Maggie. "No problem, it's the same code every time far as I can tell."

Maggie had over two hundred messages, most from her favorite stores offering discounts. Two more popped up as she scrolled down the list looking for personal messages. The day after her disappearance was announced she received three e-mails from mothers of Craig's school classmates asking if she was okay. She barely knew them. They must have found her e-mail address in the old school directory, hoped they might snag some advance gossip about her whereabouts to impress their friends, garner some of the spotlight for themselves.

Had they really expected a reply? Or was the lack of reply in itself a talking point? She imagined them sitting over coffee, shaking their heads, "still no response." Though now with the news of her murder it would more likely be "I knew when she didn't reply that this wouldn't turn out well." As if they had such a close connection that, of course, Maggie would have responded to them if she could. She couldn't remember whether they belonged to the same clique, only that they all had reputations for being two-faced and hence to be avoided whenever possible.

What would they make of her murder? The news reports quoted a few shocked friends and neighbors who could only come up with innocuous generalizations to describe her. Nice, friendly, good-natured. No fun-loving, adventurous or world-changing epitaphs. She'd led an ordinary, boring life. Or at least she had until a few days ago.

It was weird reading what your friends thought about you. Would they have said any different if they'd known she would read it? And what were they saying over their lattes and smoothies, that's what she'd really like to hear. Though, maybe she didn't really want to know.

She grinned, hovered her fingers over the reply button on one of the three e-mails. She pictured Marissa's confusion when she received an e-mail from a dead woman. A simple message— "thank you for your concern, I'm okay"—would suffice.

No. "I'm okay now" would be better, the emphasis on the now.

Marissa wouldn't dare tell anyone. She'd be beside herself. Normally she wouldn't keep something like that a secret, but she'd know chances were she'd be laughed at. What? She was getting messages from the grave? E-mails from heaven? Somebody must have hacked the account.

Tempting as it was, Maggie resisted. For it to be real fun, she'd have to witness the reaction herself and since that wasn't going to happen there was no point.

Besides, death wasn't a laughing matter, especially when it involved murder. And someone had been murdered. Beaten about the head and stuffed in a box. Somebody's baby, no matter how old. A proxy for her. A distraction for the police so that the Mastersons' henchmen could go after the real Maggie Cumberland with impunity.

So why not go to the police? They'd have to protect her once they realized she was alive. They'd see the danger she was in because it couldn't be a coincidence she'd told them about the phone call and within days the arrests had happened. Her information would have been key. And the Mastersons knew she'd gone to the police too. How was beyond her, except it had to have something to do with her disappearance. If she'd stayed like the police said, pretended to be sick for a couple more days, none of this would have happened. She'd brought it on herself. She'd let fear overrun sensibility. Or had she? Because what she didn't understand was how the Mastersons were able to keep track of her. They were obviously onto her the moment she got on the train in New York, which meant they had to have followed her from home. Which meant they had to know she had a reason for running. Which meant someone had told them. Which meant—

She shuddered. No, she couldn't go to the police. The trail started with them. To go back would be putting herself in more danger unless she could get Detective Abbot to believe there had to be a link between his department and the Mastersons. A deadly link. And for all she knew he might be that link.

He was the only one she'd spoken to. He could have got on the phone as soon as she'd left and warned the Mastersons. Not made any mention to his colleagues as to why she'd come to see him. Though, the desk sergeant on duty had seen her too. She'd told him she'd come to report a crime. He must have made the connection when he'd heard about her disappearance and murder. He should have said something to somebody.

Unless he was involved too.

Maggie groaned. The grandfather flashed a concerned glance in her direction.

She rolled her eyes and muttered, "People." She added a head shake for emphasis.

The man grinned his understanding before returning his attention to his screen.

This was like trying to solve a logic puzzle with only half the clues. Not that completing logic puzzles was one of her strengths anyhow. Keeping the strands separate was impossible. Whichever line of thought she took threw up one obstacle or another. What was she missing?

A new e-mail popped into her inbox. Another discount coupon. And another. Somebody needed to tell these stores she was dead. They were wasting their time marketing to her, but as it was most likely an automated message would they care? There had to be dead recipients on most e-mail lists of any size, nobody to know to unsubscribe on their behalf.

Another e-mail popped up.

She froze.

From Craig.

With a subject line of "Hi."

She opened the e-mail. There was no message. Did he want to chat? The green circle next to his name on her recent contacts list indicated he was still online. Dare she risk it? They wouldn't be able to physically chat while she was in the library, but they could message. She wanted so much to talk to him, but what she had to say, or write, wasn't suitable for a public place. It wasn't the message that worried her, although heaven knows that was going to be tricky enough to explain, but her ability to hold herself together.

The green circle disappeared.

Too late.

She wiped away a rogue tear. The single salutation was short even by Craig's standards. She'd hoped his overseas trip would inspire lengthy missives, give her a sense of his daily life, his observations, the people he met, but he'd turned out to be as reticent about his current life as he had been about high school.

Daniel had jokingly suggested that Craig had a template which he copied and pasted and changed a few salient details such as the weather or the name of a place he'd visited on a trip. It sounded like something Craig would do. Maggie had checked. He hadn't or at least not unless he'd varied the order of the sentences too.

Why would he send an e-mail saying hi? Had he noticed she was online too and wanted to reach out? But that would assume he hadn't heard the news. And why switch off so quickly?

She gasped.

Unless he'd started the e-mail automatically. Had some news he wanted to share and forgot he no longer had parents to share it with. She checked the recipients. Daniel's address was there too. That made sense. She pictured him sitting at his laptop ready to dash off a few lines to reassure them of his well-being or to give them details of his flight home for the funeral and then remembering no one would read them. He was on his own.

Her heart ached for him. Maybe it was that very moment when reality sank in—mother dead, father in prison. He'd meant to delete the e-mail, but in his distress hit send instead, had no idea he'd connected with the very person he mourned. If only she could reach out and comfort him, take away his pain.

The doubts she had about the wisdom of her plan disappeared. She had to let him know she was alive. She'd swear him to secrecy, but do it without giving too much away in case anyone else came across the e-mail. Somehow she'd have to convince him of its authenticity. She wrote and rewrote a draft. Told him not to believe everything he was told but that he must go to the funeral regardless. She couldn't bring herself to say *her* funeral. Then in a week or two, when the fuss had died down, because didn't it always and life continued as normal for all but the nearest and dearest, she'd make contact again somehow.

She read and reread the message, afraid of the consequences of sending it. What if Craig ignored it? Anyone could have written those words. It needed something personal, something he knew only she, or Daniel, would know. Should she mention Mr. Snuggles, the battered bear who'd shared Craig's bed every night until he started having sleepovers and now lived on the top shelf of the linen closet, not at Craig's insistence, but hers? She'd tucked him in beside Craig for too many nights to consign him to the garbage can. Stupid maybe, but one day there might be a grandchild who'd delight in Daddy's old bear. She doubted Craig even knew they still had it. He might not even remember it, childhood memories could be so fickle. Better to pick something more recent.

She searched her memory for a particular activity or trip. She wanted something subtle so a protracted "do you remember?" wouldn't do.

She hovered the cursor over the delete button. What was she thinking? It was a stupid idea in the first place. She'd gone to all this trouble to disappear and she was willing to risk it all in one e-mail. Better to send the e-mail from her new account and hope Craig didn't share it with anyone—if he even opened it. As far as she was aware he didn't know anyone called Abigail. He knew his aunt only by her second name so would have no way of connecting the dots.

She sighed.

A message box popped up on the screen telling her she only had five minutes left. She decided to take it as a sign, but her finger remained rigid on the mouse. With a minute to go she requested another half hour.

Another e-mail account. Craig had another account, his first. Halfway through high school he'd stopped using it, the moniker supercraig too childish for the cool teen image he tried to present to the world. The desire to be cool quickly wore off, forsaken for human rights, but the second account survived this transition.

She copied her draft response, deleted the original. Replaced it with, "check your old e-mail account" and hit send.

She switched to her Abigail account, pasted her original message into a new e-mail addressed to supercraig and told him not to reveal her latest e-mail address to anyone and only to contact her from the old account. She hoped he'd have the sense to obey her instructions otherwise her actions would all be for naught.

She sent the e-mail, relief mingling with disbelief, soon

turning to horror as she realized her son would be left wondering why, if his mother was still alive, she was allowing his father to be accused of her murder.

What had she been thinking? Panic surged up inside. How could she be so stupid? Was there a way to get the e-mail back? She glanced frantically around as if somebody or something might come to her rescue. The few remaining users were intent on their screens, ignorant of her distress.

She clicked on the empty inbox, willing a e-mail to appear, one returning her last message, a fortuitous error in the address, a missed dot or an extra dot or a typo. Please, surely, she was under such stress, she could easily have made a mistake.

Five minutes passed. Ten. The e-mail had gone. To hope otherwise was futile. The rejected mail message should have shown up by now. Her only hope was that Craig would ignore her reply, assume it was spam and not bother checking his other account.

She logged out of the session, grabbed her bag and rushed out of the computer room to the admonishment of voices in her head, their brutal truisms of her shortcomings bringing tears. The path ahead was a blur, people and shelves hazy objects to dodge.

She heard a voice call out, "Abigail."

She ignored it.

Let the other Abigail in the library respond and deal with the disdainful looks of the librarians and patrons at someone daring to disturb the quiet.

Another call, this time lower and much closer, and then a hand on her shoulder forcing her to stop and turn.

And face Rebecca.

Chapter 45 – Friday afternoon

The shock took Maggie's breath away. She opened her mouth to speak but no words came to mind.

"Abigail?" Rebecca's quizzical smile completed her question.

Maggie swallowed hard, but words still failed her.

"You had us worried." The obvious relief in Rebecca's voice made Maggie cringe. "Disappearing like that. We didn't know what to think."

Neil would have known. He just wouldn't have wanted to tell Rebecca the truth.

"So what did you do?"

The quizzical look became a frown. "What do you mean?"

Rebecca expected an apology, an explanation, but that could wait. She wanted to know how Neil had reacted, what he'd done, where he'd gone. Assuming Rebecca knew.

"Sorry, I hope you didn't waste time looking for me."

Rebecca scoffed. "Well, of course we did. Someone you're with suddenly disappears, we could hardly ignore it."

Maggie wished they had.

"When you didn't come back, I went over to the ladies' room, asked whether anyone had seen you. Luckily, one lady said a woman fitting your description had been in front of her, but had suddenly left and hurried toward the exit, like you were too desperate to wait."

Desperate was the right word. But not in that sense.

"When I told Neil, he suggested we finish looking at the exhibits and you'd either turn up again or we'd see you back at the hotel."

Maggie frowned. Not quite the reaction she expected from someone trying to keep tabs on her. Was she wrong about Neil? Or had he relied on her being predictable, going back to the hotel where his buddy would pick up her trail?

"When we didn't find you at the hotel and you didn't show up later, I was really concerned. I suggested we should contact the police but Neil said there was no point, they'd say you could have decided to go off on your own."

That made sense. Neil definitely wouldn't want the local police involved. Although, neither did she. They'd be looking for Abigail Thornton. Which meant she'd have to find yet another identity—no easy feat.

"So what happened? Where did you go?" Rebecca's genuine concern increased Maggie's guilt. "When I didn't get any answer from your room last night or this morning I was so worried. I even asked at the desk whether you'd checked out. They said you hadn't, but in a way that worried me more because I didn't know whether that meant you'd been missing overnight too."

"What did Neil think?"

Rebecca sighed and shook her head. "That's what made it worse. He had to leave. He got a call about work, minutes after we got back to the hotel. Literally only had time to pack up and go because he needed to meet with a client first thing this morning."

Maggie almost laughed. Good story. Rebecca would have no reason to link his need to leave with Maggie's disappearance, but at least her strategy had removed Rebecca from danger. Now all she had to do was come up with a story to explain her strange behavior yesterday.

"Where was he going?" she asked, to give herself more time to think.

Rebecca waved the question off with a flick of her hand. "He didn't say and I was so preoccupied about you I didn't think to ask." She exhaled heavily as if finally able to drain the worry out.

Maggie's guilt over the anxiety she'd caused spiked. She barely knew Rebecca but the knowledge there was someone who cared enough to worry about her threatened to bring tears to her eyes.

"So what happened?" Rebecca asked again.

Decision time. The euphoria from Rebecca's confirmation that Neil had left town, and presumably his buddy with him, made the temptation to tell the truth overwhelming, but that wouldn't be fair to Rebecca. She'd be asking her to keep her secrets. She had no right to inflict that burden on her. And she had no guarantee Rebecca would carry it.

She considered saying she'd been overcome by the heat, the earlier headache returning with a vengeance, driving her back to the hotel, the need to get somewhere cool and lie down pushing all other thoughts from her mind. Those times they knocked on her door or called the room or however they'd tried to contact her, she'd been beyond responding. But that still left the reason why she'd moved hotels unexplained.

Although did it? Rebecca had confirmed that Abigail Thornton hadn't checked out of the hotel. Could she get away with pretending she'd only moved that morning, needed to find somewhere cheaper, and had been about to go back to the hotel to check out and let Rebecca and Neil know of her decision?

"Why don't you let me buy you a coffee and I'll explain," she said.

Chapter 46 – Friday afternoon

Maggie placed their order at the counter while Rebecca selected a table. By the time she joined her, carefully balancing a tray laden with cappuccinos and chocolate cake, Rebecca was tapping away on her phone.

"Thought I'd send a quick text to Neil, let him know you're okay."

"No! Don't!" Maggie almost dropped the tray, her jerking motion sending milky froth spilling over the sides of the cups.

Rebecca glanced up, a finger poised over the screen. "Why ever not? He was worried about you too. He felt bad about having to leave when he did."

"Please, no." Maggie set the tray down. So much for her plan. "There's something I need to tell you. About Neil."

A glimmer of intrigue lit up Rebecca's eyes. She laid her phone on the table and focused on Maggie. "Okaaay," she said, in a voice that suggested she expected gossip.

Maggie took her time setting out the coffee and cake. Time for her heartbeat to subside to a more regular rhythm, for her vocal cords to unknot. A few seconds longer at the counter and the text would have gone with her whereabouts revealed. Another sign that danger lurked in the smallest detail.

She sat down. "When I told you I was separated, I wasn't being completely honest."

Rebecca leaned forward in her chair, the glimmer fading in acknowledgement of the seriousness of Maggie's tone.

"I left my husband. I…"

Maggie hesitated. She couldn't do it. She couldn't tell the truth. Whether from fear of guilt—ha! What did she have to be guilty about?—or embarrassment, she couldn't bring herself to talk about the horrible crime Daniel had been involved in. She felt tainted by association.

"I couldn't stay with him. He had… issues. Issues which I couldn't deal with."

Rebecca nodded encouragingly.

"Issues… I didn't want to talk about."

The statement garnered a sympathetic nod. Presumably Rebecca thought she meant he was abusive. It made her uncomfortable after her work at the shelter to claim such a problem as her own, but she didn't see any choice.

"I finally told him I was leaving. There was no reason to stay once my son had left home. He didn't want me to go. Said he wouldn't let me go. Said if I did, he'd harass me until I relented and returned home."

The more she spoke the easier the words came. It helped having heard other women's stories.

"He said he needed me. Claimed he loved me. Would do anything if I'd only stay. I'd heard that before."

She hoped she wasn't laying it on too thick but she needed to build it up so Rebecca would understand her concern. Rebecca appeared to be swallowing the lies wholesale.

"So you decided to flee," Rebecca said.

Maggie sighed. "I thought it was my only option, but I knew he was serious about not letting me go and that, knowing him, he'd probably pay someone to track me down."

Rebecca gulped. "Are you sure? That's an expensive

business."

Maggie sighed again. "Yes, but one he can afford unfortunately. I hoped if I didn't settle in one place, at least not at first, it would make it more difficult for them to find me."

"And a change of name would help."

Maggie froze. "What?"

"A change of name." Rebecca shook herself. Snorted. "Sorry, I'm just thinking what I would do under those circumstances." She crinkled her nose. "Though I guess that's easier said than done unless you have contacts in the criminal world."

Or your sister's New York driver's license, but that was one secret Maggie wasn't going to reveal. Rebecca only knew her as Abigail Thornton, better she didn't know any different.

Rebecca's eyes widened. "You haven't been using your credit card have you? In movies they always use them to track people down."

She paused and sat back in her seat, her expression one of somebody connecting the dots. She nodded approvingly. "That's why you paid cash in the hotel, isn't it? I thought it was odd."

Maggie tried not to scowl. She thought nobody had noticed. Though Rebecca struck her as the kind of woman who didn't miss much. Curious about everything, determined to enjoy what life had to offer. She watched as Rebecca scooped up a forkful of chocolate cake, savored it as if it were some exotic delicacy and rolled her eyes in delight.

"Mmm. Heaven." Rebecca waved her fork at Maggie. "Try it. It won't solve any problems but I guarantee it will make you feel better." She scooped up another mouthful. "If only for a few seconds."

When Maggie didn't comply she put her fork down. "Sorry, I'm not trying to make light of your situation. It can't be easy. Loving someone, discovering they're not who you thought they were and having to leave, especially when you have to leave everything else behind too. Did you tell anyone you were going?"

Maggie shook her head.

"No one?" Rebecca didn't even try to hide her incredulity.

"Not even your son? Or your sister?"

"I couldn't tell anyone. I know I'm going to have to tell them eventually." Maggie picked up her fork, toyed with her cake. She didn't want Rebecca to see her tears. "I don't even know if they know I've left yet, whether my husband has told anyone I've gone."

"Somebody must have noticed by now. How long you been away? It has to be over a week."

Maggie thought of all the people who knew. The people who didn't know her, but who would lap up the human interest story in the news. Friends, neighbors who thought she was dead. Chrissy, her hair stylist. Bryan and Amy on the front desk at the club. The cashiers at the local supermarket, her dentist, doctor, they would all now know she'd gone. And wasn't coming back. Everyone, except for the Mastersons, the very people who were supposed to think she was dead.

She stabbed at the cake. Let her fork drop to the plate with a clatter. She sniffed. Raised her tear-filled eyes to meet Rebecca's uncertain gaze. She imagined Rebecca was wishing she'd never bumped into Maggie in the library, hadn't agreed to go for a coffee. Who'd want to spend their vacation listening to another's tale of woe? She should say what she wanted to say, let Rebecca make her escape which she would surely want to once she discovered she'd almost got embroiled in someone else's marital strife.

"I think Neil was working for my husband."

Rebecca blanched. Her jaw dropped open but it was several seconds before she managed to utter an incredulous, "No!"

"Yes." Maggie assumed Rebecca had already figured out where the conversation was headed, but judging from her reaction apparently not. Unless her quick mind had already moved on to consider the potential consequences of Maggie's statement.

She told Rebecca her fears. How the coincidental meetings on the trains were anything but, in her opinion. How Neil had befriended them both, using Rebecca as a cover.

"But he appeared to genuinely like you." Rebecca looked more aghast at every supposition.

"What better way to have an excuse to stay close?"

"But he seemed such a nice guy."

"Who's to say he's not?" Maggie doubted it, but she could hardly tell Rebecca she thought he was a hit man. The poor woman was having problems enough absorbing the facts. "And I think he's not the only one."

That comment really spooked Rebecca. She glanced nervously around as if the other person might be standing behind her.

Maggie explained about the guy on the train to Washington. How she'd bumped into him in Union Station, then thought she'd seen him in New Orleans even though he'd told her he was going to Florida, but knew for sure she'd seen him in San Antonio, the previous day, talking to Neil.

She wanted to say Rebecca had been there too but that would make Rebecca think she'd been spying on her which might freak her out more than she already was. Instead she described him, hoping it might jog Rebecca's memory, result in a slew of details about who he was and how he'd linked up with them for lunch, but Rebecca didn't make the connection. There was no light bulb moment.

"I think they're taking it in turns. The other guy was sitting in the hotel lobby when I got back yesterday. That's when I really knew, knew I had to get out."

"But wouldn't he have seen you leave. Been able to follow you here?"

Maggie recounted how she got away, embellishing her story slightly, wanting Rebecca to appreciate the gravity of her situation.

"Wow, you are so resourceful." Rebecca said as Maggie explained about buying the decoy bus ticket. "I probably would have taken the bus out of town."

"I had to assume they'd check the bus station. They'd know there weren't any trains for several hours."

Rebecca shook her head.

"I still can't believe it. I was there when he got the call from his client. He was so apologetic at having to leave. He'd wanted to take us to one of the riverside restaurants for dinner. He'd booked a table." She scrunched her nose. "Asked me if I wouldn't mind cancelling it for him and … and suggested we should go anyway. Why would he say that if he knew you'd left town?"

Who knew what that kind of person would say to cover his tracks? He probably had a repertoire of stories to cover every eventuality. And how smart to suggest they go to the restaurant anyway. Rebecca had fallen for the duplicity. And under other circumstances she would have too.

"Rebecca, think about it. I disappear without warning and an hour or two later he has to leave town. You think that's a coincidence? That's no coincidence. I left. He had to leave." She grinned. "Or at least he thinks I left."

Rebecca didn't respond. She took several mouthfuls of cake.

Maggie could tell she was playing things over in her mind, trying to make sense of what she'd heard. It was a lot to take in at once.

She picked up her own fork. Rebecca hadn't lied about the cake. At any other time the moist, delicious texture would have demanded her full attention.

Finished, Rebecca emitted a satisfied sigh. But when she spoke it wasn't to praise the cake as Maggie expected.

"How can you be so sure he's left San Antonio?"

Maggie froze with her fork halfway to her mouth.

"Maybe he knows you haven't left," Rebecca added.

"But you said he left."

Maggie lowered her fork. He had to have gone. Her safety, sanity and success depended on it. It was the logical conclusion to her plans. She'd never been a devious person so why would Neil not assume she'd followed through on her actions. Buy a bus ticket, use the bus ticket. How dare Rebecca cast doubts? Point out the obvious. So obvious she'd never considered it.

She pushed her plate away and with it went her sense of well-being.

He'd left. They'd left. There was no way they could know she hadn't. The ticket clerk would have told them. About the crazy lady who didn't know where she wanted to go except it had to be on a bus leaving within an hour or two. She remembered his impatient eyebrow raising as she deliberated and he struggled to remain polite. He'd be happy to vent given the chance. Who tried to buy a ticket without knowing where they were going? Somebody crazy or desperate, one of the two. Possibly both.

She mustered all the confidence she could find.

"There is evidence I've left. None that I've stayed. He's gone. I'm sure of it."

She hoped she was right.

Chapter 47 – Friday afternoon

"What will you do now?" Rebecca scraped her fork across her plate, scooping up the few crumbs and dots of frosting she'd left.

Maggie inched her barely touched portion across the table toward her.

Rebecca put out her hand to stop her. "Don't tempt me. I've had more than enough. If I keep this up I'm going to need to buy new clothes."

She patted her flat stomach as if to make a point. "Besides, you look as if you need it more than me. You're positively skinny."

Maggie scoffed. If they stood side by side, there'd be no competition over who was more slender. And Rebecca could hardly be described as skinny. She had the kind of figure Maggie aspired to but at this stage of her life was unlikely to ever achieve, especially if she continued the junk food diet of the last few days.

"Actually, I need to go shopping." She knew that wasn't quite what Rebecca meant by her question, but with no clue as to what she should do going forward, it would have to suffice. "Turns out my wardrobe is woefully inadequate for this heat."

"Great." Rebecca beamed, no doubt relieved to switch topics. "Do you want some company?"

"Don't you have anything more exciting to do? Sights to see?" Maggie hoped Rebecca hadn't offered out of sympathy for her plight. She liked her, enjoyed her company and the opportunity to have someone to distract her from the constant soul searching that occupied her mind when she was alone.

"Not at all." Rebecca picked up her bag and stood up. "To be honest, after yesterday, I could do with a change of pace. Come on, let's go."

She headed for the door without waiting for Maggie's response.

They shopped, they lunched and then Rebecca suggested they visit Market Square to shop some more. On the way they took in the San Fernando Cathedral and the Spanish Governor's Palace, which turned out to be neither a palace nor the home of a Spanish governor.

They were the only visitors and the shady courtyard offered a welcome respite from the fierce afternoon sun. They sat on a stone bench beneath the leafy canopy of a large tree and chatted. Maggie was careful to steer the conversation away from her predicament, fearful that the peaceful, verging on religious, atmosphere of the place might compel her to confess more than she should.

They talked about their children and Maggie admitted how guilty she felt that she'd yet to tell her son that she'd left his father. To her surprise, Rebecca didn't appear shocked at her revelation and said under the circumstances she would probably make the same choice until she had decided on a more permanent plan. Why worry your kids needlessly, especially if they were far away? They might feel obliged to return at short notice, adding yet another torn apart life to the mix.

Maggie nodded her agreement. Though she'd already torn Craig's life apart. Instead of being the grounding force against whatever storms Daniel's activities eventually inflicted on the

238

family, she'd prematurely run for shelter leaving Craig to battle the tempest alone. What kind of mother did that?

She leapt up, the serenity of the courtyard shattered. Would Rebecca still want to be her friend if she knew the truth? She doubted it. She wouldn't want to be friends with a person who behaved that way.

Rebecca misunderstood her actions. She stood up too, gave a weary grin and said, "Ready for the market."

Maggie didn't want to go to the market. She wanted to rush back to the motel, sate her obsession with checking the news reports. Check her e-mails in the slim hope Craig had responded. The internet was now her only link to reality, everything else was irrelevant. Going through the motions of life to fill the endless hours between... between what? Between pathetic attempts to discover the happy ending. A happy ending she'd stupidly believed she deserved. A happy ending that simply didn't exist.

She sat down. Sank her face in her hands and sobbed.

A moment later, Rebecca embraced her, holding her tight, rocking slightly. She didn't speak, didn't issue platitudes about everything being alright. She was a mother too. She recognized the agony, the agony a stranger's words could not heal.

That evening they dined by the river at the upmarket Italian restaurant where Neil had made the reservations. The prices were higher than Maggie would have liked—for the cost of one meal she could have had two or three dinners elsewhere—but Rebecca had been so insistent and after the way she'd comforted Maggie earlier, it seemed churlish to refuse. She'd make up for it with a few fast food dinners once she and Rebecca went their separate ways.

But when it came to pay Rebecca insisted the meal was on her, saying Maggie could buy the next one because she was sure Maggie had only agreed to come to this place to please her.

The comment made Maggie wonder whether Rebecca assumed she wasn't very wealthy, hence the jeans and cheap t-shirts compared to the smart cropped pants and blouses Rebecca wore. Her purchases that afternoon would not have altered that opinion.

She'd opted for the lowest price item each time, caring only that the shorts and sundresses fit rather than the image they portrayed. The wealthy, suburban woman had died, what did it matter what she looked like? She wasn't dressing to please anyone anymore.

Rebecca paid with her credit card. When the waiter took it away to process, she excused herself and went to the ladies' room.

Maggie relaxed back into her chair, watched the taxi boats on the river, the evening crowds saunter along the riverbank. She liked the gentle bustle of humanity. Her hometown was so quiet that when she had reason to walk out after dark the only other people she would see would be dog-walkers. The village had two restaurants and a bar but with no local public transport and a layout sprawled over several miles, a car was essential for socializing.

She'd got used to it, accepted it as a way of life, but now realized how isolated her life had been, revolving around Craig's school and friends with the occasional trip into the city to see a play or visit a museum.

She'd had one of the most exciting cities in the world on her doorstep and she virtually ignored it. Not that she'd want to live in the city, it was too busy for her liking, but a place like San Antonio would be an acceptable compromise. She liked what she'd seen, the Spanish influenced architecture, the relaxed atmosphere, even the Texan drawl. Maybe she should stay here for a while, try to find a cheap apartment, some kind of job.

The waiter came back, put the tray with the check and the credit card down in front of her.

With an address and a job she could apply for a credit card. That would make life a lot easier. She allowed the image of this new life to play in her mind as she moved the tray over to Rebecca's side of the table. Rebecca's credit card was identical to the one she'd left behind, the one which would be rapidly accruing charges and interest on the unpaid balance. With Daniel in prison there would be no one to pay the bills. The mail would mount up waiting for Craig to arrive home. But what did Craig know about the family finances? She hoped he'd have the sense to visit his father in prison and take his advice.

Rebecca came back. She swore softly at the sight of the

tray.

"I'm quite happy to pay my share," Maggie offered.

"No problem." Rebecca snatched up the card. "I just realized I've used the wrong card. I get more points on another card for dining out."

She shrugged, slipped the card into her wallet. "It's no big deal. Shall we go?"

Chapter 48 – Friday night

Maggie lay in bed staring up at the red light blinking on the smoke detector. Sleep evaded her. The last time she checked it had passed midnight. Over two hours since she'd parted company with Rebecca and discovered there was no response from Craig and nothing new to learn about Daniel.

She had to face the fact that now he'd been charged the story would probably go cold until the trial. The press would find more fascinating news to report. Her funeral would generate a day or so of coverage as would Craig's return. She hoped the press wouldn't hound him too hard. He had enough to deal with. And he hated having to speak before an audience. If he had a microphone thrust at him or, worse, a video camera aimed in his direction, he'd freeze up, terrified his stutter would return. And under stress it might.

The last thing he needed was to think he'd made a fool of himself on television. He wouldn't be able to face his friends and, God knows, he would need his friends to get through this.

She rolled on her side.

But if he did appear on the news she'd have a chance to see him again. To see his face, hear his voice. Judge how he was coping. But how would she know if he was on?

She sat up suddenly, amazed she'd never tried googling Craig's name. True, there could be numerous Craig Cumberlands but with the amount of press about the human trafficking and her murder, any mention of his name should show up high in the search rankings, especially if it came from one of the major newspapers or channels.

She poured a glass of wine while she waited for her laptop to boot, the need to sleep replaced by nervous anticipation over what she would find. The wine would hopefully calm the trembling that made her hit the wrong keys several times. When she finally got the spelling correct she stared perplexed at the results.

Professor Craig Cumberland had written a paper, the title of which was beyond Maggie's comprehension. A lawyer by the same name offered to take on personal injury lawsuits. Another had been a valedictorian at his high school graduation. But of the Craig Cumberland whose mother had just been murdered, there was not a single mention. Not on page one of the results, or two or three. She eventually found her son in a link tucked away on a later page but it was in connection with a school charity event he'd attended in his senior year.

It made no sense at all. It was as if Craig didn't exist as far as the reporters knew. She couldn't remember seeing a single mention of his name in any of the reports she'd read or the videos she'd seen. Even if Craig was unaware of what had happened she would still expect the existence of her son to be mentioned if only for the added human interest angle to an unfortunate tale.

A cold shiver washed over her as the possible implication sank in. Had someone in authority ordered that his name be kept out of the news, the risk to his safety deemed to be too great? Did Daniel know that the Mastersons, not satisfied with merely exacting revenge on her, would also go after his son? Had he implored the authorities to keep his son's whereabouts, even his existence, secret? The Daniel she'd married would do that, no matter what cost to himself. Was this a sign that traces of that Daniel still did exist?

She shook her head. Either tiredness or more likely the wine made her logic faulty. They might be able to make Craig disappear, give him some kind of protection, but to wipe out his whole existence was surely impossible. What about his school friends? And the neighbors? With the number of people who'd have to be sworn to secrecy, it would be a mammoth job and would only take one loose tongue to give the game away.

She opened her e-mail account. Apart from the welcoming e-mails her inbox was empty. No surprise there. The e-mail to Craig had been her first from Abigail Thornton. Abigail had no friends or family to contact, no subscription to groups she was interested in, no stores to tempt her with discounts to spend her hard-earned money on their products. Then again, Abigail didn't have any hard-earned money either. She was a marketer's nightmare.

The empty inbox reflected the emptiness of her life. She'd never imagined having to start over in her forties and without the benefit of any of life's ritual passages, school, college, motherhood, to create a sense of belonging. And no family to share the burden with. She really was starting with a clean slate.

Out of curiosity she typed Abigail Thornton into the search box. The first few results were all related to one blog site, "Abby's travels." A title half way down the list caught her eye: "How to Take the Stress out of Relocating." Advice she certainly needed. She clicked the link wondering if it would offer any advice on how to relocate incognito.

The web-site was so slow to load she debated canceling it. She had more pressing matters to consider than wasting time on light-hearted articles written by people who only thought they knew what stress was. Maybe when this was all over—if it ever would be all over—she'd write a piece about it. "How to disappear in ten easy steps." She'd have to use a pseudonym, of course, but the advice would be based on firsthand knowledge.

Finally a page loaded, a simple format with the blog post centered under the "Abby's travels" banner superimposed over an idyllic beach scene. Maggie scanned the article, disappointed at how commonsensical the advice was. It was obviously aimed at the confident extrovert for whom new places and people were a source of excitement rather than anxiety. It provided no magical solutions for a middle-aged introvert.

She scrolled down to the bio at the end to reassure herself that the writer was a twenty-something-year-old whose reality was far removed from her own and therefore justified her reasons to discount the suggestions.

Her sister's photo appeared.

Maggie blinked.

Her sister's photo was still there.

Stunned, she read the bio. Abby was a thirty-eight-year-old New Yorker with a passion for travel who'd recently married and moved to San Francisco, now expecting her first child, but hopeful the adventures would continue.

That was a word-perfect description of Jane. But Jane didn't have a blog. And Jane hated the name Abigail, refused to use it, at one point insisting she was going to legally change her name to remove it. Become simply Jane Thornton so she didn't have to admit to being Abigail on official documents. As far as Maggie knew, Jane hadn't actually followed through on her threat, which is why her New York driver's license showed her as Abigail Jane Thornton and Maggie hadn't felt too bad stealing the Abigail identity. She wouldn't have dreamed of pretending to be Jane. It would have been too weird and possibly dangerous for her sister if the wrong people had discovered she was using her name. She didn't think Jane's close friends even realized Jane wasn't her first name.

So why had she suddenly decided to become Abby? And when? And why hadn't she told her sister she had a blog?

Maggie clicked on some of the other pages. Discovered the decision to become Abby wasn't so sudden. The blog, started back in 2011, recounted Jane aka Abby's travels in Europe and Asia, announced her marriage and, more recently, her pregnancy. Her sister's 1,641 followers knew more about Abby than Maggie did about Jane.

Maggie didn't know whether to be hurt or angry. She'd

kept Jane up to date with what was going on in their lives, or at least she had until recently. Short e-mails when there was something important to report, and the Christmas letter filling in the gaps with the more inconsequential events of the year. Jane had responded with postcards saying "brushing up on my French in Paris for a few months," or something similar, to mark her change of location. Since settling down in San Francisco she'd made do with the occasional phone call.

So why hadn't she told Maggie about the blog? Maggie would have enjoyed following it, hearing more of her sister's exploits and, perhaps, coming to a greater understanding of what drove her.

Would Jane be upset when she found out Maggie was using her name? Or rather, if she found out. Her sister was one more casualty in this fiasco, robbed of her sister and her firstborn's aunt. Maggie would never get to see her niece or nephew, never get to hold them, see them grow. There'd be no excited call announcing their birth, their weight, their name. She would exist in their lives as merely a name on the family tree, cousin Craig's mom who, sadly, died before they were born.

She cursed Daniel. She hoped he'd rot in prison. He deserved to. He'd as good as killed her, deprived her of everything she loved. Deprived those she loved of her. What did it matter if he personally hadn't committed the murder of that poor, innocent woman? His actions had been the ultimate cause behind it. She hoped he sat in his cell every day remembering what he'd given up in order to achieve whatever it was he'd hoped to achieve. She hoped every minute was like an hour, every hour like a day. She hoped he stayed in prison so long he died there. The idiot, the damned, damned idiot.

She slammed the laptop closed and burst into tears.

Chapter 49 – Saturday

Getting out of San Antonio was Rebecca's idea. Maggie had
resisted for a while but was eventually won over by Rebecca's
argument that if Neil had been part of a plot to keep track of her,
staying in the one place he'd last seen her didn't make a lot of
sense. Rebecca insisted that if she were following someone and lost
track of them she'd come back to where she'd lost them, hope to
pick up the trail again. What other choice was there? And if Neil
came back there was always a chance he'd run into Abigail. Hadn't
she?

Maggie thought that would be an amazing coincidence, but
given the number of recent coincidences, once Rebecca put the
possibility in her mind she decided it was one risk too many, no
matter how much she liked San Antonio. But where to go instead?

Rebecca suggested Los Angeles, her planned destination.
They could share a sleeper, save on costs, and the twenty-eight
hour journey would be a respite for Abigail, a chance to relax
without worrying about being seen.

Maggie argued that plan hadn't worked out too well on the

way to San Antonio. Knowing her luck she'd get on the train and trip over Neil again or his buddy. "They're like homing pigeons," she said. "And I'm their home."

Rebecca dismissed her argument with a wave of her hand. Promised she would personally walk the full length of the train checking to make sure Neil or anyone fitting Abigail's description of the other guy was on board and, if they were, she'd distract them so Abigail could sneak off at the next stop.

Maggie didn't think it was a great plan. There were several stops between San Antonio and Los Angeles. What if Neil got on at one of those?

"Why would they have any reason to do that?" Rebecca scoffed. "They're not mind readers. If Neil did discover you'd bought a bus ticket to Dallas and followed you, and to be honest Abigail, I think that's quite a stretch, why would he suddenly think you would go to Los Angeles?"

"Because that's where the trains from here are headed."

"Or Chicago. Or back to New Orleans. There's nothing stopping you from retracing your steps. Under the circumstances, that might be a less obvious idea. They probably wouldn't expect you to switch direction."

It was a valid point, but Maggie didn't want to return to New Orleans. She couldn't imagine staying there for any length of time and now she was apparently deceased and had lost Neil, the notion of finding somewhere to settle down played increasingly on her mind. She doubted she'd want to live in Los Angeles, but a smaller Californian town would suffice—maybe something on the coast. She'd never lived near the beach. The mere possibility filled her with unexpected pleasure.

Besides, it would give her a day or two more of Rebecca's company, longer if Maggie could persuade her to explore some small towns with her.

She smiled. "Let's go to L.A."

Rebecca's grin was proof enough that Maggie's decision pleased her too. "Tonight?"

Maggie nodded. "The sooner the better. In case Neil does come back."

"Okay." Rebecca finished off the last of her breakfast. She'd come to the motel that morning as planned armed with coffee and juice, muffins and croissants. "You hang out here at the motel and I'll go to the station, see if I can get a sleeper for tonight. On the way back I'll pick up a few supplies and we can have a picnic lunch."

Maggie laughed. They'd barely finished breakfast and Rebecca was already thinking about lunch.

"What?"

Maggie shook her head. "Nothing."

How Rebecca managed to keep her figure with such a voracious appetite amazed her. But she didn't know her well enough to joke about it. It might be a sensitive issue. For all she knew Rebecca might have a history of weight problems, hence the comment about Maggie being skinny. Her body image may have been so distorted that she couldn't see that she was the slimmer of the two.

Maggie's friend Tanya had a similar problem. Even after she lost fifty pounds and several dress sizes she still complained of being fat, a complaint which she regularly remarked on disparagingly in front of other larger friends. It made Maggie cringe, but calling her out on it at the time would only add insult to injury and she'd never been brave enough to take her to one side and suggest she temper her remarks according to the company.

The train didn't leave until 2.45 in the morning so once Rebecca managed to reserve the last remaining roomette, she checked out of her hotel and took her bags to Maggie's room so they could wait out the rest of the day together. As promised she also brought lunch, an enormous pizza and two chocolate chip cookies the size of side plates. Maggie wished she'd asked for a salad.

They spent the afternoon by the pool. For someone from a cooler clime Rebecca appeared totally unfazed by the scorching heat, her only concession being to slather her already evenly tanned skin with sun screen before she stretched out on an un-shaded lounger.

Maggie opted for a chair under the shade of a umbrella and

ventured out only for the occasional plunge into the pool to cool down. Rebecca ignored her suggestions to join her, leading Maggie to wonder if perhaps her companion couldn't swim and didn't want to admit it. There was so much about Rebecca that she didn't know.

She pondered the wisdom of committing herself to such close quarters for an extended period with a person she barely knew. Back home she wouldn't have dreamed of doing it. Back home she wouldn't have had to. All her usual routines were on hold now, all her should and should not's open to reconsideration and change.

The thought both terrified and thrilled her.

Maggie watched the driver take their bags from the trunk of the taxi while Rebecca did a quick check of the station waiting area to ensure Neil wasn't lurking in wait. If Rebecca didn't return within five minutes, Maggie was to take that as a signal he was there and get back in the taxi and leave. She kept her back to the building until Rebecca gave the all clear. They'd timed their arrival for as near the train's departure as possible, Rebecca ceding to Maggie's request that they limit their wait in the station to the minimum.

Once boarding commenced Maggie hurried down the platform to the sleeping car, her shoulders hunched, her cap pulled down to hide her face. Rebecca followed slightly behind—another of Maggie's precautionary requests. If Rebecca was spotted she was to pretend she was traveling on her own.

Rebecca had laughed at the instruction, said it made her feel as if she was a spy or something, but if that was what it took to make Abigail feel safe then so be it. She warned Maggie she wasn't sure how good an actor she was. Subterfuge wasn't exactly her strong point.

Maggie only had a vague notion of what subterfuge meant, but didn't like to admit it. All that mattered was Rebecca was willing to play along.

As soon as they were in the sleeper compartment, she pulled the curtains and locked the door. The beds were already made up for the night, leaving only a tiny amount of floor space. If one person wanted to move, the other had to as well. What had been spacious enough when on her own now felt horribly confining.

"Cozy," Rebecca said with a grin. "We're going to need a plan. Why don't you take the top bunk? I'll go and have a quick reconnoiter and make sure you know who's not aboard. That should give you time to get ready and tuck yourself in. Then there'll be room for me. Okay?"

She unlocked the door and was halfway out before Maggie had a chance to agree. Only then did Maggie realize that unlike the earlier train, this compartment had neither toilet nor sink. She gently slid the door open again and peered into the corridor. Several of the other compartment doors were still open, the occupants shuffling back and forth as they tried to fit their belongings into the limited space. She shut the door. The bathroom would have to wait.

She stripped off her shoes and jeans, stuffed them into her backpack which she tossed onto the top bunk, and clambered up after it. She debated using it as a pillow, but the lumpy shape made her head uncomfortable so she slid it down to the bottom of the bunk and tucked it between the wall and her legs, the reassurance of its presence outweighing the discomfort from the lack of space left for her feet.

Rebecca knew she was only using cash but some instinct warned Maggie of letting her know exactly how much she had with her.

She wished she could lock the door. She felt vulnerable up on the bunk with the door unlocked. Anyone could open it and there'd be nothing she could do. She'd be trapped, at their mercy unless she could fling herself off the bed straight on top of them, knock them down into the corridor. She was playing the scenario out in her mind when the door did open. It was all she could do not to scream.

"Phew. It's a long train," Rebecca said. "And fairly busy."

"But no Neil?"

Rebecca exhaled hard. "Not as far as I could tell. Most

people were asleep, some with blankets over their faces." She smiled reassuringly. "I'll check again in the morning."

She yawned as she locked the door. "But for now, I really need to go to sleep. I think all the sun and the excitement has taken it out of me."

She yawned again. Pulled off her shoes, opened her case and started stripping off.

Maggie closed her eyes to give her some privacy. Opened them again when she heard a grunt. The roomette was dark. Rebecca had disappeared from view, must have fallen asleep the moment her head hit the pillow, because now she serenaded Maggie with a discordant snore.

Maggie rolled onto her back. Felt the sway of the train as it raced along the tracks, sometimes with a low hum, at others with a noisy clatter. An intermittent series of horn blasts warned of the train's approach to a crossing and temporarily obliterated the noise from Rebecca.

Maggie sighed. Just what she needed. Another disturbed night's sleep.

Chapter 50 – Sunday

The journey passed without incident, Maggie growing more relaxed with every stop. As soon as the guard announced their arrival at each station she would sequester herself in the roomette while Rebecca would watch from the observatory car, searching the faces of the waiting passengers on the platform as the train slid by. Only when Rebecca gave the all clear would she venture out again to sit in the observation lounge and take in the vast expanse of scenery passing before her eyes.

Hours of Texan plains, dotted with the occasional town so tiny Maggie couldn't believe anyone actually lived there, gradually changed to sand and scrub, craggy hills interrupting the endless horizon. By the time they retired for their second night on board they were headed for the desert.

If the train had internet access, Maggie decided she could happily have stayed on board for longer, but even the lack of access became less of a concern as the day wore on. The story had unfolded in its entirety, the crimes committed, the suspects arrested. Her fifteen minutes of fame over except, no doubt, for a brief report on her funeral, but that date had yet to be announced.

She was curious as to who would turn up. Would they allow Daniel to attend? To stand by her coffin in handcuffs? To face the steely stares of her friends who thought him guilty, his grief-stricken demeanor a façade? To be embraced by Craig, unable to embrace him back? What would father and son say to each other?

Would Craig tell Daniel about the strange e-mail he'd received, an e-mail that would prove the murdered woman could not be his mother, his father's wife. It would surely start a full-scale investigation into who the victim really was and what had happened to the real Maggie Cumberland. Maybe it wouldn't be such a bad thing. Now, anything that made the Mastersons more circumspect in their search for her could only work in her favor.

She pulled the blanket over her head as Rebecca's snore increased by several decibels. Made a mental note to invest in a quality pair of earplugs for any future joint overnight journeys.

When she finally succumbed to sleep it was to a mish mash of dreams featuring problems with passports and credit cards and a sense of unidentifiable danger so vivid that the attendant's wake-up call as they approached Los Angeles brought a huge sense of relief.

She dragged herself out of bed wishing she had half the enthusiasm displayed by Rebecca whose short but solid sleep had provided her with boundless energy. Maggie managed to resist the temptation to squash Rebecca's cheerfulness with the guilt of being the cause of Maggie's grumpiness. It wouldn't solve anything.

The charm of the station raised Maggie's spirits. The white Spanish-influenced architecture encircled with spindly palms swaying in the breeze, exotic compared to the previous city stations, reinforced her sense of a fresh beginning.

During the journey she'd nervously admitted her latest plans for the future to Rebecca, aware that in the telling she was seeking both admiration and approval. The slightest hint of doubt in Rebecca's response was likely to cause her to rethink.

Rebecca gave her seal of approval, but suggested that before Abigail started her search for the perfect place to begin her new life she should allow Rebecca to treat her to a few days of sunshine and relaxation by the beach in Santa Monica. After all,

Abigail's future was a cause for celebration and how better to celebrate than with her first new friend?

Maggie wondered how to politely ask whether that involved sharing a room. She wasn't sure she could cope with another night of it. Rebecca's plan involved at least three.

Her concern was dispelled when Rebecca explained she'd booked a suite in a beachside hotel, the accommodation offering a separate living room with a sofa bed.

"Don't worry, I'm only suggesting we share the suite, not the bed," she said and laughed.

Maggie laughed along with her, relieved to be spared the awkward question but wondering exactly how wealthy Rebecca was. A suite in a hotel overlooking the beach in Santa Monica, even at discount rates, would be way out of her own price league.

Normally she would have refused, even been affronted by the offer. She wasn't a charity case. Maggie Cumberland was a benefactor, a minor one compared to some, but enough to be proud of the assistance she gave those less fortunate. If her plans failed to come to fruition Abigail Thornton might well end up needing charity. Fourteen thousand dollars would only last so long and she'd already made substantial inroads into it.

For a stranger to the city, Rebecca displayed a remarkable degree of confidence as she led Maggie through the station and out to the taxi rank, even having a conversation with the driver as to her preferred route. The woman thought of everything.

Maggie watched in awe. She'd thought she was organized.

As the taxi pulled up outside the hotel, Maggie gasped. The eight-story blue building hugged the main road, its prime spot on the sweeping cliff top only yards from both the beach and the pier.

"Awesome, right?" Rebecca said, breaking into a huge grin. "Definitely worth putting your plans on hold for a while, wouldn't you say?"

Maggie agreed. After all she had been through, this could be just what she needed.

Chapter 51 – Monday morning

Despite their early arrival, the suite was ready for them. What Rebecca hadn't told her was that it was ocean-facing. Maggie stood in the middle of the room, taking in the sumptuous surroundings, the breathtaking views, her first real glimpse of the Pacific Ocean. Down below tanned lean bodies walked, jogged and roller-bladed along the cliff top walkway. On the beach solitary figures strolled at the water's edge. She wanted to pinch herself, make sure it was real.

She turned to Rebecca. "This is so beautiful. Thank you, but I must contribute. It must be costing you a fortune."

Rebecca shrugged off her offer. "Just enjoy. You've had a rough few days. You deserve a little luxury."

A little luxury? If that's what Rebecca considered this, how had she rated the motel in San Antonio? She must have felt she was slumming.

And yet Rebecca didn't strike her as the kind of person who frequented this kind of hotel. The hotel in San Antonio hadn't been anywhere near as opulent, yet there were plenty of others that would have been.

"And I decided I did too. And where better to indulge than Los Angeles." Rebecca gave her a conspiratorial wink. "I planned this treat before I met you, so don't worry about it. It makes it more fun having company."

Her words took a weight off Maggie's shoulders. "Still, I insist on paying for dinner tonight in return."

"Okay, but nothing too expensive."

"MacDonald's okay?"

They both laughed.

For the first time since leaving home Maggie felt at ease. While Rebecca showered, she sat out on the balcony and watched Santa Monica come to life. She sank further and further into the plump-cushioned chair as the tension in her muscles seeped out and the early morning warmth bathed her body.

She closed her eyes for a moment and let the weariness from the disturbed sleep wash over her. Life wasn't so bad. She'd escaped her trackers. A reluctant acceptance of her situation grew stronger each day, admittedly by only a fraction, but bringing a frisson of pride when she considered how she'd coped since leaving home. Her problems were far from over, but her survival this far gave her a confidence she'd never dreamed she was capable of. And for now, she wasn't alone. She had a friend. And if she'd made one friend, she could make another and another. Build a new life. But that was for the future. For now she would do what Rebecca suggested and enjoy the present.

A gentle shake of her shoulder woke her up.

Rebecca smiled down at her. "Sorry to disturb you. I didn't know how long to leave you sleeping, but soon you're going to be in direct sunlight."

Maggie sat up with a start. "What time is it?"

"Ten-thirty. You've been asleep almost three hours."

"I'm so sorry."

"Hey, there's nothing to be sorry about. This is a vacation. You can do what you like."

"But you haven't been sitting waiting for me, have you?"

"Not at all. I went out for a walk after my shower. I needed some exercise after all that time cooped up on the train. I left a note in case you woke while I was gone, but I guess you needed a good sleep." She made a face. "My snoring, right? It kept you awake?"

Before Maggie could downplay it, Rebecca continued. "When you didn't say anything after the first night I reckoned I'd had one of my quiet nights. My husband used to say I didn't snore every night, but when I did he certainly knew about it. The laugh of it was he did snore every night. Between the two of us we must have made quite a racket."

Maggie hated to think what it sounded like. Rebecca alone was bad enough.

"Since being on my own, there's been no one to complain about it so it never entered my mind when I offered to share the roomette."

"It wasn't that bad." Maggie hoped she sounded convincing.

Rebecca scoffed. "Just bad enough you needed an extra three hours sleep. You're too nice, Abigail. You should have said something."

She hesitated.

"Though I'm not sure what we could have done about it."

Exactly, thought Maggie, so what would have been the point in bringing it up?

Chapter 52 - Tuesday

Daniel was dead.

It said so in black and white. Not one easily refutable report, but several, listed one after another in the search results, the headlines varied but all with the same message for her.

Daniel was dead.

Her husband, the guy who only days earlier she'd cursed and hoped would die in prison, had been found dead in his jail cell.

It wasn't possible.

She pinched herself and winced. No, she wasn't dreaming. She read the New York Times report again. If it was in the New York Times it had to be true, right?

Cause of death believed to be suicide, but no details as to choice of method. Surely the options were limited for a man in a cell who'd already been stripped of anything potentially dangerous. Did that mean it was really a murder?

Daniel was dead.

Why wasn't she shedding tears instead of being engulfed in a heavy numbness? Twenty-plus years of happy marriage had to mean something. Was it from the fear that Rebecca, asleep in the next room, would hear her weep and demand to know why?

An image of Daniel slumped on a hard cot, blood gushing from a wound, filled her mind. Where? His wrists? That would be suicide. She shuddered. Murder would be something else, a slashed throat or a fatal stab in the stomach.

She started to tremble.

Daniel. No, no, no, it couldn't be. Not her Daniel. Accepting the idea he could be a criminal was bad enough, but to know he'd died was one punishment too many.

The trembling grew more pronounced. She yanked at the blankets on the sofa bed and pulled them up over her shoulders in an attempt to ward off the ferocious chill of the air-conditioning. She should get up and turn it down, but it wouldn't have any effect on the cold sensation surging through her now.

Cruel memories flashed through her mind. Daniel smiling, Daniel laughing. Daniel gazing into her eyes with the look he reserved only for her. Daniel weeping tears of joy and awe at his first glimpse of baby Craig. That was her Daniel. That was the real Daniel. The Daniel who'd supposedly be with her until they grew old and decrepit. Not this Daniel, the one she didn't recognize, capable of callousness beyond imagination, the one who deserved to be in prison, the one who'd died, but taken her Daniel with him.

She clamped her hand across her mouth, leapt up and rushed to the bathroom, locking first the connecting door to the bedroom and then the one to the living area before turning the shower on full blast. She sank down in the corner furthest from the bedroom door, pulled the blanket over her head and allowed her anguish out as quietly as she could.

Once started, there was no stopping the tears. Five minutes passed, ten, maybe thirty before she heard the handle on the door to the bedroom click.

She froze, terrified that in her haste she might not have locked it properly and Rebecca would find her.

The door remained closed. Rebecca issued a muffled apology.

Maggie gulped back the remaining sobs. She'd have to face

Rebecca soon or she'd know something was wrong. She got to her feet and staggered over to the sink. The water she splashed on her face did little to repair the ravages the crying bout had inflicted. Puffy skin surrounded her red-rimmed eyes and the rosy sheen of her nose contrasted sharply against the pallor of her cheeks. There was no denying she had been crying, so she needed to come up with an excuse for the episode.

She could simply say she'd been suddenly overcome by the impact of the last week or so, but that would presuppose she could hold herself together going forward and, in her current fragile state, she didn't think it likely. She needed something serious enough to warrant being caught unawares by grief, but she could hardly admit her husband had died. Rebecca would expect her to want to return home immediately and that was out of the question.

Unless she pretended she was going home. Rebecca would be none the wiser, but it would require giving up the only friend she had. She'd coped alone before but the thought of doing it again, after this shock, filled her with despair.

She burst into tears again. What a mess. And was it all her fault? If she hadn't gone to the authorities, would any of this have happened? Daniel's suicide was surely a result of being charged with her murder. If she'd got in touch with the police immediately when she'd heard about the charge he would still be alive.

And Craig. He would know too. He'd blame her for his father's death. Even if he'd seen the e-mail, considered getting in touch, she wasn't sure she'd want to hear what he had to say to her.

Rebecca knocked on the door. Called out, "Abigail, you okay? You've been in there for ages."

Maggie swallowed hard several times before managing a muffled, "Yes. Sorry."

She stood under the shower, soaking her hair to make it appear she'd washed it, dried herself off roughly before using the towel as a wrap and padded out into the living area.

Rebecca had switched off the air-conditioner and opened the balcony door. A warm breeze wafted in, taking the edge off the room's chill, the refreshing scent vying with the smell of freshly brewed coffee.

Rebecca poured out two cups, held one out to Maggie.

Maggie dropped the blankets and her nightclothes onto the sofa and casually closed her laptop before accepting the cup.

Had Rebecca seen what was on the screen or had it gone into sleep mode before she came out of the bedroom?

"Thanks." She took a mouthful of coffee to give Rebecca a chance to speak first.

"Rough night?" Rebecca motioned toward the balcony. "Do you want to talk about it?"

Maggie nodded. If only Rebecca knew how much she wanted to talk. She gestured at the towel wrap.

"Give me a minute to dress and I'll be right with you." The words came out much calmer than she'd expected.

As she dressed, she decided to work on the assumption Rebecca hadn't seen the news report. Just because she might be tempted to peek at an unattended screen she shouldn't assume Rebecca would be too. And besides, all Rebecca would have seen was a random news article.

But a news article which had seriously upset her.

What she needed was an excuse as to why. Ideally an excuse which would give her cover for any spontaneous outbursts of grief and despair. And which would work whether Rebecca had seen the report or not.

As she pulled on her shorts, the answer came to her. Of course, the perfect solution, tell the story of Maggie Cumberland.

Chapter 53 – Tuesday morning

"A few days after I left home, I got an e-mail from a friend saying I wouldn't believe what had happened. This other friend, Maggie, her husband had been arrested, something to do with an organized crime ring." Maggie gave a tearful laugh. "I mean, if you'd met him, you'd never in a million years think… He was such a nice guy. I assumed it had to be a sick joke or a mistake until I checked the story out on the internet, and there it was."

She sniffed. "And if that wasn't bad enough, Maggie had disappeared." She shook her head, hoped she sounded convincing. "Just vanished into thin air. They found her car in a supermarket lot. She'd left her purse in it. The police started a search but nobody expected it would have a happy ending. Maggie was the kind of person who never went anywhere without her purse."

Maggie hesitated, genuine emotion choking her up.

Rebecca put down her cup, reached out and put her hand over Maggie's. "I'm sorry. Were you close?"

Maggie nodded, unable to give voice to the lie. She dabbed her nose with her forearm.

"Hold on a moment." Rebecca disappeared inside to reappear with tissues.

The act of blowing her nose triggered another melt-down. Daniel was dead. Dead. Dead. And because of her. Whether it was suicide as a result of being charged with her murder or murder as payback from the Mastersons learning of her involvement, if she had stayed out of it Daniel would still be alive.

Rebecca sat silently, probably at a loss for what to say or do. Picturing her wonderful, extravagant sojourn marred by another's grief, a virtual stranger's grief, at that.

"I'm sorry," Maggie said as her tears began to subside. "I don't want to spoil your vacation."

"Don't worry about it. It can't be helped." Rebecca grimaced. "I'm guessing they've found her body?"

Maggie clamped her lips together.

"I am so sorry, I can't imagine how you must feel."

"But to make it worse," Maggie reached for another tissue, "her husband was charged with her murder. They found her body in a... a box in the garage. And now..."

She gasped. Had to stop talking, concentrate on her breathing. An overpowering light-headedness enveloped her.

"And now?" Rebecca said.

Maggie exhaled hard. "And now, this morning's news is that he's committed suicide in jail."

There, the story was out. True, it was a story rather than the truth, but one which Rebecca might offer an opinion on and help sort through the myriad of conflicting decisions.

"Do they have any children?" Rebecca asked after a protracted silence.

"A son."

"How dreadful for him. What he must be going through. To lose both parents in a short space of time and in that manner."

Rebecca's words threatened to undo Maggie.

"Do you know if he has other family to turn to? Or friends?"

"He was a popular boy. Bright, kind-hearted, I think he took a gap year, went overseas, voluntary work." The tears were building up in her eyes again. "He might not know his father is dead yet."

"Oh, I'm sure he will by now. Something like that, they always notify next of kin, usually before it hits the newspapers. The last thing they want is someone learning about the death of a loved one from the press."

Maggie scoffed. She could vouch for that. It even topped reading about her own demise.

Rebecca gave her a strange look, as if she were trying to figure something out.

Maggie panicked. Had she made a mistake? Said something wrong?

"They'd get the embassy in Botswana involved if necessary. Make arrangements to get him home," Rebecca said.

The thought of Craig besieged by embassy officials distressed Maggie. It should be her guiding her son through the formalities of death, her voice he should hear the news from, her presence beside him as he navigated the path of acceptance of his new status: orphan. But then if she were with him, he wouldn't be an orphan.

What had she done?

"Will you go back for her funeral?"

"I can't. Her funeral was today." She glanced at her watch. Hoped Rebecca wouldn't look up the story and discover the lie. "Given the time difference, probably over now."

"What about his funeral?"

Maggie looked to see if Rebecca was joking. "He murdered my friend, his wife, not to mention other crimes."

"Did he admit to it? The murder I mean. Or those other charges?"

The conversation was veering onto dangerous ground. She had to change the subject somehow.

"No, but all the evidence suggests he did."

"You know what they say. Innocent until proven guilty. You said yourself it seemed out of character." Rebecca shrugged. "Maybe he was set up."

Maggie recoiled, pained that Rebecca would toss the

265

suggestion out there so casually. What would she think if she knew how close to the truth she was? And that the woman in front of her was as guilty as anyone for setting him up for the murder?

Chapter 54 – Tuesday morning

Maggie let out an enormous sigh of relief as the hotel room door clicked shut. Alone at last. Not for long—Rebecca had only gone to get them some breakfast after failing to persuade her it would be good for her to get out, try to forget about the tragedy for a while.

As if she could forget.

Maggie didn't want breakfast. Had insisted in turn that Rebecca not spoil her own day on Maggie's account, but Rebecca had been adamant that she should eat, keep up her strength, so what could she do? She couldn't insist the woman left her own suite. Although when they'd finished breakfast—she'd force down a muffin or croissant if it would make Rebecca happy—she'd try again to convince her that she'd be fine on her own and that Rebecca should go off and enjoy Santa Monica. Maybe she'd dangle the offer of a late afternoon walk on the beach as a sign that she simply needed some time on her own to get over the shock.

Rebecca had peppered her with questions about her supposed friend and her husband, presumably under the impression that it would help her mourn her loss. At times, Maggie struggled to keep her responses from a third party viewpoint, especially when the questions involved Daniel. She didn't think she'd slipped up, or not in a way that Rebecca noticed, but she had to be careful. The more she revealed, the more likely she would make a mistake and say something she shouldn't know.

Rebecca's memory was much better than hers. She appeared to remember the tiniest detail Maggie told her, some Maggie had already forgotten she'd mentioned, such as about Craig and his work in Botswana.

She felt the blood drain from her face. Craig. She'd told Rebecca her son's name. She must have done, way back on the river cruise in New Orleans. She hadn't seen any need to change his name, unlike Daniel, who she'd first only referred to as her husband but, in later conversations, by his middle name, John.

Had she used Craig's name in her story? She couldn't be sure. But even if she hadn't, if Rebecca were to see any of the news reports wouldn't she think it strange both sons were named Craig?

And that they both worked in Botswana?

She frowned.

She hadn't said her friend's son worked in Botswana, had she? She'd deliberately tried to be vague. Yet Rebecca had definitely said the authorities would get in touch with the embassy in Botswana. She remembered because it brought solace to think Craig would have someone to help him. She'd been so focused on that, she hadn't questioned why Rebecca would mention that embassy in particular.

Unless Rebecca had merely got confused and mixed one story with the other. That had to be it. But that didn't solve the same name issue.

She reopened her laptop, anxiously scanned the report for any mention of Craig. Luckily, there wasn't any. She checked a few others. Nothing there either. Again, it was almost as if Craig didn't exist.

So nothing to worry about there.

Except.

Except what if Rebecca had accidentally slipped up? What if she'd come across an earlier report on the missing woman story or the murder report, seen the similarities between the photo and Abigail and realized they were the same person?

Except why would she continue to hang out with a woman who was believed to be dead? Why would anyone do that?

Maggie frowned again.

Unless Rebecca saw an opportunity for an exposé, to sell this incredible story she'd stumbled on to the highest bidder. The gutter press would pay handsomely. And with Daniel's death, even more.

She groaned. Thought of the tale she'd spun. No wonder Rebecca was so interested in whether she would go back for the funerals. Her refusal would only add to Rebecca's doubts that Abigail was who she said she was.

What if Rebecca hadn't merely gone out for breakfast? What if she also contacted someone, a journalist or the police, and was busy organizing a face-to-face encounter with a woman believed to be dead?

She glanced around, her mind whirring. Her suitcase lay open beside the sofa bed, barely unpacked. It would take only moments to gather her things together and go. Get away before Rebecca came back. But go where? And if she did disappear yet again wouldn't that confirm any suspicions Rebecca may have had about her identity? And what would stop her going to the press anyway with her story, a story which would reveal not only Maggie's false identity but also her latest whereabouts? And the fact that she'd stood by and watched her husband be falsely accused of her murder and done nothing to refute the claim. Was that a crime in itself? An accomplice to suicide, some kind of involuntary manslaughter but from a distance?

Concentrate. She had to concentrate. On facts not fantasy. One tiny slip by Rebecca, that's all it had been. Getting one story confused with another. How often had she been guilty of the same mistake? Especially when she hardly knew someone, hadn't had time to fully absorb their back story.

Rebecca had been nothing but kind and understanding. She hadn't pushed for details about Maggie's past beyond the simple exchange of information any two new acquaintances might reveal, and her questions this morning were no different from those Maggie might ask if she'd been on the other side of the conversation. It was a motherly instinct to automatically consider the effect of any bad news on the children involved. At least it was for her. And from what she'd learned about Rebecca, it was probably the same for her.

Unless, of course, Rebecca's story was as false as hers.

She checked her watch. How long until Rebecca returned? Ten or fifteen minutes maybe, if she'd only gone out to get breakfast. Longer, if she had other tasks in mind.

Maggie replayed her image of Rebecca leaving. She'd had her phone in one hand, nothing in the other. No bag. So the bag had to be in the bedroom.

Did she dare?

The idea of going through another's personal possessions was abhorrent, but it could give her the reassurance she needed. Or not. If anyone searched through her bag they wouldn't find anything to suggest she wasn't Abigail Thornton, although the lack of bank or credit cards in this day and age would strike them as strange.

The bedroom door was closed. Maggie didn't want to risk Rebecca returning and realizing it was open so she went in via the bathroom. She left the door into the living area slightly ajar, but the second door into the bedroom wide open to give her the best possible chance of hearing if Rebecca returned.

Rebecca's belongings were strewn around the room. The sight surprised Maggie. She'd assumed Rebecca would be the neat and organized type, an assumption which she realized she had no evidence to base on, except that the woman always appeared well-groomed.

She shivered. Hoped this wasn't the first of many other wrong conclusions she'd jumped to.

She spotted Rebecca's bag wedged between the bed frame and the nightstand. She tried to imprint a strong image of it in her mind so she could put it back the way she'd found it, the shoulder strap falling to the right over the slightly rolled, closed opening.

She searched through the cluttered contents, found a wallet.

She swallowed hard, her mouth dry from fear and guilt. She let out a gasp of relief as the first fold revealed a driver's license in the name of Rebecca Harrison with a photo that looked more like Rebecca than Maggie did with Abigail's. Behind the fold there was an array of credit cards, Bank of America, Chase and several store cards, each one in Rebecca's name. If she was traveling under a false identity she'd done a much better job than Maggie. She also had some hotel loyalty cards and a thin wad of dollar bills, nothing to be suspicious about.

Maggie put the wallet back, pushed it down where she'd found it and removed Rebecca's passport. She opened it to the detail page. A younger Rebecca stared out from the photo. The date of birth showed she'd been correct in her assumption that Rebecca was older than she was, but wrong by how much. Rebecca must have been many years younger than her husband if he'd been near retiring age when he died.

She idly glanced at the other details. Birthplace: Richmond, Virginia.

She frowned, her jaw falling slack as the implication dawned. The passport was black not maroon; American, not British or European. The color difference hadn't registered, not even when she'd seen it fall out of Rebecca's bag on the train. She hadn't given it a moment's thought. Nor to the fact that Rebecca's driver's license was identical to hers in style. She'd concentrated solely on the photo and the name, blinded herself to the issuing authority.

She pulled out the wallet again and confirmed her doubts. The license was a New York license, the credit cards from American banks, the store cards from American stores. Rebecca might be Rebecca, but she was American not British. Why would she claim otherwise?

Her hands shaking, Maggie put the wallet and passport back, bent over to return the bag to its rightful place, and heard the hotel room door slam.

She shoved the bag back and dashed into the bathroom, closing the connecting door behind her as quietly as she could. She glanced in the mirror. Cringed at the sight of the ghostly pallor of her face. Hopefully Rebecca would put it down to the shock. She must never know Maggie had discovered her secret.

She scoffed. How ironic. Two women with something to hide. Both too scared to admit the truth. And they ended up together. What was the likelihood of that happening?

She scowled at her reflection.

Highly unlikely.

She needed to keep her wits about her until she could either find out what Rebecca's secret was or get as far away from her as possible.

She stuck her hands in her pockets to hide their shaking and shuffled out of the bathroom to face Rebecca.

Chapter 55 – Tuesday morning

Rebecca had found a bakery nearby which had such a wide selection of delectable items she'd been unable to make a choice and ended up buying more than they could possibly eat.

"We can finish any leftovers tomorrow," she said, brushing off Maggie's protest over the quantity.

"And the next day and the day after that." Maggie tried to sound light-hearted.

Rebecca shook her head. "That's what you think."

"How do you manage to stay so slim?"

"Good genes, I guess. Both my parents were slim. Plus a mega dose of nervous energy."

What exactly did Rebecca have to be nervous about?

"Besides I can't get pastries like these back at home. I need to make the most of this opportunity."

Maggie saw her chance. "Where did you say home was again?"

"Richmond." Rebecca arranged the last pastry on a plate and crumpled the bag in her fist.

Which one, Maggie wanted to ask. Though she knew what the answer would be. Despite her claims she wasn't good at acting, Rebecca was obviously skilled at this deception business. She'd fooled Maggie to this point. Even her accent was consistent.

"There's a Richmond in Virginia, isn't there?" she asked casually.

"State capital," Rebecca said without a moment's hesitation. "Can you bring the juice and cutlery out?"

She picked up the plate and headed for the balcony. Maggie did as requested and followed her out.

"I'm impressed you know that." Maggie put her load down on the table, started sharing out the cutlery. She paused, looked innocently at Rebecca. "As a Brit, I mean. I'm sure many Americans would struggle to answer the question."

Rebecca's brow furrowed.

Maggie smirked. She'd caught Rebecca out.

But Rebecca laughed. "It would be pretty remiss of me not to know. I spent a couple of days there on my way down the east coast. Nice city. Lots of history."

There was a strange glint in Rebecca's eyes. Did she know Maggie had tumbled on the truth or was she merely enjoying spinning her lies?

"Family, too." Rebecca bit into a blueberry scone. "On my mother's side. In fact, I was born there."

The offhand revelation stunned Maggie. "But you said you were British."

"I've dual nationality. My father was British. My parents met here but moved to England soon after I was born. I grow up there, was educated there, so I consider myself more British than American.

"So that's why." Maggie hesitated. If she mentioned the passport Rebecca would know she'd been snooping. "Why you were so eager to do this trip. Haven't you been back since?"

Rebecca shrugged. "I barely know the American side of the family. My mother only had one brother and they weren't particularly close. And my maternal grandparents died when I was quite young."

She gestured at the food and remarked, "you're not eating," before continuing on with the family history.

Maggie transferred a cranberry pastry to her own plate, but made no attempt to eat it. The dual nationality might explain the passport, but not the credit card and driver's license. She distinctly remembered Rebecca saying she'd only been in the States for six weeks before they met.

"Abigail."

The interruption to her chain of thought annoyed Maggie. "What?"

"You look miles away. And you still haven't eaten." Rebecca hesitated. "I know you're upset about your friends but has something else happened?"

How to answer? Keep on pretending? Or reveal her full-blown paranoia? She couldn't deal with both her grief over Daniel and the endless sense of insecurity. Something had to give. The constant tip-toeing around the truth had to stop. She'd been as honest as she could be under the circumstances with Rebecca. If Rebecca was keeping secrets too, it was time for her to be honest with Maggie.

"Why do you have an American credit card?"

"What?" The question obviously startled Rebecca. Good. She'd be less likely to come up with a glib answer.

"Your credit card. I noticed at dinner the other night your card was the same as mine. Issued by an American bank." She faked a smile. "I just thought it was weird given you live in England."

"What a strange thing to notice." Rebecca laughed. "American banks have branches in London too, you know."

She laughed again.

"Besides, I wanted to make sure I didn't have any problems using my card or drawing cash while I was here, so having an American bank card seemed the safest bet." She squinted at Maggie. "Are you sure you're okay?"

Maggie didn't answer. Rebecca was definitely lying. While her response made perfect sense, it didn't explain the driver's license. The obvious explanation for both was Rebecca had lived in the States at some point, but she'd easily avoided answering the earlier question of whether she'd ever been back before. Deliberate? It had to be. For some reason Rebecca didn't want her to know that she'd lived in America.

Maggie wished she'd thought to check the dates on the license. It would have given her some indication of how old it was. It would also have had an address.

A New York address.

So Rebecca must have lived in New York long enough to need a license. Possibly even worked in New York. But she didn't want to admit it. Why?

"Abigail."

Maggie watched for Rebecca's reaction. Saw a look of fear in her expression. Fear of being found out? Or was it born of concern? Fear for Maggie's well-being after this latest shock.

Maggie stood up, excused herself, and dashed into the bathroom and locked the door.

New York. Rebecca had lived in New York. Apparently. Or she had fake New York ID. But why would she do that? So, assuming it was real, they both had New York connections. Coincidence? Of course, New York was huge. But what if it wasn't? By their nature, trafficking organizations tended to be international. Mastersons could have links in the UK. Maybe with her dual nationality Rebecca had been some kind of link, an intermediary.

She sat down on the side of the bath. Closed her eyes. Did she really think Rebecca was part of something so horrendous? The woman appeared to express real horror at the story of the Mastersons and the Cumberlands.

Yet she was lying about something. And Maggie had no idea how to find out what.

She grimaced. Opened her eyes. Took in the opulent bathroom. It was too bad, but she'd have to leave. She couldn't risk Rebecca being on the wrong side, however miniscule the risk might be. She'd beg off whatever Rebecca had planned for the day, say she needed time alone to grieve and as soon as Rebecca left, she'd pack up and go. She could leave a note. Say she decided she should go back to New York after all, needed to be with her other friends at this difficult time. Where she'd go, she had no idea, but until she picked on somewhere to settle down, she'd avoid letting anyone else into her life. It was just too damned complicated.

She returned to the balcony. Rebecca was on to her second, possibly third, pastry.

"Sorry about that." Maggie mumbled as she sat down. "My emotions are a little too close to the surface."

"Nothing to be sorry about. It's only to be expected," Rebecca said between bites.

"I think I'll eat later. I really have no appetite."

"At least drink the juice."

Maggie gave her a wan smile. Picked up the glass.

"Okay, but I think I'm going to stay in the room today." She shook her head. "I don't feel up to going out. I'm sorry. You should go ahead and do whatever you were planning."

"No problem. Don't worry. I' m going to go across to the beach." Rebecca grinned. "Paddle in the Pacific for the first time. I'll come back at lunchtime and check on you."

"You don't have to do that," Maggie protested. Ideally she wanted several hours to elapse before Rebecca discovered she'd gone.

Rebecca seemed in no hurry to leave. She prattled on and on. She might think she was distracting Maggie with her idle chatter but couldn't she see Maggie wanted to be alone?

Maggie tried to drop a hint by barely responding but Rebecca kept talking, long after Maggie had finished both her coffee and juice.

Maggie yawned.

Rebecca grinned. "What do you think?"

About what? Maggie realized she'd switched off from listening. "I don't know," she said through another yawn.

She stood up. Much more of this and she would be dozing off. She needed to get Rebecca out of the suite as soon as possible. She picked up some of the dishes. "You go and get ready for the beach. I'll clear these up."

Rebecca hesitated.

Please, Maggie thought, just go.

Rebecca merely shrugged and went inside. She was still in the bathroom when Maggie finished putting away the leftovers. How long did it take for someone to change into a swimsuit?

Or was her impatience playing tricks with time? Maggie yawned again. She sank into the armchair, struggled against the overwhelming desire to close her eyes. Just a little longer and she could give in to the exhaustion inflicted by shock and grief, safe in the knowledge she'd removed herself from all possible threats.

What was taking Rebecca so long?

Daniel used to complain about the time it took her to get ready, couldn't understood the need for all the primping before going out in public. Used to tell her she was beautiful without the make-up.

She swallowed hard. Blinked away tears.

Daniel.

How could you hate someone and love them so much at the same time?

Daniel.

She yawned, the action so pronounced it hurt her jaw.

Daniel. Dead.

Chapter 56 – Tuesday evening

Maggie woke in an unfamiliar room. As her eyes adjusted to the dark, the vague shape of a bureau topped with an oversized television screen opposite the foot of the bed came into focus. For some reason she was sprawled, fully dressed, in the center of a king-sized bed.

Momentary panic set in when the location of her whereabouts failed to come to her mind. The panic intensified when she realized she couldn't remember the previous day at all, whether she'd taken a bus or a train, whether she'd headed north or south or east. Yet she remembered that had been her plan.

She sat up.

And she remembered why.

She reached out to the nightstand, fumbled for the light switch.

The unfamiliar room became familiar. She sat up, confused now by the knowledge she'd journeyed only from the living room to the bedroom of the suite. But how was that possible? She recalled sitting on the balcony talking to Rebecca, but the memory stopped there.

Had she fainted? She rolled her eyes. Talk about bad timing. And if she had, how had Rebecca got her into bed? Had she called a doctor? Or at the very least hotel security? How embarrassing.

A tiny sliver of light filled the gap where the drapes didn't quite meet at the top. Daylight, but early morning or early evening? The bedside clock proclaimed six-thirty with no indication of whether it was a.m. or p.m. Whichever, she'd been out for hours and she couldn't say she felt well rested for it, more like she was on the cusp of a hangover.

She wondered whether Rebecca had felt obliged to hang out in the suite, afraid to leave her friend alone. She would have felt guilty leaving Rebecca alone if she had been unwell. Of course, if Rebecca had skipped the beach on her account, she'd feel guilty about that too. Sometimes there was no winning, guilt followed at every turn.

She listened for sounds of life from the other room.

Nothing.

She eased herself off the bed, straightening up tentatively, not wanting a repeat performance of whatever had made her black out earlier.

She hesitated at the door, uncomfortable at having to face Rebecca after her moment of weakness. Stupid, she knew, but first the outburst of tears and then the fainting—she was disintegrating in public. This wasn't how she wanted to be. This wasn't how she needed to be if she was going to survive.

She needed to be strong. Her plan to leave may have suffered a setback but there'd be another chance. If necessary, she'd wait until Rebecca was asleep and then sneak away. Until then all she had to do was act normal. Give Rebecca no reason to suspect anything was up.

She yanked open the door, breezed out into the living room, prepared to apologize for the inconvenience caused.

Rebecca wasn't there. Nor was she on the balcony or, from what Maggie could see through the wide open door, in the bathroom. Maybe she had gone to the beach or to the shops. She must have let housekeeping in at some point. The sofa bed had been transformed back into a sofa and all the dirty cups and plates had vanished. Maggie's suitcase, laptop and backpack piled neatly in a corner were the only indication the room was occupied.

Maggie frowned. Headed back into the bedroom to confirm her fears. The floor was clear. Rebecca's clothes had gone from the chair, the nightstand bare of anything personal. She inched open a drawer. Empty. Tried another. Empty. She checked the closet. The case stand stood neatly folded against the wall. Spare blankets on the high shelf, but no personal possessions.

Dazed, she wandered into the bathroom, the marble vanity bare except for her meager toiletries and a piece of paper anchored by a water glass.

In the note Rebecca apologized for her sudden departure. A family emergency demanded her immediate attention, but Abigail should know the room was paid for another two nights so she might as well stay and enjoy it.

Maggie read the note several times, puzzled by its brevity. No mention of Maggie's fainting spell. Whether a doctor had been involved or at least someone alerted to a possible medical problem. What if she'd never woken up, the loss of consciousness caused by some bodily flaw that stopped her heart? She shivered, imagined housekeeping coming in the following morning to find her cold body in the bed.

This certainly wasn't how she'd handle the situation. She'd... she'd... She didn't know exactly what she would do, but she wouldn't have abandoned Rebecca. She would have sought help, made sure she was in good hands, and then disappeared.

Rebecca's emergency must have been a matter of life or death. She hoped it wasn't something to do with Rebecca's children or grandchildren. A momentary pang of guilt assailed her for thinking if it was at least it had nothing to do with her own current situation.

Still, maybe the safest bet would be for her to leave too, in case there was an ulterior motive behind Rebecca's suggestion she stayed for the two nights.

She wandered back out into the living area, glanced

wistfully around. It was really too bad to have to leave, it was unlikely any future accommodation would be so pleasant. Was she being stupid? Throwing away two nights' free accommodation on the basis of potential paranoia? For every doubt, she could summon up a contradictory riposte, but the reassurances rang hollow. She wanted to stay. It was the easy option. Anything else required action and in her current state that was asking too much.

She'd compromise. She'd stay one more night, leave in the morning when she'd had time to make a plan, had more time to assimilate Daniel's death. The decision did little to ease her fears. She double-bolted the door and put on the safety chain, aware that if anyone came for her, she'd be trapped. The only option would be to go on the balcony and scream for help and worry about the consequences later.

If there was a later.

On second thoughts, best to go now. She grabbed her backpack, its lightness instantly noticeable, a lightness that couldn't be explained by the absence of her laptop.

Barely able to breathe, she unzipped one of the side pockets. The contents were intact, except for the wad of cash. She searched another pocket and another, her movements more and more frantic. Every single bundle had gone, even the notes she'd slid into the cell phone and sunglasses pockets.

She clasped her hands on her head, desperate to retrieve a memory of moving the cash herself. But she knew she hadn't done that. She went through the pockets again, ripping the other contents out, flinging them on the floor, unable to accept the truth.

Rebecca had robbed her.

Chapter 57 – Tuesday evening

Maggie tossed the empty backpack aside. The money was all she had to fund her fresh start. Without it, what was she supposed to do? She dug in her pockets, pulled out a few crumpled notes. Just over a hundred dollars. Thank goodness Rebecca hadn't taken it too, but how long would a hundred dollars last? She'd be homeless, forced to find soup kitchens. She knew leaving wouldn't be easy, but never imagined it would come to this. She doubted her ability to survive on the streets.

She wanted to scream at her idiocy, her naiveté. What possessed her to trust Rebecca? Lies, lies, lies, and she'd lapped them up. How Rebecca must have laughed. Utter a few kind words, flash money around, and reel in the next victim. When Rebecca heard Maggie's story about her husband, she must have realized Maggie had to have cash somewhere, so she'd stuck with her, like a limpet, waiting for her chance.

That's why she'd left. By saying there'd been a family emergency and suggesting Maggie stay, she'd probably hoped it would be a while before Maggie realized the money had gone. And she would have been right if Maggie hadn't decided to leave. She'd already removed everything from the bag that she needed. It might have lain untouched until Thursday.

Rebecca was obviously an accomplished con artist if she could afford such luxurious accommodation. She'd need scams much bigger than this one to maintain her lifestyle.

Unless…

Maggie phoned reception, her heart rebounding against her chest as she waited for someone to answer. The clerk asked her to repeat her breathless, nonsensical query twice before finally understanding.

"Yes, Ma'am. The room is fully paid until your Thursday check-out. Did you wish to extend your stay?"

"No!"

"Is there anything else I can do for you today?"

Maggie swallowed back a sob. Or she hoped she did. Taking her frustrations out on the receptionist wouldn't help. She managed a strangled, "Thank you," and hung up.

So she did have somewhere to say for two nights, a heady relief, something to be grateful to Rebecca for, although she'd give it up in an instant if she could have her cash back.

She spent the evening online, trying to figure out what options were available for someone with only a hundred dollars to their name, a false name at that. She'd need to find a job, but without a local address it would be almost impossible. And without money for a deposit she wouldn't be able to find anywhere to live.

By taking a false name and staying silent in the face of the reports detailing her disappearance and murder, she'd cut herself off from any friends or acquaintances who might have been willing to help her. Assuming she could persuade them Maggie Cumberland wasn't dead, who among them would be willing to perpetuate the lie by helping her out? And what right did she have to ask them to? Or to demand their silence with regard to their conversation if they did refuse?

The risk would be so great it would be easier to turn herself in. At least if she was arrested she'd have a roof over her head and food. She snorted. Couldn't believe she was actually thinking like that.

And had she committed a crime? She'd used a false ID, but not for any illegal purpose. She'd failed to come forward to refute reports of her disappearance and death, wasting police time on investigations into her whereabouts, possibly, no make that probably, prompting Daniel's suicide and definitely obscuring the identity of a genuine murder victim. Did the fact she never intended any of this to happen, or at least not the suicide or murder, excuse her behavior? And would her fears for her life be an adequate defense?

And would the police be willing to handle this in a way which would keep her safe from the Mastersons?

The irony of her situation hit her full on. Running away had been the biggest mistake or, at least, running when she did. If she'd waited until after the arrests she would have had access to all their savings. She could have hired bodyguards, even moved to an undisclosed location while the trials were underway and then sold the house and used her share of the proceeds to fund a decent lifestyle. One divorced from Daniel. No matter how much she loved him she couldn't forgive him for what he'd done.

She could have reverted to her maiden name and, if she wanted to make it doubly difficult to track her down, she could have adopted her middle name, Frances, instead of Maggie. All legal and above board and she wouldn't be in this huge mess of her own making. In the heat of the moment she'd let panic overrule commonsense.

Was it too late now? Did Daniel's death change everything? She was now his widow. Once she proved her existence, she'd be entitled to his estate and his pensions. She knew what was in his will. They'd both prepared their wills at the same time. The surviving spouse would inherit all but a few thousand dollars set aside for Craig, who would be the sole beneficiary after the death of the remaining parent.

Which meant at the moment, technically, Craig was in line to inherit everything.

She logged in to her e-mails. Still no response from Craig. If she could only get in touch with him, this could be the answer to her problems. Assuming he was willing to forgive her. He surely wouldn't want to think of her being out on the streets, would he? And yet at the same time he would surely see the logic in her remaining dead to the world, wouldn't he?

Or would he hate her so much, he wouldn't care what happened to her. Refuse to perpetuate her lie. After all, if he did he'd have to lie too, for as long as she lived. Pretend he was an orphan when he wasn't, deny any children he might have of their grandmother. He would have every right to be angry and she could hardly blame him for it. Nor could she bear to complicate his life any further.

Either she had to remain dead to him or turn herself in. There was no other option. And hope the police would understand her motives, the Mastersons would never hear about it, and her family, what was left of it, would just be pleased she was still alive.

And hope she could be strong enough to ride the storm of disapproval she would unleash. It had to be easier than being on the streets.

And maybe she'd be able to attend Daniel's funeral. Say a final goodbye to the man she knew and loved, the only Daniel she'd known until a few weeks ago. They had been happy. What she'd learned recently had shattered her illusions, but nothing could alter her perception of the past.

The decision made, Maggie felt remarkably calm. She sat out on the balcony as daylight faded. The day-trippers were replaced by dog walkers and evening joggers, the throngs on the pier slowly dissipating, as she made her plans.

Before she went to the police, she would go to San Francisco, make contact with Jane. She needed to know someone else knew the whole story as she saw it, an outside point of contact if she became embroiled in criminal charges or merely to back up her claims she was Maggie Cumberland. Who better than a sister to act as a witness? She and Jane shared so many memories that a fake Maggie Cumberland could not possibly know.

She didn't necessarily expect Jane to agree with what she'd done, though what a relief it would be if her sister at least understood why she'd felt the need to act as she had.

Jane, no doubt, would offer a much more logical option, one that would have been obvious if Maggie hadn't panicked at the first sign of a problem and acted on impulse.

Maggie sighed. She'd happily put up with Jane cataloging the mistakes she thought Maggie had made in return for her sister's support, support which she should have reached out for immediately. What had she been thinking to believe she could do this all on her own?

She checked the fares to San Francisco. She had enough money to get there providing she didn't spend too much on food. Thankfully there were the leftover pastries, not exactly high nutrition but better than nothing. She hoped Rebecca didn't think a few pastries were recompense for taking off with her money.

As she pondered her choices, whether to have the chocolate croissant now or for breakfast, she decided to enhance her makeshift dinner with a bottle of wine from the mini-bar. The check would presumably be automatically charged to Rebecca's credit card.

She grinned as she considered her choices. She could have a miniature bottle of champagne for an extortionate price, but she didn't really like champagne. And the white wine was a chardonnay, not her favorite. She was about to ditch the idea when she spotted the room service menu. Glancing through it, she found a half bottle of Sauvignon Blanc which was suitably expensive. And that was before the service charges.

She hesitated as she made to pick up the phone. She was being ridiculous. She didn't need to have pastries for dinner. She could have a full dinner at Rebecca's expense. She ordered the most expensive fish dish on the menu, a salad and a tiramisu, the bottle of wine and a pot of coffee. She felt suitably guilty as she replaced the receiver but managed to stop herself from calling back to cancel. She deserved this. It had cost her thousands of dollars.

She burst into tears.

Chapter 58 – Wednesday morning

A persistent banging woke Maggie from a fitful sleep. It took several seconds for her to figure out someone was hammering on the door.

Room service, angry at discovering her ruse with Rebecca's credit card, wanting immediate payment for a meal which cost more than her total wealth?

She burrowed down the bed and pulled the blankets over her head. They'd have to give up and go away eventually.

The racket continued, the culprit showing scant consideration for guests in nearby rooms.

The police?

Didn't they normally announce their presence with "police" and "open up"?

She burrowed further down.

Someone from the Mastersons?

Unlikely, not with the noise they were making.

The knocking stopped. Maggie slithered back up the bed, poked her head out of the blankets and strained for the slightest sound of someone trying to open the outer door. The door handle squeaked but the door remained closed.

Housekeeping? But didn't they too announce themselves before trying to get in? Besides, it was early for housekeeping.

Curiosity got the better of her. She needed to know who was on the other side of the door. Her life might depend on it.

She slid out of bed and crept toward the door, slowly inching her head up until she could peer through the spy-hole. All she could see was empty corridor. Whoever had knocked had either left or was standing to the side of the door out of her sightline. And she could think of only one reason anyone would do the latter.

She tip-toed back from the door, considered calling security, expressing her concern that someone was loitering outside her door. So what if she was making a mountain out of a molehill. Better safe than sorry.

She reached for the room phone. Jumped with fright as it rang before she could pick up the handset.

Should she answer it?

The ringing stopped. For a few seconds. Started again. The pattern repeated over and over, the caller presumably cutting the call and redialing each time the message service cut in.

Someone was desperate to contact her. But who? What if it was hotel security, aware of the disturbance outside her room, calling to check she was okay?

She snatched up the receiver.

"Abigail! Open the door."

Maggie almost choked. Rebecca?

"Abigail. The door. You've got the deadbolt on. I can't get in."

"You can't get in?" Maggie sniggered. Raised her voice. "You stole my money."

"No, I didn't."

The audacity of the woman. Did she think Maggie was stupid?

"Who else could have taken it? And besides, whatever happened to the so-called family emergency?"

A heavy sigh came down the line. "Look, let me in and I'll explain everything."

Maggie shook her head. This had to be a trick. Whatever Rebecca was up to, it couldn't be good.

"Are you on your own?"

"What?"

"I said, are you on your own?"

Rebecca hesitated.

Maggie scowled. That was it. Rebecca had sold her out. She knew it. Why hadn't she listened to her instinct?

"You're not alone are you?"

Before Rebecca could answer, Maggie continued, "Who is it, Rebecca? A journalist? Did they promise you a substantial pay off? Or was my money enough and you thought you'd be a solid citizen and go to the police?" She scoffed. "Why would I want to let you back into my life again? Haven't you done enough damage?"

"I'm not trying to hurt you."

"Really? You expect me to believe that?"

"Please, open the door."

"No."

"You're going to have to open it eventually."

Maggie had no answer to that.

"And the room's in my name. I could get hotel security. Tell them you won't let me into my room."

"Do that. And I'll explain how you stole my money."

"I told you. I didn't steal your money."

"Well, where is it then?"

"Let me in and I'll tell you."

"Oh, so you do know where it is, do you? Well, since I don't, if that's not stealing, I don't know what is."

"Abigail. Please."

Maggie hung up.

She paced back and forward, her mind racing. Rebecca was right. She'd have to leave the room eventually, so somehow she needed to deal with this now. Think logically.

The phone rang again.

Maggie snatched it up.

"Please don't hang up again." Rebecca's plea made Maggie hesitate; her intention had been to do just that.

"Look, I need to explain something to you. I understand you might be annoyed with me."

"Annoyed?" Maggie snorted.

"You've a right to be suspicious. After all you've been through. So how about we meet in a public place and I'll explain everything. I'm in the hotel lobby. Come down and we can talk."

Maggie stayed silent.

"And I'll tell you where your money is."

A trap if ever she heard one.

"What do you say?"

Maggie didn't say anything.

"I'll be here for fifteen minutes," Rebecca said. "Please come."

The line went dead.

And after fifteen minutes, what would Rebecca do? Marshal her troops—hotel security, the police, hit men for all she knew—and storm the room?

Fifteen minutes.

Time enough to dress, grab her belongings, and slip out of the hotel. But Rebecca must realize that too. So there had to be a catch.

She scrambled to dress while she ran through the possible options. There wasn't a decent one among them, but at least she'd be fully attired.

She peered through the spy hole again. Recoiled as a figure flitted by. She took another look. Couldn't see anyone but heard the murmur of voices. She strained to listen. Female voices, two or more, and not English. The voices came closer and the end of a housekeeping cart appeared in view.

Maggie sighed with relief. The housekeeping staff. They'd surely be curious if anyone was loitering in the corridor or they heard a woman scream, which she would do if someone tried to grab her as she left the room. Create an almighty raucous. She released the deadbolt, unlatched the security chain. Waited until she heard the voices again—she wanted the women to be in the hallway so they would see her—and opened the door.

A man stepped into her line of vision. He gave her a tentative smile.

She yelped and slammed the door in Daniel's face.

Chapter 59 – Wednesday morning

She'd seen a ghost.

Maggie backed away from the door as if any moment she expected Daniel to emerge through it. She gulped, the act of breathing suddenly needing concentration. She was going crazy. That was the explanation. She didn't even believe in ghosts. The trauma of the last few days, it had induced first paranoia and now hallucinations. Daniel was dead. She didn't want Daniel to be dead, not really, but she'd wished it on him and now she was conjuring him up in her mind.

If she opened the door again, she'd see there was no one there. No one but housekeeping and they were probably rolling their eyes at the crazy lady in the suite.

But she didn't dare open the door. What if he was still there? Wearing a smile that said, "look what you did, Maggie"? She couldn't bear it.

Afraid her legs would give way she slumped down into the nearest armchair, put her head between her knees and told herself to get a grip. Something had temporarily unbalanced her. Maybe the fainting episode the previous day had made her imagination run riot. Maybe she'd even imagined the conversation with Rebecca—some kind of wild dream—her troubled mind desperately trying to right all the wrongs. As if Rebecca would steal her money and then give it back.

She needed to see a doctor.

She couldn't afford a doctor.

The door clicked.

She froze. Realized too late she'd failed to double lock the door or use the chain.

She held her breath, praying it was someone from housekeeping.

Daniel stepped into the room. He closed the door gently behind him. Made no effort to come any closer.

"Maggie," he said.

He looked remarkably fit and well for someone who'd died in prison less than forty-eight hours ago. He had no obvious scar marks on his wrists or neck and, if she wasn't mistaken, he sported more of a tan than the last time she'd seen him.

"Maggie," he said again. "I'm sorry."

He took a few paces toward her, hesitated as if unsure how to continue.

That made two of them.

Maggie wanted to speak. Ask him what he was sorry for exactly. She could think of so many things he should be sorry for.

Including turning up like this out of the blue and rendering her speechless.

And scared.

And confused.

He wasn't a ghost. Which meant everything she'd thought and believed since… since when… had to be false. She frowned. And everything she'd read.

Which meant this Daniel was still not her Daniel. Her Daniel wouldn't dream of putting her through the agony and uncertainty she'd had to bear.

And then just say sorry.

If she dashed into his arms would he hold her tight? She

wanted to. But she also wanted to pummel him, make him suffer for the fear and frustration that had filled her days.

Instead, she did nothing. Stood there like a statue, mouth gaping.

Daniel seemed to sense her conflict. He perched on the edge of the sofa, leaned toward her and began to talk.

Her Daniel had been living a lie for some time. To the Mastersons he was their Chief Financial Officer, a subservient type who, for the appropriate amount of salary and benefits, would happily massage the financial records, no questions asked, to give the appearance of the company being above board. To the Organized Crime Division he was their inside informant tasked with secretly digging beyond the paper trail to find the evidence needed to bring the company down. And he'd succeeded.

But before the police could act on the information he was able to provide about a forthcoming delivery, Maggie disappeared. The disappearance coincided with a report that filtered through to the bureau of her visit to the local police station to express her concerns, an action which not only put the operation into jeopardy, but also increased the risks that Daniel's role would be revealed.

Daniel had already taken steps to ensure their safety as the operation came to a conclusion. He'd employed bodyguards to watch the house and, in particular, shadow Maggie. He smiled ruefully. The bodyguards didn't report on Maggie's every move so it wasn't until too late that he learned of her return to the house the night he'd relayed the delivery information to the police or that she'd taken a trip to the town hall the following day.

"You had someone following me?" Maggie was aghast. "Why didn't you tell me?"

"I couldn't. Because I couldn't tell you why. The operation's success depended on as few people as possible knowing about it."

"But I'm your wife." She broke off, as the truth dawned.

"When I left, they must have seen me go, correct? Did they follow me to the station?"

She paused again. She hadn't seen anyone.

"So you knew, and the police knew, that I'd got on a train

to Manhattan. And yet the reports said there was a big search."

Daniel nodded. "All part of the cover up,"

He gestured helplessly. "Look, you're not going to like this, but there was a contingency plan in place in case something went wrong while I was undercover, the Mastersons found out about it or anything else that might have put us in danger."

"A contingency plan?"

Daniel exhaled hard. "Word would go out we'd both been killed in a car crash. We'd be given a new identity and helped to start fresh elsewhere."

Speechless, Maggie gaped at him.

When she found her voice, she exploded. "I'm not going to like it? Too damned right, I'm not going to like it. How could you agree to such a ridiculous scenario without consulting me first? Didn't it occur to you that I might want a say in whether I was willing to uproot my life because of your desire to play... to play..."

She shook her head. Had she ever known this man?

"I wasn't playing, Maggie. This was serious business. Someone had to do it."

She stood up. Moved away. "It didn't have to be you."

"No. I grant you that. But it was something I was capable of doing, something I wanted to do, and I thought that given your work with abused women you would understand why. How many times did you complain that somebody had to make a stand against human trafficking?"

Maggie bit back her retort. Not at the risk of putting our own lives on the line, she'd nearly blurted out. But he was right. Without the courage to follow through on convictions how could anyone really make a difference? Her work with victims was important, but the problem would only really be solved when the source was stamped out.

She spun back toward him. "And what about Craig? Where did he fit in your grand plan?"

"Calm down, Maggie. You're not making this easy for me."

"Easy for you. Ha! Did you stop to think about me for a moment? Fearing for my life, hearing my husband had been arrested, jailed and accused of my murder. You're telling me this was all fabricated?"

Daniel nodded. He told her how her leaving had forced them to come up with a different plan that would detract from any suggestion that he had been involved in the bust by pointing the finger of suspicion at him, first for her disappearance and then her murder. Later, they could use his guilt over the crime as a justification for his apparent suicide.

All loose ends tied up nicely, for her and Daniel, but what about their son? Had they abandoned him for the sake of a lie?

"He knows," Daniel said.

"He, what?"

"As soon as we knew how we were going to handle the situation, I contacted him. Gave him the briefest details and told him to stay out of the picture. Make it seem that the authorities couldn't contact him in time for him to fly back for the funerals. We kept his name off the radar as much as possible. He won't go back to New York, not for a while, and he's already agreed that he'd want to change his name to whatever we pick. That way he won't have to pretend to be an orphan."

"It's a lot to ask a nineteen-year-old."

"It is. But he understands."

"And yet, you didn't think I would understand. What? You thought I'd go blabbing to my friends on Facebook?"

"On the contrary, you did a great job of keeping yourself incognito. Using Jane's old license was a masterstroke."

"But what made you so sure I wouldn't blow your plans by reappearing to refute the reports of my disappearance or my death? It crossed my mind several times."

"And why didn't you?"

What? Now he wanted her to justify her actions?

"Because I was scared of the consequences. I thought the arrests were a result of my information. I thought if it got out..." She scoffed. "I guess I gave myself too much credit. I should have known better."

She scowled.

"You took a gamble that's how I would react, didn't you?"

He shrugged. "It was a fairly safe gamble. I know you well enough. You couldn't live with an injustice. You'd do the right thing even at your own expense. Besides, we had people following you the whole time. They would have interfered if you'd shown any signs of heading back to New York."

"Let me guess. Neil and another guy?"

Daniel nodded.

"But I lost them in San Antonio."

"No, you didn't."

Maggie smirked. "Yes, I did. I snuck out of the first hotel I was staying in, walked straight past the younger guy without him noticing. Haven't seen them since."

She smiled smugly.

"How do you think I knew where to find you?"

Maggie froze. "I didn't lose them?"

Daniel shook his head. Explained how Rob, the younger guy, had put a tracking device in her suitcase when he'd helped her with it when they arrived in Washington, DC. From the moment she'd stepped off the train, they tracked her movements from location to location. Neil had slipped one into her purse on the train to New Orleans when they realized she was better at subterfuge than they'd imagined.

He grinned proudly at her as he said this. "I had no idea you had it in you, Maggie."

She glared at him. "Fear has a strange way of concentrating the mind. And subterfuge is a skill I could happily live without learning. Especially under circumstances like this. Do you have any idea what you put me through?"

Daniel didn't answer.

"I thought you were dead. Deserved to die. Do you know how hard that was? And then you turn up like some resurrected do-gooder and I'm... what ... expected to welcome you with open arms? Trust you with my life again after you've played with it so casually?"

She spewed her words at him in a torrent of anger and guilt until the dam burst and the tears flooded out. She brushed off his attempts to comfort her. Her emotions toward him were too raw to accept his embrace. She could see the hurt in his eyes at her rebuttal, a sight which added to her pain, but her sense of being used was so great she refused to give him a moment's relief.

All the moving around, all the caution, the fear, had been for nothing. Her apparent enemies had been her allies. What a difference it would have made to have known that.

Daniel countered her arguments at every stage. They didn't know she was going to leave. Would she have believed Neil and Rob were on her side if they'd told her so, or would she have assumed they were lying to get close to her?

And at first, they'd figured it was safer for her to keep moving, especially in light of the sightings called in to the local police. They'd had to open a hotline when they announced the search, it would have looked weird if they hadn't, but they hadn't been able to shut it down until they'd announced they'd found her body. Some retired detective had phoned several times adamant he'd seen Maggie, although claiming she was using the name Abigail. They'd had to act quickly, create a diversion to take her out of the picture as far as the Mastersons family was concerned. The main culprits were in jail, but who knew what contacts they had outside.

Maggie blanched at the confirmation that her fears had been genuine.

Daniel insisted everything they'd done was with her safety in mind.

It was a lot to take in, more so with the realization that her actions had inadvertently been the cause of much of the problem. She could understand the need for secrecy, but if Daniel had taken her into his confidence, none of this would have happened. He was as guilty as she was for the mess.

Imagine if he had told her from the beginning though? She would have been terrified, worried every day he went to work that he'd be found out, wary of any stranger that approached, any car that followed her more than a block. Each time they kissed, hugged, made love, she'd wonder whether it would be the last. And Daniel knew her well enough to know this and that this would be one issue she wouldn't happily cede to his choice as she'd done with most major decisions in the past. He'd banked on her love for him being great enough to forgive his huge transgression, but was it? Her love had been based on trust, their mutual trust, and he'd shattered that. What other secrets might he keep from her in the future?

She paced back and forth, deliberately avoiding looking at him. He expected a response and she didn't have one.

Chapter 60 – Wednesday morning

A knock at the door interrupted the silence. Daniel leapt up to answer it as if he'd been expecting someone.

"Everything okay?" Rebecca asked as Daniel stepped aside to let her in.

"You too?" Maggie glared at her. "You were in on this too?"

Rebecca gave her a mea culpa grimace, her discomfort at the level of tension in the room obvious.

"We assumed you'd be less suspicious of a woman. And that it wouldn't seem odd given we were both traveling alone for me to suggest we travel together. It made it a lot easier to keep tabs on you." Rebecca sighed. "I have to say, you were very convincing with your story. If I hadn't known it wasn't true I would have believed you. And the way you explained the news of your husband's death as a friend's story—that was inspired."

Maggie blushed, embarrassed at being praised for being an accomplished liar.

"I think you told a few lies too. Had me fooled."

"Part of the job. Turn myself into whatever is needed to make our female clients feel comfortable. My husband says sometimes he thinks I'm too good at it. Which one is the real me?" She laughed. "He's joking. I think."

"So you're not a widow? Even that was a lie?"

"Yep."

"And the part about being British?"

"Now, that is true. Though I've lived in the States for the last twenty years. Since I married Neil."

"Neil." Maggie parroted the name back at her. "You're married to Neil?"

Rebecca nodded. "And in the interests of full disclosure, Rob's my brother. And this is yours."

She held out a small nylon duffel bag. Maggie didn't need to open it to know what was inside.

"Why did you take it? I thought you'd robbed me."

"I needed to make sure you stayed here. We didn't want you taking off again. And ruin the planned grand reunion."

Daniel butted in. "You were never supposed to think I was dead. I was supposed to be here yesterday morning before you had a chance to see the news reports of my death. But the weather worked against us. Huge storms along the east coast shut down the major airports for hours. I couldn't get out."

"Which left me in the awkward position of having to deal with your reaction to the news, knowing it wasn't true," Rebecca said. "When you came out with that story, I thought we might be okay, but then you started acting suspicious of me, asking all those questions."

Maggie explained why. It was Rebecca's turn to look embarrassed.

"That's the problem with lying. The smallest thing can give you away."

"If I hadn't been so paranoid I probably wouldn't have noticed your slip up."

"I wish you hadn't. I had a feeling you were on the verge of running again. As we were hoping Daniel's flight would get in late afternoon, I decided the best way to make sure you stayed put was to slip a sedative into your juice. That worked a treat, but the weather refused to cooperate. Latest estimates were that Daniel wouldn't arrive until this morning. I suggested we tell you everything but Daniel said it was too dangerous, you wouldn't believe me. So I had to find some way of ensuring you stayed here until this morning."

Daniel again. Making decisions on her behalf. Thinking he knew best. How dare he?

She strode over to him, raised her hand to slap him but he was too quick. He grabbed her wrist, encircled her waist with his other arm, and pulled her to him. He held her in a tight embrace, squeezing her against his chest as if he were trying to pull her inside of him. Their faces were inches apart, his eyes fixed on hers, his expression intent.

"Six young women, Maggie. That's how many we saved. In one cargo! How many other shipments have we prevented? How many other young lives saved?"

Out of the corner of her eye Maggie saw Rebecca slip out of the room.

"I know you're mad at me. And you have every reason to be. But we've made a difference. A small difference."

"And ripped our lives apart in the process."

"But we can start again. A fresh start. You always said you'd like to change things up when Craig left home."

Was he serious? "I didn't mean like this."

Daniel grimaced. "And I hoped it wouldn't come to this. Faking our deaths was supposed to be a last resort. But it's happened. And we can't go back." He released his grip, held Maggie at arm's length.

"So please, say you'll go forward with me. You can pick. Where we live, the house we buy, everything."

"Our new names?"

Daniel's smile disappeared.

"Daniel?"

He reached into his shirt pocket. Pulled out a driver's license and handed it to her. A Californian license in the name of John Daniel Thornton.

She raised her eyebrows.

He pulled out another, this one for her. This one, Frances Margaret Thornton.

She couldn't hide her surprise. "You took my name."

"Well, you took mine twenty-two years ago. It only seems fair. The Cumberlands are dead. Long live the Thorntons."

He leaned forward and planted a kiss on her lips.

She pushed him away. Saw the disappointment in his eyes. He knew he'd lost her trust.

She had a choice. She could let him earn it back or she could walk away. And the choice was hers to make.

Whether to start her new life single or as a married woman. Whether her new life would be as a clone of Maggie Cumberland, the dutiful wife and mother, or incorporate the newly discovered aspects of Frances Margaret Thornton's personality, a woman in her own right.

She'd been happy with Daniel. She couldn't deny that. She had no reason to think they wouldn't be happy again providing she didn't let the events of the last few weeks fester. Ultimately, Daniel had made a moral choice, one she could be proud of, secretly. Neither would be the same again, but that didn't mean their love for each other needed to change.

A woman in her own right. She liked the sound of that. Maybe Daniel would like it too. There was only one way to find out.

Other Books by Mel Parish

Motive for Revenge

For over three years kidnap victim Jake Cornish (Ulterior Motives) has struggled to put the memories of his ordeal in the Philippines behind him. Not even his wife Beth knows the full truth and he wants to keep it that way. However, on their first family vacation since returning to the US, a chance sighting of one of his kidnappers inflames his need for closure. When attempts to learn more about his kidnappers' new lives coincide with a brutal attack on their family, Jake becomes entangled in the ensuing police investigation. Now, not only have his actions jeopardized his marriage, but if his secret is revealed he will hand the police the one piece of information they are missing – a motive for revenge.

Ulterior Motives

Kidnapped while on vacation in the Philippines expatriate Jake Cornish struggles to retain his dignity in the face of the humiliating circumstances imposed by his captors. As his wife's chilling silence to the ransom demand continues, Jake's futile attempts at escape and defiance are met with a degree of hostility and brutality that suggest his chance of survival is grim—until his captors suggest another use for him. Their outrageous new demand not only pushes him to unparalleled levels of despondency but also causes cracks in their unity, laying bare ulterior motives and revealing the true nature of the kidnappers themselves.

A story of ordinary people in extraordinary circumstances, Ulterior Motives tells of life stripped bare of daily comforts, where desperation drives motivation, and loyalty and love may lead not to happiness but unimaginable consequences.

Silent Lies

During a police investigation into the whereabouts of his young assistant Katy Shore, the decision to withhold information that could get him into trouble is an easy one for accountant Cal Miller. That is, until he discovers Katy's deceptions far outweigh his own. Now, not only is Cal's reputation as a newcomer to small-town Leyton's business community at stake, but also his already fragile marriage and his freedom. With detectives deaf to his claims that no crime has been committed, Cal's impulsive and secretive nature threatens to alienate even those who could help him, as the ensuing scandal brings to light issues that suggest that his secrets are darker and his past more blemished than he is willing to admit.

The Anniversary

Detective Paul Rigby's role in his girlfriend's death has haunted him since that tragic event almost one year ago. With his dreams of marriage and a family already destroyed, Rigby's guilt now threatens to sabotage the one thing left to him: his once promising career.

That career would already be in ruins without the intervention of Chief of Police Jim Pearson. Reluctant to lose his best detective, Pearson is forced to resort to ever more devious methods of keeping his young protégé under control as the anniversary approaches.

Sidelined following a spontaneous act of violence, Rigby finds himself at increasing odds with his mentor but is determined to prove that he is still worthy of Pearson's trust. A manpower crisis within the department offers a chance of redemption during what should be a straightforward case, but when repercussions from his punch-up and his unorthodox handling of the investigation collide with devastating results, Rigby discovers he has a lot more to lose than he thought.

About the Author

Mel Parish grew up in Newcastle-upon-Tyne, England, lived for many years in London and Hong Kong and now currently resides in New York. Mel is also the author of *Motive for Revenge*, *Ulterior Motives*, *Silent Lies* and *The Anniversary*.

Mel talks about life and the activities that inspire her writing on her blog *Food for the Author: Books and Travel* at www.melparish.blogspot.com. She would be delighted to hear from you if you would like to drop by.

For more information on Mel's books, please visit her website at www.melparish.com

If you would like to be notified of new releases and subscriber-only special offers sign up for my occasional newsletters at http://bit.ly/melparishnews. Your email address will never be shared and you can unsubscribe at any time.

Made in the USA
San Bernardino, CA
20 April 2017